"Your buddy Seminov took the hard way out."
Randal waved his gun in the direction of the
body lying in the driveway. In the half light
Bolan recognized the Russian cop. Dark
pools of blood were forming under his body.

The Executioner was pushed into one of the SUVs.
Doors slammed, and the vehicles rolled away from
Trechenko's house. As they turned onto the road, a
series of heavy explosions sounded behind them.
The house was engulfed by flame and smoke.

"He wasn't going to need it much longer anyway,"
Randal said from the front seat.

He turned to smile at Bolan. "Ain't life a bitch,
Belasko? Ain't life a freakin' bitch?"

Don Pendleton's Mack Bolan.

Circle of Deception

A GOLD EAGLE BOOK FROM

WORLDWIDE.

TORONTO • NEW YORK • LONDON
AMSTERDAM • PARIS • SYDNEY • HAMBURG
STOCKHOLM • ATHENS • TOKYO • MILAN
MADRID • WARSAW • BUDAPEST • AUCKLAND

First edition November 2004

ISBN 0-373-61499-3

Special thanks and acknowledgment to
Mike Linaker for his contribution to this work.

CIRCLE OF DECEPTION

Printed in U.S.A.

Count it the greatest sin to prefer life to honor,
and for the sake of living to lose what makes
life worth living.

—Juvenal
c.50–c.130

Never surrender, no matter how high
the odds are stacked against you. Always
defy those who would beat you down.
Always fight back. It's the only way to live.

—Mack Bolan

PROLOGUE

The strike team came in from the sea, six men clad in wet suits, wearing scuba gear and carrying weapons and explosives. It was a half hour before dawn when they stepped from the water and made their way up the sandy slope, their objective directly ahead of them.

They had left their seagoing motor launch three miles out, and swam toward the Colombian coastline and their target—the dock and warehouse facility belonging to Hermano Salazar.

THE TEAM WAS made up of former Soviet military personnel who had moved into the free enterprise market, specifically into the employ of Fedor Trechenko, one of Moscow's leading drug traffickers, a self-styled Russian mafioso.

While the American Mafia affected a persona of being honorable men who followed the age-old traditions, Trechenko had none of those traits. He was known and feared as a ruthless individual who accepted no interference in his sphere of operations. He would mete out punishment to his own people for infringements as quickly as he would to his enemies. Trechenko was a driven man, with a confidence that had led him to take on ever more risky enterprises in order to increase his wealth.

Always ready to push into new markets, Trechenko had formed an alliance with a Jamaican drug lord named Deacon Marley. Together they were ready to challenge the Colombian narcobaron, Hermano Salazar, for the enviable position of supplier to the immensely lucrative American market, determined to push Salazar out of Florida.

Trechenko's supplier of high-quality heroin—Razak Khan—controlled Afghan poppy fields that produced the raw material. The Russian's organization, via its Afghanistan-Tajikistan pipeline, brought the poppy flowers to his processing plant and from there the refined heroin was moved by various routes, using his own people and well-paid officials, to the distribution points for shipment to Jamaica, where Deacon Marley's operation took over. At Marley's distribution center the heroin was repackaged into blocks that would be smuggled into the U.S. and sold on the streets.

Salazar's cartel became increasingly agitated when his people found out what was happening. Their response was direct and uncompromising. In one month they killed three of Marley's couriers and destroyed two of his seagoing vessels. It was a stark warning to the new alliance that its presence wasn't going to be tolerated. If Salazar had expected his hits to deliver the nail in the alliance's coffin, he was mistaken.

The input from the Jamaican's Russian combat team, plus knowledge of his enemy's country from his own home team, gave Marley the intelligence and the means of getting them to the Colombian coast and Hermano Salazar's dock facility.

PALE LIGHT CHASED AWAY some of the night shadows as the team eased its way along the rocky base of the dock, staying within the thick forest of massive pilings. Water lapped at the men's feet and splashed against the lower levels of the dock. The dank smell of seaweed tainted the air.

The Russians moved silently; each knew his task. Detailed plans of the dock and the warehouse had been studied and memorized. Each man had a specific part to play, and true to his training, he went about his task without additional instruction.

From where the team was situated everyone could see across the natural harbor around which the dock and warehouse had been constructed. There were two vessels moored at the loading docks—cargo ships that would be loaded with both legitimate and illegal cargo. Salazar's normal business was conducted from here, as well as his drug trafficking. On this part of the coast Salazar was in total charge. He harvested his cocaine up-country, had it refined, transported it to his packing plants and then down to the coast, where it was loaded onto cargo ships. His influence and his vast fortune allowed him to buy off the necessary officials. If that didn't work, there were other means of persuasion.

The cargo ships leaving Salazar's dock set their course for any number of destinations. His delivery of drugs crisscrossed the sea-lanes. In many instances the drugs were off-loaded at sea, yet others were simply dropped overboard in sealed containers that would be picked up later by divers working from high-powered speedboats. Simple ship-to-ship deliveries were used, as well. There were also aircrafts used to carry consign-ments, making drops into the ocean, sometimes as far as the Florida Everglades. Salazar's operation was ever-changing in order to confuse the authorities. It was a flex-ible, highly organized operation. There were seizures that Salazar accepted as part of his business, but what he might lose could easily be made up for very quickly due to the mass production of the base drug. A loss in profit was swallowed up and recouped on a daily basis.

The dock facility was Salazar's main distribution point, which was why the Russian strike team was here. Their intention was to hit the dock facility hard and de-stroy as much as they could in order to create confusion and delay in Salazar's operation. Both the vessels tied up were to be hit, as well as the warehouse that housed the final processing and packaging section.

Moving quickly now, the strike team breached the main dock area and the selected targets.

Three armed guards were on patrol. One drove around the dock area in an open Jeep, a 7.62 mm FN MAG swivel-mounted machine behind him. The other guards roved the docks, carrying handguns and SMGs. Each man was equipped with state-of-the-art communications.

The driver of the Jeep was taken out first. He had halted his vehicle briefly, checking out the area with powerful field glasses. Satisfied, he lowered the glasses and reached out to start the vehicle again. A suppressed 9 mm bullet hit him in the back of the skull, driving him forward against the steering wheel.

Simultaneously, both of the roving guards were killed with the same type of weapon. The corpses were left where they lay as the Russian team moved on. They had limited time to complete the rest of the operation.

Team A was assigned to the main warehouse. Around their waists they carried sealed waterproof bags. Each bag held a dozen explosive charges that consisted of plastic compound already assembled with digital timer and detonator. These would be placed around the warehouse and processing plant. The combined destructive power of these charges would level the warehouse and destroy everything inside.

The moored vessels were the targets of Teams B and C. They also carried bags holding explosive charges. The only difference was that these charges were fitted with magnetic plates capable of holding the charge to the metal hull of the ships. The charges were to be placed around the hulls of each vessel, below the waterline, so that the vessels would be severely damaged. The detonations would open up the hulls, allowing water to flood in. The cargo in the holds would be destroyed and the vessels would sink to the bottom of the harbor, creating wreckage that would be costly in both time and money to remove.

As the Russian strike teams began to close on their respective targets, they found themselves confronted by a large force of armed men. There was momentary confusion and then reaction from the Russian team.

They were trapped, surrounded by the opposition, and they knew there wasn't going to be an easy way out. With the determination that had been trained into them, they did the only thing they could, and made a vain and desperate attempt at fighting their way out.

The firefight was short and bloody.

In the conflict, five of Salazar's men were killed and an equal number sustained severe wounds.

The Russians, outnumbered and outgunned, stood their ground until there were only two left standing. Both had suffered wounds, though neither was life threatening. In the event they might have been luckier to have died like their comrades. They weren't allowed that luxury. Overpowered and stripped of their weapons and explosives, the two Russians were removed from the dock and taken inside one of the smaller warehouses. Here they found themselves face-to-face with Hermano Salazar.

If circumstances had been different, Salazar could have made a good living as an actor. He was a fit, handsome man in his midthirties. In his private moments he had great success with women, due to his charm and personality. Even at this time in the morning he was clean-shaven, dressed in expensive casual clothing that emphasized his tall, athletic figure. He watched the two Russians as they were brought to stand before him, a pleased smile on his lips.

"I wish we had met under better circumstances, gentlemen. However, let me welcome you to my country. Needless to say you will not be leaving it. As you have undergone great efforts to find us, the least I can do is bury you here. You showed much initiative but unfortunately no success because we knew you were coming. I was informed days ago. Trechenko and that idiot Marley believe they can take over my business. They are wrong. I realize they will try again. A pity. Men like you dying for nothing."

Salazar turned to his people and gave instructions, then again faced the Russian captives.

"I have told my men to show you our special place. Where we entertain *guests*. After all, you deserve special treatment. The idea is to see who can stay alive the longest. My people are very skilled at this procedure. It will be extremely unpleasant, of course. And very painful. My people are very strong on payback when they see their friends hurt, and you did kill a number of them.

So I am afraid you must be prepared to accept the punishment." Salazar turned to his men. "Take them away."

After the struggling Russians had been removed, Salazar beckoned to one of his lieutenants.

"Call our friend in Moscow and give him my thanks. Tell him it has gone well and let him know that my gratitude will be expressed in the normal manner. He will understand."

Salazar stepped outside and stood on the dock, breathing in the cool air of the new day.

It was good to be alive, he decided.

Then he turned and made his way to the entrance leading to the steps that would take him to the basement chamber. He wanted to see how the Russians were faring.

In fact, he heard them before he saw them....

CHAPTER ONE

Washington, D.C.

Mack Bolan knew his man as much as Leo Turrin knew him. They had gone the course in the past, coming to a mutual respect that transcended the spoken word and didn't depend on anything as superficial as reciprocal ego bolstering.

Turrin sat down, relaxing in the low leather armchair. He looked well, the only sign of passing time a little graying in his hair around the temples. As always, he was smartly dressed in a dark suit, white shirt and deep blue tie. His shoes held a shine that almost begged the observer to wear shades. He took a few seconds to appraise the man facing him. He was aware of Bolan's continuing battles against evil, a definitive expression that covered a multitude of transgressions. It was enough to cover the spectrum, and it told Leo Turrin that

Mack Bolan, aka the Executioner, was still the man to turn to.

"I'm heading up an investigation into illegalities in DEA activities. Namely a team we have working alongside the Russian OCD in Moscow. Your name, actually the cover name you were using at the time, came up. You had dealings with the OCD during that mission."

Bolan nodded. He remembered that mission, and a Russian cop who had been his partner during it until she had died. A beautiful young woman named Tanya Danovitch. She had given her life in the name of justice.

Yeah, damn right he remembered that mission.

"The main man you dealt with at the OCD was Commander Valentine Seminov."

He was Danovitch's boss, a big man who had reminded Bolan of Hal Brognola.

"I know him. We only met once. Not long enough for me to get his first name."

"Well, he's our liaison. The man believes he may have people in his department in bed with our rogue DEA operatives."

"What's the deal?"

"When the Taliban was taken out of the picture in Afghanistan there were assumptions that the poppy-growing fields would be destroyed. Unfortunately that hasn't exactly happened. Despite government efforts the business is still thriving, and the Afghan growers have a new partner. The Russian Mafia is buying opium poppies and processing them into heroin. Here's the twist. We have a link between the Russian Mob and a Jamaican trafficker who supplies U.S. dealers and is looking to expand his empire."

"That isn't going to please the Colombians."

Turrin smiled. He'd been right. Bolan had seen the added complication immediately. His perception of the drug culture was exactly on track.

"We could have a drug war on our hands if this thing really gets rolling. The Jamaicans are falling over themselves to up their percentage of the trade. They know the Colombians will hit back, but they believe they can handle them. The Russians have promised them all the help they need. It's in their interests. Our source tells us the Russians have plans to import hit teams into Jamaica. The Jamaican heading this up is a top drug lord named Deacon Marley. Lives with big style and has connections all over the Caribbean. He's a scary guy according to what we've heard. And smart."

"And the U.S. is going to be their dumping ground," Bolan said.

"Mack, if this DEA involvement proves out, it's going to make it a damn sight easier for the traffickers to get doors opened for them. We need to shut this pipeline down, both ends and the middle, and deal with these rogue DEA agents. If we let this all run free, we could have drugs being shipped in with DEA help. Plus the likelihood of an open war between the rival factions. If that happens, it'll spill over from the Caribbean onto the mainland."

"Where do I come in?"

"I need you to follow this through. If we have rogue DEA agents involved, I want their heads. Same with the other players, Mack. I need someone in the game who can deal out instant justice on this. Not get bogged down in endless legalities and plea bargaining. If it gets into legal hands, we're screwed. You know the way it works. Restraining orders, delays, stalling. All to give the bastards time to crawl back under their rocks and out of our sight. Mack, dig the bastards out of the shadows and shut them down." Turrin raised his hands. "Hell, I don't need to tell you what needs to be done. Truth is, I need someone on this I can trust. Not some guy who might be on the other side."

"Seminov?"

"He asked for a meet. Says he'll only talk to you." Turrin leaned forward, a slow smile on his lips. "He trusts you, Mack. Whatever you did last time around left an impression."

Bolan recalled his meeting with Seminov. It had lasted all of thirty minutes.

"You joining the party?" Turrin asked finally.

"It would be bad form to refuse your invitation."

Turrin nodded. "Back to the hellgrounds?"

It was Bolan's turn to smile.

"Back, Leo? What makes you think I ever left?"

Turrin passed over a thick envelope. "I had these worked up for you," he said. "In case you said yes. Passport, visas, credit cards. The usual package. ID has you down as a Justice Department special investigator, working with the backing of my department for a Senate hearing. You'll go in on a remit to assess how well the DEA-OCD tie-up is running. No cleaning house or making life hard for the DEA. Let them think you're just there as window dressing. Any problems, all you do is call the number on the card. It gets you through to me and we'll field any queries."

Bolan opened the envelope and checked its contents. As well as the expected paperwork, he found a couple of thousand dollars in hundred-denomination notes, plus a sizable amount of French francs. There was an airline ticket to France and a reservation for a Paris hotel.

"Seminov is attending a law-enforcement convention in Paris. He figured a meeting on neutral ground might be the best way to kick-start this mission."

"Okay."

"Your commercial flight leaves tomorrow, so we have time for dinner tonight, and I'm not in the mood for you to say no."

Bolan smiled. "No problem, Leo. I've said yes, so it looks like I'm working for you. I don't need to get on your wrong side first day on the job."

"Mack, I can't do anything about weapons at the moment. Once you reach Moscow I can do something. As Seminov has requested your help, there shouldn't be a problem. But you know the French. They'll scream bloody murder if you try to take a gun into the country. That going to be a problem?"

"Let's hope not."

Paris, France

LATE-AFTERNOON Paris lay under a bank of heavy gray clouds. Thin, chill rain made the buildings and streets glisten.

Bolan had spent most of the flight reading the detailed files Leo Turrin had provided. The complexities of the various parties involved might have defeated a newcomer to the game, but Mack Bolan was far from that. His involvement with the drug world went back to his beginnings, to the days when he had fought the mafia, and beyond as he took on a wider and more disparate overall campaign of attrition. In Bolan's eyes the purveyors of evil wore the same uniform. Drugs, rackets, prostitution, call it what you would, it all amounted to the same thing: the degradation of those involved and suffering—in one form or another—for the civilian casualties. They carried the burden of others' greed, and it was Bolan's obligation to stop those transgressions.

Midway through the flight Bolan had closed the files and placed them back in his briefcase. He had enough of the written word to last him for the rest of the flight. Tipping back his seat, he relaxed, content to watch the attractive flight attendant serving his section of the plane. She provided innocent enough distraction from what lay ahead. Bolan had no illusions. Paris might have been known as the city of romance. It was the last thing Bolan would be thinking about once he arrived.

Once he was through French customs and outside the

airport, Bolan hailed a taxi and gave instructions to be taken to his hotel. The driver turned out to be Algerian, and once he realized Bolan's nationality, spent the entire trip regaling his passenger about his two years in New York. The driver had family there and had driven a New York cab for most of his stay. He had only returned to France because the woman he wanted to marry refused to leave Paris.

"What can you do?" the driver said.

"Look at your choices and decide. Is she the woman for you?"

"Of course."

"And?"

"We will get married next month."

"Seems to me you made the right choice."

The driver shrugged, then gestured at the city unfurling in front of them. "You have been to Paris before?"

"A few times."

"Business or pleasure?"

"The city is always a pleasure."

Bolan didn't elaborate. The driver considered the implications.

"And this time?"

"Most likely be the same."

BOLAN'S HOTEL ROOM was clean and comfortable. He barely had time to settle in before the telephone rang.

"A call for you, Monsieur Belasko."

"*Merci.*"

The line clicked as the call was put through.

"Mike Belasko?"

Bolan recognized the Russian accent. "Commander Seminov."

"Did you have a good flight?"

"Tolerable."

Seminov laughed. "I will not be done until this evening. This damn conference is taking longer than I anticipated. Policemen are the same all over. They love to talk. This group more than usual. I should be free about seven. Join me for a meal. I took the liberty of making reservations for us on one of the Bateaux-Mouches. Meet me at the landing just after seven-thirty."

"I look forward to it, Commander."

"Valentine, my friend."

ONCE HE HAD FINISHED talking to Seminov, Bolan called in. His connection to Leo Turrin went via satellite, the signal being rerouted a couple of times before Bolan heard the distant phone being picked up.

"I'm meeting our friend this evening. Depending on what he tells me I could be moving on fairly quickly."

"Anything you need?"

"Nothing right now. Only thing is, I'm feeling a little lightly dressed."

"I had another try at getting around the French laws. But no go. Sorry."

"I'll live with it, Leo."

"I hope you do."

BOLAN SAT across from Seminov. The glass-canopied Bateau-Mouche, the floating restaurant, moved slowly down the Seine, floodlights on the embankments highlighting the famous landmarks. They were sliding by Notre Dame as the waiter refilled their glasses with red wine.

"In the old days this would have been a black mark against me," Seminov said. "Allowing myself to become seduced by the decadence of the West."

"It's a cross we all have to bear."

Seminov raised his broad shoulders. "I will try to live with myself."

"You were saying your suspicions were confirmed a couple of weeks back?"

"Yes. Too many coincidences. Every time we seemed to be closing in on a suspect they would change location, cancel deals that had been set up much earlier. I watched and waited, even set little traps with paperwork and evidence. I made careful observations. And I was proved correct. Documents were replaced incorrectly. Some evidence items vanished. Small things, I suppose, but when I added them together they pointed to someone in my department interfering with the drug cases. Nothing else was involved. Only matters relating to the ongoing trafficking investigations."

"Our people in Washington believe there are rogue DEA operatives working some kind of deal with the traffickers. That *might* include the team working out of your Moscow department."

"That makes it even more difficult. Watching my

own people is hard enough. I have to be careful when it comes to the American team."

"That's my job, Valentine. When we get to Moscow I'll handle the Americans."

Seminov smiled. "I remember last time you were in my country and went after those people in the Pamir Mountains. You *handled* them if I recall."

"At a high price," Bolan said.

"Danovitch?" Seminov sighed. "A great pity. She had the makings of a good officer." He raised his wine-glass. "To Danovitch. Good memories."

Bolan drank. This time the wine seemed to leave a slightly bitter aftertaste in his mouth. Seminov watched him and leaned forward.

"It could have been you who died, my friend. Instead it was Danovitch. You cannot carry the burden around with you for life. Celebrate that you are still alive, Mike Belasko. Tanya Danovitch would not have expected you to carry her death with you."

"The drug trail that starts in Afghanistan. Do you have enough solid evidence to move against it?"

"Evidence? Yes, but problems dealing with it. The poppy fields are inside the country. There is nothing we can do about that. Too many people involved. Local officials on each side of the border. Money changes hands on a regular basis. Bribes. Payoffs. A blind eye at a checkpoint. And the country up there is very difficult to police. So many places where even a fleet of trucks can be hidden. Secret trails. Ah! If I could commandeer a few planes and load them with bombs I could destroy the damn poppy fields and blow up the processing plants. But my hands are tied by bureaucracy. One of the ills that has not vanished since we became Westernized."

Bolan considered Seminov's remarks.

"Do you have any idea who might be working against you from your department?"

"Each time I look around the office I think first this one, then another. No, I can't point the finger yet."

"We need to act as if we don't have anything. Let them stay free so they carry on working, contacting their people. We watch and let them do the finger-pointing for us. Same with the DEA suspects. We let *them* make the running."

Seminov nodded as he picked up his glass.

"That is for when we reach Moscow. Now, let us have some more of this wine."

LATER BOLAN and Seminov walked along the embankment of the river. They had disembarked from the Bateau-Mouche at the end of the trip along with the other passengers. As the crowd dispersed, Bolan and the Russian decided to walk back along the Seine, ignoring the fine rain drifting in from the night sky.

They still had things to talk about, and the comparative silence and scarcity of people made it easier to discuss mutual matters.

They had little chance to discuss very much. Their

privacy was invaded without warning as they walked beneath the arches of one of the Seine's many bridges.

There were three attackers. Moving like wraiths out of the shadows thrown by the massive pillars supporting the bridge, they closed on Bolan and his companion like hyenas moving in for the kill. In the dim light beneath the arch of the bridge the blades of killing knives glittered like steel fangs in the hands of the three attackers.

Seminov muttered in Russian as he leaned forward, his powerful arms extending in a defensive curve. Despite his bulk, he moved lightly as he poised himself in anticipation of the strike that was coming.

Bolan had already initiated his own defense, turning toward the closest of the attackers, his eyes fixed on the man. His adversary moved awkwardly, slightly thrown by Bolan's confident stance. No one had told them their victims might be skilled fighters themselves. They had accepted the contract because the money was good and they had been told that the victims would be alone and not expecting to be confronted. The odds had seemed to be in their favor at the outset, but the wheel was turning in a different direction. There was nothing to be done now. The contract had been taken and money had changed hands. The kill team had to honor the agreement. If they reneged, their days would be numbered.

The man facing Bolan lunged, then changed direction, twisting the blade of his knife as he stepped in close. It was a maneuver he had used many times, always with success because it fooled the victim into believing the knife was coming from a different angle. By the time the victim realized his mistake it would be over and he would be on the ground with his blood—

The attacker felt excruciating pain in his wrist. He glanced down and saw his victim had gripped *his* wrist, turning it, then applying pressure that bent it against the natural line of the bone. The pressure increased, becoming unbearable. Something snapped and the knife dropped from limp fingers. A brutal blow to the attacker's face crushed bone and flooded his mouth with blood. He felt himself being swung around, helpless to resist. A moment later he was slammed against one of the stone pillars with stunning force. His head snapped forward, crunching against the ancient stone and his world exploded in sickening pain. A hand caught hold of his hair, drew his head back, then drove it forward into the pillar again. The front of his skull split like an eggshell and he slumped to the ground, unconscious.

Bolan heard a scuff of boot leather on the stone flags behind him and whirled, catching a glimpse of a second attacker rushing at him, knife slashing the air. The soldier let the guy get close. Almost too close. He saw the crooked smile edging the man's thin mouth as he sensed victory, then Bolan struck out. His right fist swung around and caught his adversary on the point of his jutting chin, slapping his head around, blood flying in dark flecks.

As the guy stumbled, trying to reconnect, Bolan's left hand clamped around his adversary's knife wrist as he stepped in close, pivoting, bringing the guy's arm over his shoulder. He twisted the arm, hauling it down over his shoulder and dragging it down until the bone splintered, drawing a shrill scream from the attacker's throat. Bolan swiveled again, swinging around and slamming his right elbow into the guy's throat, crushing it. The guy fell to his knees, clutching his broken arm and gagging against his ruined throat. Bolan brought his right knee around and whacked it against the side of the attacker's head, driving him to the ground in a single moment of destructive energy.

Bolan turned and saw Seminov hauling his own adversary into a crippling bear hug. The big Russian lifted his attacker off the ground, his massive arms encircling the guy's body and closing down with relentless force. The man arched his back, eyes wide, mouth open in a soundless yell moments before there was a soft crunch and the attacker became limp. Seminov held him for a few moments longer, then let the guy slip from his grasp. The man dropped to the ground without a murmur.

Bolan stepped over the motionless form, his eyes scanning the area, searching for any movement. Beyond the cover of the bridge the embankment flanking the Seine was deserted, the ground wet from the rain drifting in across the city.

"Belasko," Seminov said, his usually deep voice softened.

Something in his tone drew Bolan's full attention.

"Valentine?"

"It appears I did not move quite fast enough."

Bolan saw the Russian had his right hand pressed to his side. Moving closer, he spotted the moist gleam of blood seeping between the Russian's fingers.

"Is it deep?" Bolan asked.

"My coat will never be the same again," the Russian replied, "but I'll survive. Nothing to make a fuss about."

"With you bleeding all across Paris?"

"We can go to the Russian embassy. They will have someone there who can tend to this. Call a taxi."

"We need to check these guys out to see if we can find out who hired them."

"I will do that while you find a taxi."

Bolan made his way up from the embankment and onto the street. The traffic was still brisk and it took him no more than a couple of minutes to catch the attention of a cruising Renault taxi. Bolan leaned in at the window and spoke to the driver.

"My friend is a little ill. I need to get him to where he can recover."

The driver shrugged in typical French fashion, then he glanced over Bolan's shoulder.

"Is this your friend?"

Bolan turned to see Seminov appearing at the top of the steps. The Russian crossed to the taxi and climbed in as Bolan opened the door.

"Where to?" the driver asked.

"Russian embassy," Seminov said, "at 40 Boulevard Lannes."

The car pulled away from the curb, merging effortlessly with the late-evening traffic. Beside Bolan the Russian cop sank back in the seat, favoring his side.

"Don't worry. We have a good doctor at the embassy." The Russian stared out the car window. "We will leave for Moscow tomorrow," he said. "The sooner we get back there the better."

"There a reason for this sudden haste?" Bolan asked.

"Later."

At the Russian embassy Seminov used his rank and influence to get things moving. The embassy doctor took him away to tend to the knife wound in his side, leaving Bolan alone in a small office with a desk, endless pots of Russian tea and curious faces peering around the door to see if he was comfortable. Bolan took it in stride, using the time to go through the personal belongings Seminov had taken from the trio of attackers.

There wasn't a great deal to see on first examination. Only one of the men had owned a wallet. It was worn and frayed at the edges; leather that had seen better days. It held an identity card that told Bolan the man was a French citizen named Dubois. He had been born in a suburb of Paris, and the card gave his age as thirty-two. The wallet held a sheaf of high-denomination euros. Bolan did a rough calculation and worked out that there were at least ten thousand U.S. dollars. He dropped the cash on the desk he was using and went through the rest of the wallet's contents. Dubois seemed to have a lot of contacts, names and telephone numbers written on numerous strips of paper. None of them meant anything to Bolan.

He checked out the other items Seminov had taken from the corpses. More cash. ID cards. Packs of French cigarettes. Lighters. One was a battered Zippo that looked as if it had been around the block a great many times.

Bolan leaned back in his leather chair and stared at the belongings spread across the desktop.

"Nothing?"

He glanced up and saw Seminov framed in the doorway. The Russian cop came into the room, pushing the door shut. He took a seat across from Bolan and poked a finger at the items strewn across the desk.

"How's the side?"

Seminov grunted. "Sore. Full of stitches. So? Have you found anything?"

"Only that this guy, Dubois, has a lot of contact numbers," Bolan said. "None I recognize."

Seminov scanned the numbers. He reached out and picked one up, a smile creasing his face.

"This one I know. This will get us a number in Moscow."

"Maybe where Dubois gets his orders."

"I will look into it once we get back."

Bolan glanced at his watch. "It's hardly worth checking into my hotel."

"I will arrange for someone to pick up your things. It might be safer if you stayed here tonight."

Bolan wasn't in the mood to argue the point.

Moscow

THEY WERE in the air late morning, on board an Aeroflot jet. Only a handful of passengers were on the flight, so Bolan and Seminov were able to talk freely.

"The fact that we were attacked in Paris proves my suspicion that there is a leak within the OCD," Seminov stated. "What I can't be sure of is if it comes from my people or the DEA team."

"Could be both. Someone from your department tying in with the DEA. We're talking deals that offer so much money it makes it too easy for people to turn. How much information was there on your meeting with me?"

"Very little. I told only two people from my office. Gregor Rostov and Shemel Barinkov. Both men I have worked with for many years."

"It often turns out to be someone you trust with your life, someone you wouldn't doubt."

"I understand that."

"The phone number might be a link."

LATE AFTERNOON they were in a taxi crossing Moscow. The city lay under a gray blanket of cloud that threatened rain. Bolan sat back and watched the view go by. The drabness was relieved occasionally by an oasis of light, usually from an imported franchise that brought some Western glamour to the Russian backdrop of muted colors.

The OCD was still in the same building Bolan remembered from his previous visit. The dark, soot-streaked building looked out across the sprawl of Byelorusski Station. The location was far from glamorous, but the OCD was an independent working unit, not a showcase for the Moscow police.

Bolan followed Seminov up the stone steps and into the building. The office he was led to was crammed with desks, computers and fax machines. Telephones were ringing continuously. About a dozen people were carrying out their routine tasks. Seminov's office was at the far end, partitioned off from the main room, with a glass upper section that allowed for uninterrupted viewing of the floor. A layer of cigarette smoke hovered just below ceiling level.

"Nothing ever changes here," Seminov observed as he led Bolan through the bedlam to the comparative calm of his office. As he pushed open the door, a man seated behind Seminov's desk stood up self-consciously. "I am not dead yet," Seminov said in English. "Any rumors about my demise are definitely misreported. So you can't have my job yet, Gregor Rostov."

Rostov was a lean, dark-haired man in his early thirties. He grinned at Seminov.

"I was trying to complete my monthly report, boss. It is quieter in here. You know what our supreme master is like."

"That is no way to talk about the district commissioner of the OCD."

Seminov smiled at Bolan. "My boss, Vladimir Korsov. The man at the top."

Rostov glanced across at Bolan. "Is this our guest?"

Seminov nodded. "Mike Belasko is from the American Justice Department. He is here as a representative of a Senate committee to monitor how the OCD-DEA setup is functioning."

Rostov held out a hand and shook Bolan's. His grip was firm.

"I hope you find what you are looking for, Mr. Belasko."

"So do I."

"Commander, how was Paris?"

"Surprisingly crowded," Seminov said, giving Bolan a sideways glance.

Bolan smiled briefly.

"Haven't I seen you before?" Rostov asked, examining Bolan's face. "You came to see Commander Seminov. Yes?"

"I've moved jobs since then."

"No matter."

Rostov gathered up papers from Seminov's desk and backed out of the office, offering more apologies until Seminov told him to shut up and go.

Bolan stood looking through the glass partition at the men of Seminov's department.

"Rostov doesn't miss much."

Seminov grunted a reply.

Bolan continued to watch the activity beyond the glass partition.

Was there a traitor out there? Or more than one.

"Which is Barinkov?"

Seminov took a quick look. "That's him talking to Rostov."

"They look chummy."

"Chummy?"

"Sorry. It means they seem to have a close relationship. Good friends."

"They have been with me for almost three years. Both are good men who are not afraid to put themselves in danger if the situation calls for it."

"Any suspicions where they're concerned?"

"The way things are happening I have suspicions about everyone in this office and Moscow in general."

"Are your telephone lines secure?"

"We do the best we can with the finances we are given. I'm sure you understand that."

"Same all over."

"Your DEA people have the floor below. Are you ready to go and see them?"

Bolan nodded and Seminov led the way out of his office and across the main room. They reached a lower landing, and Seminov made his way along a short passage to an open door. He tapped on the frame, sticking his head inside the room.

"I have your visitor, gentlemen."

The Russian stepped inside with Bolan close behind.

The single large room held less furniture than Seminov's main office: three desks all pushed together, a pair of computers and the same number of telephones. The walls were dotted with charts and maps. A coffee percolator bubbled gently on a small table against one wall.

Three men were in the room, and they turned their attention on Bolan the moment he appeared.

Seminov introduced them, pointing out each man as he gave his name.

"Martin Reckard. He is in charge of the team."

Reckard was in his midthirties, a lean, fit-looking man with an open face and neatly trimmed blond hair. He wore a shoulder rig over his light blue shirt.

"William Tanberg."

Dark-haired and sporting a deep tan, he looked younger than Reckard. He wore a dark suit that looked as if it had just come back from being pressed. Even his shoes had a deep shine. He smiled easily at Bolan.

"And this is Asa Randal."

There was no smile on Randal's face. He concentrated on checking Bolan over from behind the black-framed spectacles he wore. Bolan judged him to be in his late thirties, a solid, cautious man who wouldn't take anyone on trust. Randal had broad shoulders and a deep chest that suggested he worked out and kept himself in shape. He wore a shoulder rig over a white shirt and had his sleeves rolled up to his elbows.

"Come to check us out?" he asked tersely. "I guess you have some kind of ID?"

Bolan took out his badge holder and passed it over. He also showed the official letter that Turrin had prepared for him.

"Sorry about this, guys," he said amiably. "I work for the government, too. I don't pick my assignments."

Randal made a low sound in his throat as he handed Bolan's credentials to Reckard.

"He checks out with the data they e-mailed us."

The tone of his voice suggested he was disappointed.

"Don't let Asa get to you," Reckard said, handing Bolan's ID back to him. He stuck out a hand. "Welcome to the DEA. Moscow chapter."

"I'll try not to get in the way," Bolan said.

"Hey, you want a cup of coffee?" Tanberg asked. "All the way from the U.S. of A. No offense, Commander Seminov, but—"

Seminov held up a hand. "Don't worry about it. Your coffee is better, but we beat you when it comes to vodka."

"Can't argue that," Tanberg said.

Randal caught Bolan's eye. "Where does the head office get off checking us out? We're clean."

"You got the information," Bolan countered. "If you read it, you know why I'm here. If you don't like it, Randal, that's your problem. All I want is to do my job and get back home. Any grievances, you talk to your people, not me."

"Hey, come on, guys," Reckard said, intervening. "We all have a job to do. Asa, don't hassle the man. Mr. Belasko, we'll cooperate. No problems."

"That's fine. I'm not going to get in the way."

Randal turned away, obviously still not convinced. He crossed to one of the desks and logged on to a computer.

Tanberg brought Bolan his coffee. "Don't let Asa get to you. He tends to be protective of the unit and doesn't take too kindly to outsiders. Especially if he thinks they're here to watch over him."

"Guess I'd feel the same." Bolan tasted the coffee. It was good. He stood next to Tanberg. "How do you like being here in Moscow?"

"It's different. Nothing like home."

"Where's that?"

"Chicago, originally. My dad was a construction engineer, so we moved around a lot. Ended up in Florida. After college I joined the police force. Ended up in Dade County and that was where I applied for the DEA."

"You like it?"

Tanberg grinned. "Well it sure beats the hell out of being a shoe salesman."

"Anything particular you need to see, Mr. Belasko?" Reckard asked. "Just sing out."

"Right now I just need to look around to see how you operate. Like I said, I'm not here watching you so I can give you a hard time. Just carry on with your routine as if I weren't here."

"We couldn't be that lucky," Randal muttered.

Bolan ignored the remark. He made a show of wandering around the office, peering at things. He was aware of being watched by the DEA team. They were sizing him up, making their own judgments on why he was here—and what he had come to look at. Bolan wanted that to happen. If he created suspicion, someone might be pushed to reacting. He wanted to draw out the guilty. It was a dangerous game. He was placing himself in the firing line, offering himself as a target.

Reckard joined him after a short time.

"How are things between you and the OCD team?" Bolan asked.

"Fine. These people are good. We're just offering our experience. They catch on fast."

"They understand this is an ongoing thing? The DEA knows it. Chop down one trafficking organization another takes its place."

Reckard shrugged. "Same in any law-enforcement department. Drugs. Extortion. Gambling. You can't stop it for good. A man would be a fool if he thought he could. All you can do is keep hitting them, reduce their profits and make life harder for them."

Bolan could accept that. His own battle against evil was endless. He fought and won, moved on and faced yet another threat. It would have been easy to stand back and admit defeat, to see his recurring battles swamping him with the specter of defeat. Bolan could have put aside his weapons and passed the torch to others, letting them fight on. Even as the thought crossed his mind Bolan dismissed it. He would never do that. Not as long as he was mentally and physically able to carry on. His conscience wouldn't let him quit. His choice had been made a long time ago. His lonely crusade was for more than just himself. He was fighting man's eternal war against evil. In all its forms.

"It makes a man wonder if he should take their money and run."

Bolan glanced across at Randal. The man's remark had been tossed out in a moment of bravado, a flip comment on the temptations being placed in front of DEA agents.

"You make a bust in some back-street apartment. The place is filthy, overrun with cockroaches. And what do you find? Thousands of dollars being counted on the kitchen table, spilling over onto the floor. Next time it's the hold of a motor launch packed with plastic-wrapped bundles of paper money. I'm talking millions here. Enough to run a small country."

"It must be tempting."

Reckard nodded. "A man would have to be dead not to think about it. What the hell. You think about it for a minute, then you make the call for the collection team to roll in and take over."

Randal rubbed his thumb and a finger together.

"Mo-ne-y," he whispered and walked away.

"He's okay," Tanberg said. "He can be a pain in the ass, but he's okay."

"I'll take your word."

Bolan finished his coffee and made his excuses, following Seminov out the door and back to his office. As Seminov sat at his desk, Bolan took a chair set against the wall where he was able to see the outer office through the partition.

"Now you have seen everyone," the Russian stated.

"I need to go to my hotel. I'm expecting a delivery from the U.S. Embassy later. Something I might need, especially since our little interruption back in Paris."

Seminov frowned slightly but made no comment. He went through to the main office, Bolan following, carrying his bag. Seminov had a word with Barinkov, who nodded to Bolan, and they made their way outside. Seminov moved in the direction of the line of department cars parked in the yard outside.

"Valentine, why don't we take a taxi?"

There were a couple of stands nearby. Seminov hailed one of the waiting taxis and they climbed in. The Russian cop gave the name of the hotel and the driver pulled out into the traffic.

"So?" he said to Bolan.

"So now they'll know we're not going to discuss anything in front of them."

"We were in my office."

"There is an old saying, Valentine, about walls having ears."

Seminov sighed. He pushed his bulk into the corner of the seat.

"In other words don't trust anyone?"

"Only a man's mother can be trusted."

Seminov laughed out loud.

"Belasko, you haven't met *my* mother."

"Hope mine hasn't forgotten my care package," Bolan said quietly.

Seminov frowned at the American's comment. He thought about it, working out the meaning.

"Very quaint," he said. "I got it."

"Stick with me, Valentine, and I'll have you talking like an American before you know it."

The Russian sat back in his seat.

"I don't know whether that would be a curse or a blessing."

THE KOSMOS HOTEL, built by the French, was located away from Moscow's center. Bolan dumped his bag and stretched out on one of the twin beds, staring up at the ceiling. He glanced at his watch. Time for a shower and to relax before Seminov returned to pick him up. The Russian had dropped Bolan at the hotel, leaving to check something out before they got together later in the evening.

Bolan rang room service and ordered a pot of coffee. While he waited for it to arrive he opened his bag and hung up his clothes. As always, he traveled light, bringing along clothing that he might not even use and due to sudden changes in circumstances, might have to leave behind. His transient lifestyle made it necessary for him to equip himself with disposable items. All objects he could leave behind without regrets.

If he had been a man who sat back and reflected on life's injustices, Bolan could have been excused if he had allowed self-pity to cloak him. Yet there was never a moment when he actually regretted his path. The way he had chosen. None of it had been forced on him. It had begun with a personal need for settling a family matter and had escalated from there, growing in form and substance until it became his way in life. Without realizing it, Mack Bolan had taken on the burden of his War Everlasting with the natural ease of a born soldier. It was his way because there was no other path he could have chosen because of circumstance. Now he was doing the only thing he could because there was no one else as willing, or as capable, of doing it.

The coffee arrived. Bolan set the tray on a low table and poured himself a cup of dark, rich Turkish coffee. He stood at the window and stared out across the darkening city, his thoughts centered on the people he had met at the OCD offices.

Faces and names. They flitted back and forth across Bolan's conscious mind.

Who? Reckard? Randal? Tanberg?

One? Or all of them?

And what about Seminov's squad?

They were at that stage, nothing more than faces and names.

A knock at his room door brought Bolan away from the window. He stood to one side of the door.

"Yes?"

"Mr. Belasko?"

The voice was American, the accent precise, modulated.

Bolan opened the door, still to one side. He saw a

young, well-dressed man in his early thirties, carrying a black leather carryall.

"Eugene Reisner, Mr. Belasko. I'm from the U.S. Embassy. This came in for you today, via the diplomatic service, sir."

Reisner held out the carryall.

"Come in," Bolan said.

He closed the door as Reisner entered. The young man placed the carryall on the floor beside one of the beds. Crossing to the dresser, Bolan produced his Justice Department badge, clipped to the leather holder. Reisner examined it, nodding to himself. He also checked out the U.S. passport Bolan handed him.

"Thank you, Mr. Belasko. Is there anything else I can do for you?"

Bolan shook his head.

"Nothing right now, but thanks."

"If you need me my number is on here," Reisner said, handing a neatly printed card.

"Thanks again," Bolan said.

When Reisner had gone, Bolan lifted the bag onto the bed, broke the diplomatic seal and unzipped the bag. Inside, wrapped in soft cloth, was a Beretta 93-R and a Desert Eagle. There was also a shoulder rig for the Beretta and a combat harness, complete with holster, for the big Desert Eagle. Also in the carryall was a blacksuit, boots and thin leather gloves. A sheathed knife lay alongside fully loaded ammo clips for both handguns.

The weaponry and clothing had been sent via Leo

Turrin and Hal Brognola through official government channels. Bolan checked out both pistols. He loaded them and placed the Beretta in the shoulder holster. That done, he had a second cup of coffee, stripped off his clothing and headed for the bathroom, where he had a shave and then took a long hot shower. When he had finished, he dried himself and dressed, then repacked his other gear, including the Desert Eagle, in a compact backpack he could carry with him. A couple of spare clips for the Beretta went into a zippered pocket of his leather jacket. He laid the jacket across the back of a chair, next to the backpack, then stretched out on one of the beds and closed his eyes.

The telephone roused him. Bolan glanced at his watch as he reached for the phone. It was just midnight. He picked up and heard Seminov's voice.

"Be ready. I will be outside the hotel in five minutes. I hope your mother didn't let you down, because our night out looks as if it is going to be a busy one."

CHAPTER TWO

Bolan stepped outside the hotel and scanned the area. It was dark, the air cool. He heard the sound of an engine and looked around to see an unwashed Toyota sedan rolling to the curb in front of the hotel. Seminov was behind the wheel. Bolan opened the front passenger door and climbed in, dropping his backpack onto the floor at his feet. Seminov drove away from the hotel, cutting through traffic once he was on the main street. They had been driving for almost five minutes before Seminov spoke.

"I have an informant named Kishka. I've used him for years. He's always been reliable. He called me just after I got home and said he had information about one of my undercover operatives in Afghanistan. It was one of the things I was going to discuss with you this evening. I wanted to give you all the information I have so there would be no misunderstanding between us."

"Why should there be, Valentine?"

Seminov glanced across at the American. He shook his head.

"This whole damn affair has become so full of suspicion. You see how it is at the OCD. I'm ashamed to say I can't even trust the people I work with because I don't know *who* to trust. Why do you think I am driving myself tonight and not using my usual driver?"

"You believe you can trust me?"

"Well, of course… Damn you, Belasko, yes, I do trust you. Why did I bring you all this way if…?"

"Valentine, *we* have no problems."

"Okay. Well, there is my undercover man—his name is Benin—who has worked for me two years now. Brilliant man. He has never been to the department. We always work via telephone, or by meeting. So he has no contact with my people, nor they with him. I believe you would call him a deep-cover man. Yes?"

Bolan nodded.

"Two months ago Benin joined up with the traffickers who are allying with the Afghans. He is from the border region so he can pass easily among them. He worked for weeks, very patiently, until they accepted him and then he started to infiltrate the higher echelons of the drug ring. We were both aware it might take some time before he managed to get close enough to pass back useful information, so I didn't hear from him for a long while. Then I began to receive messages telling me he suspected there were things happening. First information about foreign visitors. I later established he was talking about the Jamaicans. Two weeks ago I had a call from him telling me there was an American at the current meetings. I had started to have my own concerns about our DEA friends by this time. There were too many trips out of the city. Unexplained at the time but until I had enough to go on what could I do? I had my hands full with our own cases and we were having too many failures. It was only later I began to link the two things together. By then it was too late because I had no one to confide in."

"What about your man Benin?"

"I lost contact with him a few days ago. His last message was that he had to lay low for a while. He thought there might be someone watching him. So he was going to stay in his undercover role and do nothing until he was certain any threat was over."

"And now you hear he may be in trouble?"

Seminov nodded.

"Have you considered this might be a trap?"

"I'm always suspicious."

"You just told me your man is deep cover. You've told no one about him."

"No one."

"So how come your informer knows he exists?"

"Because…" Seminov began, then fell silent. He kept driving, staring straight ahead. "Kishka has always been a good informant. His information is always genuine. He has never fed me anything false or of no use."

"So you believed him this time because you had no reason not to? But your man Benin isn't known to anyone but yourself."

"Damn! What an idiot I am. Yes, I took his word, and forgot that he shouldn't even know about Benin."

Seminov swung the wheel and rolled the car to a stop at the side of the road. He climbed out of the car and walked away a few yards, hands thrust deep into his coat pockets. Bolan left him alone for a while, then opened his door and joined the Russian.

"Don't beat yourself up over this, Valentine. You said Kishka has always come through for you. He could be genuine. Information comes from all kinds of sources. Could be Benin needed to get through to you but couldn't use the regular way. Maybe he's in trouble. Did Benin know about Kishka?"

"It's possible. Benin has been around for a long time. He worked Moscow for a couple of years so he could have come across Kishka and heard he fed me information."

"Where are you supposed to meet him?"

"Behind a nightclub we always use. Kishka lives above it."

They returned to the car. As Seminov drove on, Bolan stripped off his jacket, removed the Beretta and the shoulder rig from his backpack and slipped it on. With the rig adjusted Bolan put the jacket back on.

"So your package *did* arrive, eh?"

Bolan nodded.

"Does this Kishka know I'm coming along?"

"I didn't tell him anything about you."

THE CLUB WAS situated in a maze of back streets. The area was shabby, and many of the surrounding buildings were shuttered and in darkness. Seminov parked the car and they stepped out. The Russian paused to light a cigarette.

"Not exactly the most pleasant part of Moscow," he said.

The garish frontage was adorned with flickering red neon lights. From deep inside the building they could hear pounding music. Seminov walked to the alley that ran down the side of the nightclub, where there was little light.

"At the rear is a delivery area and the back door of the club. Metal stairs lead up to Kishka's apartment."

Seminov took a cell phone from his coat and punched in a number. He spoke into the phone, then shut it off.

"Kishka will be waiting for us."

Bolan stayed a few steps behind the Russian, keeping a check on their rear. He had opened his jacket so the 93-R was available for swift access. As always, he treated the situation as potentially hazardous. Despite Seminov's assurance that Kishka was reliable, Bolan viewed the clandestine meeting as risky. Caution had kept him alive this far. He saw no reason to change his attitude.

They reached the rear lot of the nightclub, and Seminov walked to meet Kishka as he moved out of the shadows and into the thin light. He spoke to him in Russian and the man replied, nodding.

Kishka was a lean, dark man with shoulder-length hair that brushed the collar of his crumpled coat. His face, even in the dim light, was bony, eyes recessed in his skull. There was something about him that Bolan felt uneasy with. Kishka glanced at the tall, silent American, then turned his attention back to Seminov. It was as if he had dismissed Bolan as unimportant. Kishka began to talk to his contact, his voice low.

Bolan eased his hand under his jacket, gripping the butt of the Beretta as he folded his arms. He was still trying to get a grip on his feelings for Kishka. A small stir of suspicion began to grow inside Bolan.

What the hell was it?

Just what had Kishka done that had unsettled him? The informant didn't even know Bolan. Had never met him and probably didn't even know who he was.

Yet despite the secrecy of the meeting with Seminov, the informant had barely acknowledged Bolan. Merely looked his way before going back to Seminov. No questioning who Bolan was, or why he was present. In Bolan's experience informants were nervous types, given the delicacy of their profession, and if there was one thing they guarded, it was their anonymity. Kishka had shown no alarm at Bolan's presence. If anything, he had made a show of not making any kind of fuss.

Why?

Kishka hadn't been alarmed because he knew Bolan would be there. He knew because he had been told, which alerted Bolan to a setup.

He and Seminov had walked into a trap that had been arranged by people aware of Bolan's presence in Moscow.

"Valentine, back off," Bolan snapped, urgency in his words. "This is a setup."

Bolan's hand slid the Beretta free. He saw Seminov reaching for his own pistol, turning as Kishka made to step back.

The ratchet of weapons being cocked froze Bolan. In the periphery of his vision he saw dark figures moving out from the darkness beyond the throw of the light. Figures of men wielding SMGs that were trained on himself and Seminov. Bolan counted four of them.

The rumble of a powerful engine reached their ears. A dark-colored SUV drove into view. It screeched to a stop just short of Bolan and Seminov. The armed men closed in. The Beretta was snatched from Bolan's hand. Seminov was disarmed, as well.

Orders were given in Russian, then he and Seminov were herded to the SUV and pushed into the rear. The armed men, silent and hard-faced, crowded in on either side. The doors were closed.

Kishka and another man joined the driver in the front. As the vehicle merged with the thin line of traffic, Bolan caught sight of Seminov's car falling in behind them.

He wondered how long a trip they would have, and what lay at the end of it.

THEY DROVE for a couple of hours, leaving the city behind, heading south and pushing deep into the country. The driver knew his way, never hesitating at junctions, keeping a steady speed.

Bolan remained silent. There was no point questioning his captors. His arrival in Moscow had caused a swift reaction. There was no doubt that Seminov had been correct when he had stated there was a leak.

But why such a rapid reaction? Was something due to happen that Bolan's presence had upset? Negotiations? The anticipated transport of a cargo? Bolan had no idea at this juncture.

The SUV made a sharp turn, bumping from the road onto ribbed concrete. Bolan saw distant buildings, low to the ground, some shaped like aircraft hangars. An airfield? The SUV headed directly for the cluster of structures. They passed a double line of steel barrels. Fuel drums. Bolan stored the location.

The 4x4 rolled inside one of the hangars and across the littered floor. There were no aircraft, only a car, an SUV identical to the one that had brought them here. A few strip lights hung from the steel rafters, throwing dim illumination to the floor.

As the SUV came to a stop, Bolan made out a number of figures standing beside the parked vehicle. He also saw a number of weapons. The SUV's doors were opened and Bolan and Seminov were pushed out, their armed escort moving them to face the waiting group.

Seminov's car appeared, coming to a stop near the other vehicles.

A tall man with a long black leather coat draped over his shoulders stepped forward. He had a mean expression on his tanned, handsome face. He reached up to adjust the hang of the leather coat, and Bolan saw he wore a number of gold rings on his long, manicured fingers.

"So good to see you, Commander Seminov," he said in English. "And this will be your American friend, Mr. Belasko. How are you finding our hospitality?"

"Give me time and I'll tell you."

Seminov leaned toward Bolan.

"Ivan Kirov," he said. "Enforcer for Fedor Trechenko. One of our local traffickers. On the evolutionary scale they come lower than cockroaches."

"Valentine, you hurt my feelings," Kirov said. "I believe we know each other well enough now not to stoop to insults."

"Kirov, I haven't started to insult you yet."

Kirov smiled, but his eyes flickered in the direction of one of the armed men standing behind Seminov. The man leaned in close and struck Seminov hard behind his ear, using the steel barrel of his autopistol. The blow put Seminov to his knees.

Kirov ordered the man back, then turned back to confront Bolan.

"My man will do the same again if Valentine says anything else to upset me."

"I'd better choose my words carefully, then," Bolan said.

Kirov spread his hands. "You are our guest, Belasko. A representative of the American Justice Department, I hear."

"Does that mean I can leave when I want?"

Kirov laughed. "I don't think so. You see, your presence here in my country has come at a difficult time. I have to leave very shortly. Business, you understand. Negotiations that are at a delicate stage. We cannot afford to have anything happen that might upset them. Before I go I need to understand why you are here and what you have learned."

"I haven't had time to learn anything. I only arrived today."

"But you were in Paris with our good friend Seminov. I doubt you were there to discuss the state of French politics."

"We got little chance to discuss anything because we were interrupted."

Kirov smiled again. "I heard about that little problem you had by the Seine. It must have come as something of a surprise."

"Nothing surprises me where your kind is involved."

"My kind, Mr. Belasko? What is my kind?"

"You don't need me to describe what you are."

"Oh, the drugs. Let me explain something, Belasko. Pure and simple, we are businessmen. We supply what our buyers want, and they sell to their customers. Even you must agree we are living the American dream. The very stuff of capitalism. Supply and demand. Is there anything so wrong with that?"

"You call what you do business? Supplying drugs that kill, that destroy lives and families and nourish crime?"

"Don't leave out the money part."

Bolan stayed silent. He saw no reason to debate the issue with a man like Kirov.

"So, Belasko, now that we have established that you don't approve of our business ethics, shall we find out why you are here in my country?"

"To see how the OCD team is doing. It's as simple as that."

"Of course." Kirov stepped in closer. "Do I look stupid to you? You are not here for any such purpose. Our good friend Seminov personally requested your presence. Belasko, or whatever your real name is, we are not fooled by your pretense. You are here in Russia to spy on us and try to interfere with our business."

"So why ask?"

"We need to know how much information your employers gave you about us. Call it self-protection."

Bolan's gaze didn't flicker. He faced Kirov until the trafficker averted his own gaze.

Kirov snapped out an order in Russian. Bolan was pushed deeper into the hangar, gun muzzles grinding against his flesh. He was taken to a room at the far end of the building and shoved inside. The door was closed and bolted on the outside. After a short time there was a rap on the door.

"I will give you time to think about what I have said. Do not be fooled, Belasko. If the need arises I *will* kill you."

Bolan checked out the room. It was solidly built, no windows, a solid concrete floor. A single low-wattage bulb behind a metal mesh cover was embedded in the ceiling. There was no furniture in the room. The soldier crossed to the wall opposite the door and sat down.

And waited.

SEMINOV WAS TAKEN and placed in a room identical to Bolan's.

After a half hour Kirov pulled a cell phone from his pocket and touched a speed-dial number. The call was answered and Kirov recognized the voice of his employer, Fedor Trechenko.

"Well?"

"We have them both. Nothing yet."

"What are you doing about it?"

"They are locked in separate rooms. I'm giving them time to think."

"Don't give them too long. I need to leave early. Ivan, when the time comes do not leave any of them alive. Including Kishka."

"He might be of future use."

"No. Kishka is unreliable. It didn't take much to buy him off from being Seminov's informant. He's too much of a risk. He betrayed Seminov. He will betray us. Yes?"

"You're right. I will see to it."

"No mistakes, Ivan. We cannot afford any interference at the moment. Now deal with them all."

Kirov broke the connection. He glanced at his watch, turning to look in the direction of the rooms where Belasko and Seminov were being held.

"Bring them out," he ordered. "Let's get this done."

THE MAN CALLED Kishka had been sitting on an upturned wooden crate, unsure of his position. No one had said a word to him since the end of the drive from Moscow, and the informer was starting to feel a little uncomfortable. He tried to console himself by thinking about the money he was going to receive for bringing Seminov and the American into Kirov's hands. It was a great deal of money. More than he had ever seen before in his life. More than he could ever have made through informing, and it was in U.S. dollars. Kishka realized he could go a long way on such a sum of money. What happened to Seminov and the American had nothing to do with him, Kishka decided. Seminov, like all the others before, had used Kishka for his own needs. He took the risks getting the information and for his trouble he received very little. Cops like Seminov were always bleating on about how little they could afford to pay, yet at the same time they were always demanding more information. Now that was ended. Kishka would take his money and leave Moscow, probably leave Russia, too.

Footsteps intruded on his thoughts. Kishka saw it was Kirov.

"We are going to have a long talk with those two now," Kirov said. "It's bound to become unpleasant. Time for you to go."

Kishka stood, nodding in agreement. Relief washed over him. Kirov was smiling. He leaned toward Kishka, putting his left arm around the informer's bony shoulders.

"Yes. Time for you to leave us, Kishka."

Kirov's right hand came into view from where it hung at his side. His grip on the informant's shoulders tightened, trapping him.

Kishka saw Kirov's hand move quickly. Then he felt a solid blow just under his ribs. He wondered why the man had punched him, then felt the sharp pain inside, felt the tearing of flesh and organs as the mobster twisted the blade of the knife he had thrust into Kishka's body. He struggled to free himself from Kirov's embrace, but the pain was swelling. He felt wetness down his front. Looking down, he saw a heavy flow of blood, soaking his clothing and spilling to the floor. His blood. The knife was yanked up his torso, the heavy blade slicing open his flesh. Kishka felt a strange surge of movement in his body as Kirov pulled the knife clear and a torrent of bloody entrails pushed out of the extensive wound. Weakness engulfed him. It was as if his life had drained from him along with his organs. He slumped to his knees as Kirov let go, arms around his body as he tried to push his intestines back inside. He curled up on the cold concrete, his blood forming a great dark pool around him.

The mobster stepped away from the dying man. He felt no emotion. In his mind he had simply eradicated a possible threat to the organization. Nothing more. It was of little consequence to him.

This was the sight that greeted Mack Bolan and Valentine Seminov as they emerged from their locked rooms.

CHAPTER THREE

A hand pushed Bolan forward, past the huddled, still moving body of Kishka. He glanced in Kirov's direction. The trafficker was still holding the bloodied knife he had used on the informer.

"You understand now?" he asked.

Bolan understood. Kishka had been nothing more than a means of showing Kirov's intent. The man's life held little importance to the trafficker, but that failed to surprise Bolan. Sanctity of life had little meaning in any situation where the drug dealers were concerned. Russian or American, Colombian or Jamaican, the dealers in death had no compassion for anyone who stood in their way. The Executioner had faced these human vultures on many occasions and had reached the stage where he was never surprised at their lack of humanity.

He was aware that his presence in Russia had been compromised. Somewhere information had been passed to the drug traffickers, warning them of his arrival, and they had panicked. Just why he didn't know—but he would find out.

Bolan offered no resistance as he was escorted across the hangar. He was weighing the odds. Including Kirov, seven men made up the opposition. One each behind Bolan and Seminov. Kirov wasn't carrying a gun. Four others ranged loosely around Kirov, holding weapons that weren't trained on either captive.

"No more time to waste," Kirov stated.

Bolan said nothing. He was bracing himself to make a move. Silently he was agreeing with Kirov. There was no more time to waste. Whatever needed to be done, it had to be done *now*. Bolan hoped Seminov would back his play.

He turned suddenly, his move spinning him to the right. It took him away from the muzzle of the weapon at his back. Bolan completed his turn, hands reaching to grab for the SMG—a 9 mm Uzi. He slid in behind his guard, left arm encircling the man's throat, his right clamping over the guy's trigger hand. The soldier slid his finger through the trigger guard, pulling back. The SMG crackled with full-auto fire, Bolan directing the stream in the direction of Kirov and his phalanx of protectors. One went down with a torso stitched through with 9 mm slugs. He toppled backward, crying out in shock. Bolan nudged the SMG, spraying the area with more fire. He saw Kirov driven to his knees as a burst cut through his long coat and cored into his right hip and thigh, shattering bone as it went through. The trafficker dropped his knife, grabbing for his leg as he crumpled to the floor.

The armed man behind Seminov had turned in Bolan's direction the moment he saw the American's move. He began to yell a warning—too late—then yanked his own SMG away from Seminov, pulling it down on Bolan.

Seminov threw a quick glance at the American, saw his one chance and reacted with speed surprising for a man of his bulk. He twisted, his left arm swinging down to deflect the guard's weapon. He followed through with a hefty right fist that cracked savagely against his adversary's jaw. The crippling blow lifted the trafficker off his feet. He let out a strangled cry from a shattered jaw, spitting blood and teeth. Seminov drove in at him. His left knee hammered into the guard's groin, crushing everything in its path. The screaming guard went down on his knees, all thoughts of hostility driven from his mind by the white-hot pain engulfing his lower body. Seminov snatched the SMG from the man's hands and turned the weapon on him. The short burst drove the trafficker to the hangar floor in a mist of red.

Kirov was down, bloodied and in agony, and one of his protectors was sprawled dead on the concrete.

The survivors scattered as Bolan kept up his autoburst. The guard he held was struggling against the restricting hold over his throat, attempting to draw air into his lungs, but failing. The soldier had a hold on his collar and used it to increase his grip. As he pulled ever tighter, the inside of his wrist pressed hard against the jugular, cutting off the flow of blood to the brain. The move was based on a judo choke hold. Once the blood stopped flowing the victim would lose consciousness very quickly if the pressure wasn't released. Bolan held until the guard went limp, then let go, backing up as he sent further bursts at the scattering traffickers.

Seminov added his own fire, facing the enemy gunners as he retreated after Bolan. They ducked behind the parked vehicles. The closest was the SUV they had been brought in. Seminov yanked open the driver's door and hauled himself inside. He had spotted the key still in place.

Bolan sprinted around to the passenger side and climbed in as the Russian fired up the powerful engine, dropped into gear and rammed his foot against the accelerator. The 4×4 fishtailed as the tires fought to get a grip, Seminov hauling the wheel around and hitting one of the armed traffickers as the guy recklessly stepped out from behind the cop's own Toyota. The impact picked the guy up and threw him across the floor, arms and legs flailing as he tried to control his movements.

"Can you get us out of here, Valentine?"

The Russian glanced across at his American companion.

"Is a duck waterproof?"

Seminov swung the wheel and pushed the 4×4 toward the exit.

The sound of autofire reached them, followed by the dull clang of bullets peppering the body of the SUV. A window blew in, showering the men with fragments. Seminov pulled the wheel left and right, taking the speeding vehicle on an erratic course. More autofire followed them.

Bolan picked up the Uzi Seminov had thrown down. He twisted in his seat, picking a target as one of Trechenko's men broke from cover, racing in at an angle so he could get a clear shot. Bolan wound down his window, dropping the Uzi's barrel against the frame. He tracked the running man, stroked the trigger and sent a short burst into the closing figure. The impact slapped the trafficker into the concrete hard, twisting him over and over.

Bolan jerked himself away from the side window as Seminov took the car through the hangar doors, close enough to scrape paint from the side of the vehicle. Then they were in the clear, but only for seconds. Glancing back over his shoulder, the soldier saw Kirov's other 4×4 come screeching out of the building. It fell in behind them, closing fast as the powerful engine gained speed.

Bolan scanned the way ahead, seeking something, anything, they could use to slow their pursuer. He spotted the rows of heavy fuel drums they had passed on the way in, recalling the neat lines of stacked barrels.

"In there, Valentine. Between the drums."

The Russian cop offered no protest. He swung the vehicle and took it down the narrow alley formed by the stacked drums. Bolan leaned out the window and fired off short bursts that punctured the drums as they hurtled past. He was trying a desperate move in the face of a deadly threat from Kirov's gunmen. Glancing in the rearview mirror, he saw the 4×4 in pursuit. The heavy utility vehicle was hitting drums as it sped in pursuit, toppling the lines on either side, the driver intent on staying in sight of his quarry.

"Give me your lighter," Bolan said.

Seminov passed it across without a word.

"Soon as you clear the stacks, let me out."

Seminov grunted, concentrating on his driving. He held the 4×4 steady as they neared the end of the stacks....

Bolan grabbed the door handle, letting the Uzi hang from its shoulder strap. He freed the door, held it shut. Seminov swung the wheel as they cleared the drums, taking the 4×4 in a sliding turn. Bolan let the door swing open and jumped clear. He raised the Uzi and triggered more shots, puncturing the drums. The smell of fuel reached his nostrils as he fired up Seminov's lighter. Dropping to a crouch, the soldier touched the flame to the pooling fuel and saw the vapor ignite. He pulled himself away the instant the fuel caught, almost losing his balance as the volatile liquid flash fired. In seconds the gap between the drums was lost in a writhing, swelling burst of fire. It traveled back along the lines of drums, enveloping the pursuing 4×4.

Seminov pulled the SUV clear, braking hard and exiting the vehicle. Bolan himself had moved away from the blazing drums, waving off Seminov.

One of the drums blew in that instant, the dull thump of the blast trailing after the fiery object as it launched off the ground, clearing the SUV and hitting the ground in a splash of fire.

The other SUV burst from the raging tunnel of fire, a shivering tail of flame engulfing its back end. It roared past Bolan, forcing him to step away from the heat. Smoldering tires left black marks on the concrete as it jerked to a badly controlled stop yards beyond Bolan and Seminov. Doors were booted open and a pair of coughing figures stumbled from the smoke-filled interior, only to be met by the withering fire from Bolan's Uzi. The traffickers were decimated in those savage moments, bodies jerking under the impact of 9 mm slugs. As the last man went down, Bolan's Uzi cycled dry.

"Let's go!" Bolan yelled. "The rest of those drums are going to blow."

They raced across to the 4×4 and piled in. Seminov took them across the concrete apron. Behind them the stacked drums began to blow, many of them exploding skyward, rising on fiery tails. Others simply burst apart, spreading the gallons of fuel across the concrete.

"You think Trechenko has insurance?" Bolan asked.

"On the field?"

"On his life."

"Why do you ask?"

"It's time to cancel his policy."

Seminov swung the SUV around and drove back toward the hangar. The day was breaking with surprising speed now, the details of the area becoming more distinct with each passing minute.

"What is this place?" Bolan asked.

"An old military airstrip," Seminov said. "Abandoned years ago. Ideal for Trechenko's operations."

"Could he fly in and out from here? It would be handy for flights to his meetings."

Seminov smiled. "In the new Russia anything is possible if you have either of two things—the right connections or enough money. In Trechenko's case he will have both."

Seminov braked and brought the 4×4 to a stop yards away from the hangar. They exited the vehicle and paused at the door.

The silence was broken by the sound of a man moaning.

Bolan indicated for Seminov to take the right side. As soon as the Russian cop was in position, Bolan stepped inside, moving to his left, tight against the inside wall where the shadows were able to conceal him.

Across the hangar he saw Seminov's Toyota. The bodies of Kirov's gunners lay where they had fallen. Blood stained their clothing and pooled on the concrete floor.

Kirov lay feet away from where he had fallen. The trafficker lay in a hunched position, one leg straight out from his body. He was nursing his broken hip and thigh with hands that were red with the blood pulsing heavily from his wounds. His expensive clothes were soaked with more blood and filth from crawling across the dirty floor.

Seminov appeared on Bolan's right. He moved quickly across to where Kishka lay, kneeling beside the man. He bent over the informant and Bolan heard him speaking in Russian.

As he walked in Kirov's direction, Bolan picked up one of the abandoned Uzis.

The man glanced up as Bolan's shadow fell over him. His ashen face glistened with sweat. When he recognized Bolan his expression changed to one of sheer terror.

"What are you going to do?"

"It's already done."

"You must help me."

"A little while ago you were letting me know you were a big man, Kirov. How you had money and the power to make things happen. What happened?"

"You shot me. Now you have to help me. I can give you anything you want."

"Like you help the addicts? The kids you sell your poison to? That kind of help?"

"For God's sake, man, I'm bleeding and I can't stop it. I could die."

"I'll hold you to that," Bolan growled.

Seminov beckoned and the soldier joined him.

"Kishka is dead, but he talked first."

"A touch of conscience?"

Seminov smiled. "If it was, I didn't give him the satisfaction of absolution."

"He tell you anything useful?"

"He told me that my undercover man *has* been exposed and is a prisoner of the Afghan traffickers. He heard Kirov talking about it to his men."

"Do we know where?"

"An old outpost. Something left behind when the British were involved in Afghanistan. The traffickers use it to store drugs and weapons."

"It's a start."

"Belasko, what are you thinking?"

"That your man may have good information on the organization, the people behind this alliance. He might even be able to confirm your suspicions."

"If he's in the hands of the traffickers, any information he has is no use."

"Unless we bring him home."

"Are you serious?"

"Valentine, I didn't come here to make notes. If this deal goes through, we're going to have a chain that stretches from here to Jamaica, and on to my country. Right now another drug trail is something we don't need."

"There are some Afghans who helped Benin. They are against the traffickers because of the problems they have brought to the area. If you can get to their location they might be able to show you where Benin is being held."

"Sounds promising."

Bolan crossed to where the dead traffickers lay and searched them until he located his Beretta. As he straightened, the sound of a single shot rang out. Bolan turned to see Seminov standing over the still body of Kirov, his autopistol in his hand.

"He isn't suffering now," the Russian cop said. "It's more than he would do for any of the poor bastards dying from using his drugs."

There was no arguing that point, Bolan realized, so he didn't say a word.

CHAPTER FOUR

Tajikistan-Afghanistan Border

Mack Bolan watched the robed figures detach from the rocky terrain and walk forward to meet him. He had stepped out of *Dragon Slayer,* Stony Man's state-of-the-art combat chopper, twenty minutes earlier. The moment Bolan had gone EVA Jack Grimaldi had powered the helicopter into the bright morning, turning back for the border base fifteen miles away. Grimaldi's brief was to remain on standby until he received the call from Bolan for tactical backup.

Bolan was in full combat mode. Blacksuit and harness, complete with Beretta and Desert Eagle, a sheathed knife on his belt and a 9 mm Uzi hanging from a shoulder strap. He also had four fragmentation grenades clipped to the harness. He carried extra ammunition and wore a compact backpack. Clipped to his belt was a transceiver that worked via a satcom link.

The Executioner was kitted out for war, and he was ready physically and mentally.

Valentine Seminov had engineered a message through to the Afghans who were operating in the area and who had been in contact with Benin before his capture. The Russian cop had spoken with the leader of the group, asking then to assist Bolan. He had been given a grudging assurance that they would give the American some help, but they hadn't said *how* much. It would be down to Bolan to convince them of his sincerity.

He studied the tight group of six as it approached. They were clad in the traditional garb of the Afghan mountain people—thick tunics and trousers, leather boots. Each man also wore a robe held closed by a thick leather belt. Their headgear was a flat, peakless wool hat, or a turban with loose ends that could be used to cover the face. It was clothing worn to protect them from the inhospitable environment. The mountainous terrain at that time of year was hot and dry, plagued by recurring winds that filled the air with dust and seared the skin.

Bolan's visitors were also well armed. Each man carried a Russian-made Kalashnikov, either an AK-47 or an AKM. The autorifles were old but well cared for, and Bolan had no doubts as to their efficiency. The Afghan warriors prized their weapons and barely if ever let them out of their sight. Bolan noted, too, that the men also carried curved daggers, sheathed and tucked behind the wide leather belts around their waists.

Bolan remained where he was as the Afghans closed in. One moved slightly ahead of the others, his gaze fixed on Bolan. He was an impressive figure, taller than his companions. His brown face was bearded, eyes hard and bright as they regarded the figure of the tall American. He stopped a few feet away, still looking Bolan over.

"You are Belasko?" he asked.

Bolan nodded.

"I am Jahangar Arik. I have been asked to assist you. Can you tell me why I should?"

"I was told you are a man of great honor. That the name of Jahangar Arik is known far and wide as a warrior of great compassion. One who would not allow a brave man to die." Bolan slipped a small photograph from his pocket. It was a head shot of Benin that Seminov had provided. "This man. Do you know him?"

Arik nodded, considering Bolan's words as he stroked the tip of his beard. He turned his head to look at his companions, speaking to them in his own tongue. They inclined their heads, the moves giving away little of what they were thinking. After a few moments Arik turned back to Bolan.

"What a man says can have many meanings. I have learned to listen to the true feeling behind a man's words. Whether he speaks falsely, or from the heart. And I have also heard what Commander Seminov feels about you."

"He's a good man."

Arik pursed his lips, considering what Bolan had just said.

"Yes, a good man—for a Russian," he said grudgingly.

"Do you still consider them enemies?"

"Twenty-five years ago the Russians invaded Afghanistan. You remember that, Belasko? They did terrible things to my people while they occupied the country. Now we are trying to cooperate with each other to fight a common enemy. Is that not strange?"

"These drug traffickers are the enemy of every right-minded person, Jahangar Arik. What they do affects us all. The drugs they trade poison everyone and everything they touch. In America, the misery these drugs create is there to see. People lie and cheat to get the money for their drugs. They steal and murder. Families are destroyed. Even children are being drawn into the drug culture. Fed when they are young so that they grow up needing more. And the circle continues. It never stops, and it never will unless something is done."

"We try to destroy the trade, but the traffickers have wealth and the threat of violence on their side. Those who refuse to work for them are killed as examples to the others. Others look upon the money they are offered and go the way of the traffickers."

"It's a war that has to be fought," Bolan said.

"And why do you do it, Belasko?"

"Because I can't stand by and let it go on without doing something."

"But you are one man."

"I have my victories."

"And how long will you make this war against them?"

"As long as it takes. As long as Jahangar Arik fights to free *his* country."

Arik smiled, teeth gleaming white against his dark beard.

"I like that answer, Belasko." He slapped Bolan on the shoulder. "Come, we have a long walk to our camp."

Arik called out to his men, waving a hand in Bolan's direction, and one by one the Afghans approached Bolan and shook his hand.

THEY WALKED for three hours under the hard sweep of the sky, the heat pressing down on them. Arik gave Bolan a long scarf to fashion a turban to protect him from the sun. The loose folds covered Bolan's mouth, helping to filter out some of the dust that their traveling raised. They stopped twice during the trek, once simply to rest, the second time to rest and to drink a little water from a thin spring issuing from a rock face. The water was cold and fresh. Bolan took only a little, past experience having taught him that taking in too much in such conditions could lead to harm.

Watching the American and his careful drinking, Jahangar Arik nodded to himself. His assessment of this quiet, confident man had been correct. Belasko was no novice. The way he handled himself, aware of his surroundings, the terrain that had to be respected, spoke of a man who was no stranger to this life.

The true warrior's life.

THEY REACHED the concealed camp in early afternoon. There was no outward indication of any site. Bolan might have missed it himself if he hadn't been watching the way the Afghans moved in concert toward a seemingly barren section of the undulating landscape of rock and dust. He saw them dip into a shallow slope that led to a deep overhang of solid rock and at the last moment he saw the dark opening that took them inside the rock.

It was a cave entrance. Arik led the way. Almost immediately they were sheltered from the merciless heat. The thick walls of the cave brought a coolness that was close to being pleasant. They walked in for a few hundred yards, the light fading behind them until they were in near darkness. Then they rounded a bend in the cave formation and stepped into a larger cave. It rose above them for almost sixty feet, the smooth walls coming together at the apex to form a cone shape. There was an opening in the ceiling that allowed light to dispel the gloom.

"Welcome to our base," Arik said.

Bolan saw blankets, a small cache of supplies, boxes of ammunition. There was a small fire pit in the center of the cave, with a scattering of utensils. Hanging from outcroppings were animal-skin water bags.

"How long have you used this place?" Bolan asked.

"We have used it for almost two years. Overall it has been used by various groups for many years. When the Russians were here it was a base for the mujahideen. From here they would go out and kill the Soviets, then hide here until the searches were over. The Russians never found them. My father told me many tales of the battles he had."

"He was with the mujahideen?"

"Oh, yes. A great fighter."

"And now his son carries the war to another enemy of Afghanistan."

"I thank you for that. Tell me, Belasko, are you as skilled with your weapons as you are with words?"

"Yes," Bolan said simply, making no great show of his admittance.

Arik pointed to the holstered Beretta.

"May I see this gun?"

Bolan held out the 93-R. The Afghan took and examined it carefully. His men gathered around, as well. Bolan explained the workings of the Beretta—its 3-round capability, the under-barrel handle that could be locked down to give greater control over the weapon when it was cycling 3-round bursts. The Afghans were impressed by the pistol, reaching out to touch it, fingers stroking the smooth metal.

"It is a powerful weapon," Arik said, returning the pistol to Bolan. He held up his own Kalashnikov. "This was my father's own. He took it from the first Russian he killed. Then used it to kill many more. Belasko, do you know what my father used to shoot the Russian?"

"I'd say a Lee-Enfield .303."

Arik nodded.

"Yes. A .303 that had been in my family for generations. It hangs on the wall in my home now. And it still works well. But now we use the Kalashnikov because it has more firepower and it is easy to get ammunition for."

While one of his men prepared food, Arik and Bolan squatted on the floor of the cave and discussed the coming operation to free Benin. Arik produced a rolled-up drawing of the outpost that had become the base for the drug-trafficking group that was the focus of Bolan's attention.

"These traffickers have been very busy for months now. Ever since they started dealing with the foreigners who come to see them."

"What do you know about them?"

"We have seen them only from a distance. It was Benin who told us where they came from and what he suspected they were doing. Is it true they are making a pact between them? To take drugs to this Jamaica and then to send them to your country?"

"Simply put, that's it. The Afghans supply the drugs to the Russian Mafia. They ship them out to Jamaica, and a man named Deacon Marley handles the smuggling into the U.S."

"And from this they will make great fortunes."

"By the time the heroin reaches America, its value will have gone up many times. The only ones who suffer are your people who grow the poppy flowers and the users in my country. All the others just sit back and watch the money roll in."

"These Russian gangsters are bringing only misery to my country. While they buy the drugs my people will grow the poppy flowers for them. The Russians grow rich and my people starve. When we should be building for the future this trafficking is crippling Afghanistan. Have we not suffered enough? Our history is one of sadness. The people made to live under foreign powers. The British. The Russians. Then we were made to live under Taliban rule. When the Americans and the British came and broke the power of the Taliban we hoped things would change." Arik allowed himself a gentle smile. "Look at us, Belasko. Are we free now? I am not sure. It seems we have exchanged one war for another."

"At least you are fighting for something you believe in, Jahangar Arik. To rid your country of these traffickers. Afghans and Russians."

"A difficult war to win, Belasko. Cut off one supply and they open another."

"I've seen that a lot," Bolan said. "There's no quick end to it, but it has to be done."

They returned to the sketch map.

"This is the north approach," Arik explained. "Here is the main gate, and to the right is the cell block where Benin is being held. It is built against the northern wall and has been dug out of the stone so the block is below ground level. On the south side of the compound and partway along the west wall are living quarters and the place where they store the heroin until the trucks come to carry it across the border into Russia. Here is the southeast corner of the compound. In the stone building they keep their armament. Ammunition."

"How do they get their power? Lights. Electricity."

"Here against the east wall is a generator that makes the electricity."

"How many men?"

"They come and go. Lately more than usual because of their visitors. I would say you will find at least two dozen. Maybe less. Maybe more."

Bolan studied the sketch until he had the details committed to memory. His prime objective was to get Benin out of captivity. He would deal with the uncertain odds against him as and when necessary. He was hoping that Benin was still alive. The encounter with Trechenko's traffickers at the abandoned airfield outside Moscow had been akin to the first shots in an upcoming war. If news of that skirmish had been relayed to this outpost as a warning that hostilities had been started, the Afghan traffickers might have decided to eliminate Benin, giving them one less enemy to worry about. Bolan realized he was extrapolating, maybe worrying over something that hadn't happened yet. He simply hoped that Seminov's undercover man hadn't paid the ultimate price for his courage.

"Jahangar Arik, you have brought me this far. All I ask is for you to take me to this place. Show me where Benin is being held so I can free him. Do this for me, and I'll be in your debt."

The Afghani studied Bolan, and it was plain to see he was considering something of great importance.

"Let me talk with my men."

Arik withdrew to the far side of the cave to confer with his group, leaving Bolan on his own.

He waited patiently, aware that he was on a time limit. The possibility of Benin's life ending became stronger as time passed. The thought troubled Bolan but in his current situation there was little he could do until he had a location for the outpost.

Arik finally crossed the cave and squatted in front of Bolan.

"Belasko, we will take you to the den of these traffickers. And we will also help you to free the Russian Benin. This we have agreed to do."

THEY ATE SPARINGLY, then rested through the heat of the afternoon, conserving their energy for the walk to the outpost. Even though the Afghans had only a small food supply, they shared it with Bolan. Afterward Arik sat with him and they talked.

Jahangar Arik was a man who both loved his country and carried a sadness concerning its past and future. He had let go of the bitter memories, realizing that they would do nothing but cloud his mind and his judgment. He looked to a future where Afghanistan might yet step out from the shadows of what had been, and into better times.

"I understand the difficulties of this world, Belasko. The path to peace is a hard one. There are great pits to fall into. Each is like a snare that tethers you with the ropes of hatred and deceit. To free yourself you must overcome everything holding you back—those who smile upon you, with a dagger behind their back, the ones who want only to steal away the good years of our children. It would be so easy to let it happen. To do nothing. But this would not be the true way. I would consider myself less than a man if I fell to this. So here I am, with my brothers. And we will fight this new enemy as my father fought the Russian army."

"Then the enemies of Afghanistan have much to fear."

THEY REACHED their destination just as dawn slid pale slivers of light across the rocky slopes, pushing away the deep shadows. In silence they settled themselves in rocky depressions, where they could look down on the decades-old outpost that had been first built by defenders of the Afghan nation and was now being used by traffickers in heroin.

Bolan shared a spot with Arik. He studied the outpost below, guided by his companion's low tones as the Afghan described the place.

"Are they getting ready to ship out a consignment of heroin?" Bolan asked.

Three dusty trucks were being loaded with sacks brought from one of the buildings inside the outpost.

"Those trucks will travel along the drug trail into Tajikistan, protected by the traffickers. At the border there are guards who can be bribed. The traffickers know them and pay them great amounts of money."

Bolan watched the activity for a while. He was

considering a thought that grew rapidly into a feasible plan.

He removed his backpack and took out the powerful transceiver that would connect him, by sat link, to Jack Grimaldi in *Dragon Slayer*. As soon as he heard the pickup, he keyed the transmit button.

"You hearing me, Jack?"

"Loud and clear, Sarge. You ready for pickup?"

"Not yet. But I need you to create a distraction for me." Bolan outlined the situation.

"Activate the homing signal so I can locate you." Grimaldi waited until he received the incoming. "Okay, Sarge, I've got you."

"How long?"

"I can be over you in thirty."

"Jack, I need those trucks hit while they're still close to the outpost."

"Understood."

JACK GRIMALDI GLANCED at the computer screen readout, checking the pulsing GPS homing signal beaming down from the satcom link. He adjusted course slightly to bring the combat chopper back on line. His time readout told him he had twenty-six minutes' flying time recorded, which meant he was not far from his rendezvous with Mack Bolan.

Grimaldi keyed his microphone and made contact.

"*Dragon Slayer* to Infiltrator. ETA closing fast."

"Targets have just left the outpost. Moving north,

about a mile from the outpost. Three trucks. Plain canvas tops, dark green paint jobs."

"Let me try and locate."

Grimaldi employed all of *Dragon Slayer*'s electronic surveillance equipment as he swooped in low over the rocky, bleached-out Afghan landscape. There was a warning clatter from one of the sensors. The Stony Man pilot switched to visual and his infrared imaging brought him three hazy shapes, in line, moving slowly. Taking the chopper down in a high-speed descent, Grimaldi made out the winding ribbon of the narrow, uneven road snaking through the undulating landscape. He made a low-level flyby and was able to make out the trio of slow-moving vehicles.

Green cabs and bodies with dun-colored canvas sheeting over the backs.

"Target confirmation, Sarge," he reported, then added, "I see the outpost, too. Just over a mile behind them. Higher elevation."

"And I'm on higher ground beyond the south wall. I see you, Jack."

"What do you want me to do?"

"Take out the road ahead first. Let's make it hard for these bastards. Then deal with the trucks. I don't want a grain of that heroin left."

"Understood, Sarge."

Grimaldi cut the contact. He powered *Dragon Slayer* over the convoy, then brought the helicopter around. Hovering, he activated his weapons system and tapped in for high-explosive missiles. Grimaldi used his helmet's slave system to lock on to target and fired off two missiles. He saw the thin vapor trails as the deadly rockets leaped from the stub wing pods and curved in toward the distant road. They struck no more than twenty feet in front of the lead truck. The twin blasts threw up a cloud of debris and dust, obscuring Grimaldi's vision. As the debris pattered to earth and the dust drifted away, Grimaldi saw that his missiles had opened a wide crater. One side of the road had caved in and slid down the steep slope that bordered it. Rock from the higher side was still tumbling down the gap.

Men exited the trucks as they slammed to a stop. Grimaldi saw winks of flame from the autoweapons they carried as they fired up at *Dragon Slayer*. They only wasted their ammunition. Grimaldi was well out of range. He didn't reject the thought that they might have rocket launchers, so he took *Dragon Slayer* away in a wide curve that brought him up in the rear of the convoy.

The Stony Man pilot didn't waste time. He made target acquisition and loosed off more missiles. The first one hit the rear truck, blowing it apart in a maelstrom of flame and smoke. Grimaldi did the same with trucks one and two. He backed away, his last image one of total devastation. The convoy had been reduced to blazing wrecks.

Grimaldi keyed his transmit button. "Job done, Sarge. Standing by."

BOLAN AND ARIK'S group started moving the moment they heard the first missile explosion. By the time Grimaldi called in to confirm he had dealt with the trucks, Bolan was crouching at the base of the south wall.

"We will go around and make for the gates," Arik said. "They will have to open them to go and see what has happened."

Bolan nodded. The moment Arik and his men moved off, the soldier tackled the wall. He slung his Uzi, leaving his hands free for the climb. The rough wall offered plenty of hand and footholds, and he made the top of the wall with little difficulty. He remained just below the top of the wall, waiting as he picked up the soft footfalls of a patrolling sentry, only moving when the man had passed by and made his way farther along the walkway. Hauling himself up and over, Bolan paused to check the position of the sentry. The man had his back to the soldier as he stared out across the interior compound of the outpost, one hand shielding his eyes as he looked in the direction of the smoke rising from the convoy's position. He was shouting questions to others down below. The sentry carried a Kalashnikov rifle, slung muzzle down.

Bolan eased himself over the top of the wall, landing softly. He moved quickly behind the sentry, a darkclad bringer of death, swift and silent.

He clamped a big hand over the sentry's mouth, shutting off any possible cry of alarm. He caught hold of the man's robe and spun him to face him, shoving the sentry against the wall, his hand still over the man's mouth. The Ka-bar fighting knife in Bolan's hand flashed briefly in the sunlight before the blade slipped in under the ribs and into the heart. Bolan pushed hard with the knife, twisting the blade.

The sentry stiffened against the keen stab of pain. He struggled, but Bolan had his feet braced apart and leaned his whole weight against him to prevent any break for freedom. The hand over the sentry's mouth remained in place, pushing the man's head back, bending the upper body over the top edge of the wall. He maintained the pressure until the sentry ceased to struggle and became limp. Bolan lowered him to the walkway, drew the knife from the body and put it away. He checked to see if there were any other guards on the walkway, but there were none. Most of the traffickers were down below, already heading for the gates, too busy wondering what had happened outside.

With the Uzi in his hands Bolan moved along the walkway, keeping low behind the inner wall until he reached the stone steps that led down into the compound itself.

He conjured up an image of the map Jahangar Arik had shown him. He knew where he had to go. The row of cells, housed within a narrow run, was to his left, no more than twenty feet from the base of the steps. Bolan went down the steps fast, flattening against the wall at the bottom.

He could see the cell block from where he stood.

Bolan scanned the area he had to cross. It was open ground. He took a breath and broke away from the base of the steps, reaching the cell block without any challenge.

Bolan sprinted to the door set in the end wall of the cell block, checking the thick wooden handle. The door opened without resistance. Bolan eased it open wide enough so he could slip inside, pulling it shut behind him. A long passage stretched before him, with a door similar to the one Bolan had used set in the far end wall. A powerful stench reached Bolan's nostrils. The smell of human waste. The air was heavy with it. Bolan moved forward, seeing the steps that led deeper into the cell block. The level was around six feet below ground, dimly lit by oil lamps hanging from hooks in the stone wall. In the sooty light Bolan saw the line of barred cells. He counted seven of them, six with their doors open. Bolan moved along the line.

He found Benin in the fifth cell. The Russian OCD officer stared at Bolan through the barred door. His clothing was torn, dirty and bloodied. Heavy bruises marred his face, and his torn lips were bloodstained. He spoke in Russian.

"My English is better," Bolan said.

"Who are you?"

"Seminov's good fairy."

Benin, despite his haggard condition, managed to smile. He crossed to the cell door.

"Do you have a magic spell that will open this damn door?"

Bolan shook his head.

"No magic. Just this." He indicated the Uzi. "Get away from the door."

Benin backed to the far corner of the cell as Bolan raised the Uzi and fired off a short burst that blew the ancient lock into jagged shards. He dragged the chain away from the bars and kicked open the door.

"Let's go," Bolan said.

Benin followed close on Bolan's heels. They made for the door. The soldier paused long enough to hand Benin the Desert Eagle, then pointed to the distant steps leading to the walkway.

"Our way out. Don't stop for anything."

They sprinted in the direction of the steps. Bolan took out his transceiver.

"*Dragon Slayer*, I need a pickup at the top of the north wall. Soon as."

"You got it."

"And Jack, we have friendlies outside the wall. Six of them."

"I see them."

Raised voices reached them; armed figures began to gather in the compound.

"Keep going!" Bolan yelled.

He paused and freed a grenade from his harness, pulled the pin, counted down, then hurled the grenade across the compound. It bounced across the ground, coming to rest in front of a trio of armed figures. The blast put two of them down and left a third clutching a bloody arm and shoulder. Autoweapons opened up, slugs whacking the ground well short of Bolan and Benin. The soldier kept close behind the Russian undercover man, laying down two more grenades that scattered the armed traffickers.

The suddenness of Bolan's appearance had caught the enemy off guard. They had been so certain of their immunity that they had allowed themselves to relax, to the point where they had lost their edge. The unexplained occurrence with the truck convoy and now this attack on the outpost had created a great deal of confusion.

To add to the general unrest there was a sudden crackle of gunfire from beyond the open gate.

Arik and his group, Bolan realized.

AUTOFIRE REACHED from the shadows behind them, bullets chipping the stone wall they were running alongside.

Bolan used his last grenade to scatter the unseen shooters, then fell in behind Benin. They went up the steps fast.

A figure appeared at the top, laying down a burst of autofire that threw chips of stone against Benin's legs. The Russian cop didn't hesitate. He raised his pistol, firing on the move, and hit the shooter in the left knee. The trafficker gave a shrill cry, falling back as his knee gave way, blood quickly soaking his pants. As Benin stepped over the downed man, he turned the gun on him and hit him with a double tap in the skull. The guy flopped back.

Bolan saw the kill. He kept moving himself, shouting for Benin to head along the walkway.

At Bolan's back, boots thudded on the steps. The soldier turned, crouching, and opened up with the Uzi, catching his pursuers as they reached the halfway position on the steps. His burst cored into their exposed bodies, wrenching them off their feet and toppling them over the edge, bodies twisting as they fell.

As Bolan hit the walkway, he heard the familiar whine of *Dragon Slayer*'s turboshaft engines. The thwack of the rotors filled the air as the sleek black combat chopper swept in to hover just short of the wall.

"Come on, Jack," Bolan said into his transceiver. "What do expect us to do, jump?"

Grimaldi was smiling as he eased the helicopter up to the wall and opened the passenger hatch. Benin stepped up on the top of the wall and took the short step into the chopper. Bolan was close behind. The moment his feet hit the deck Grimaldi pulled the machine away from the wall and closed the hatch. It sealed shut with a solid thump.

Bolan joined Grimaldi, dropping into the bodyform seat next to the pilot.

"Lay down some firepower into that place."

"You want demolition?"

"Sounds good," Bolan said. "Go to it."

Grimaldi brought *Dragon Slayer* in a wide circle. He lined up on the walled outpost and loosed off a number of HE missiles that streaked in across the compound and brought buildings down in clouds of smoke and balls of fire. One hit produced an even larger explosion, streaks of fire arcing into the sky and filling the area with orange-and-white flame.

"That will be their munitions cache," Benin called from the passenger compartment.

Grimaldi put the chopper back on line and flattened the remaining buildings.

Bolan tapped him on the shoulder.

"Put me down."

Grimaldi did as he was asked. The second the hatch opened Bolan jumped out, waving for Grimaldi to clear, then sprinted across to where Arik and his men were moving in on the open gate. The Afghans were firing as they went, driving the dazed traffickers back inside the compound.

Bolan's Uzi joined the battle, taking out one man as he broke free from the smoke-filled compound. The trafficker went down in a loose sprawl, his body trembling in the last throes of death.

Arik led his men through the gate, weapons firing as they dealt with the remaining traffickers. There was no hesitation as they cornered the survivors and cut them down. Bolan followed them in and stood beside the Afghans as they surveyed the devastation Grimaldi's missiles had caused.

"This will give them much to think about," Arik said. "What we have destroyed today will set them back many months. The new crop of poppies will not be ready for harvesting for weeks. And I have plans to do something about that."

"Will they come after you?"

Arik shrugged. "There is no one alive here to say *who* did this. If any survived from the trucks, all they saw was a helicopter. From where?" The Afghan smiled. "Confusion in our enemies' midst, Belasko. Sometimes as deadly as a bullet. Yes?"

"It helps." Bolan keyed the transceiver and spoke to Grimaldi.

He watched the combat chopper circle in and make a landing, the rotor wash dragging up dust. The hatch opened and Benin stepped out. He crossed over to where Bolan stood with the Afghans.

"Good to see you again, Jahangar Arik."

Arik merely inclined his head.

Benin walked to the open gate and stared in at the smoking remains of the outpost.

"This will piss them off," he said with great relish. He jerked a thumb in the direction of *Dragon Slayer.* "If we had half a dozen of those we could wipe out every poppy field in Afghanistan." He glanced at Bolan. "Any chance?"

"That is a one-off," the American said.

"Pity," Benin said.

Bolan turned to Arik. "We should all get out of here. Leave this for the rest of the traffickers to see."

Arik raised his hands. "A short acquaintance, Belasko. One I will remember for a long time."

"As I will." Bolan held out his hand, gripping Arik's tightly. "Fight your war well."

"And you, Belasko. Go with God at your side."

Bolan turned to leave, then paused. He removed the shoulder rig that held the Beretta 93-R, adding his remaining 9 mm clips, and handed it to Arik.

"For you, Jahangar Arik."

They clasped hands over the holstered weapon, warriors sharing a moment that both of them would remember. Arik stepped back, nodding briefly, then turned and rejoined his men.

Bolan crossed to *Dragon Slayer* and climbed inside, Benin close behind. The hatch slammed shut and Grimaldi powered the chopper off the ground. Bolan peered through the canopy as the aircraft rose into the air.

The figures of Arik and his men dwindled swiftly out of his vision as Grimaldi tapped in the request for a return course. The onboard computer fed the data to the chopper, and *Dragon Slayer* corrected herself for the flight back toward the border.

"Nice gesture," Grimaldi said. "Giving him the Beretta."

"He deserved it."

"Lucky I have a spare in the locker back there. The way you go through ordnance, the arms industry will never go out of business."

Bolan smiled as he went to the locker and opened it up. There was a selection of pistols. He removed a Beretta 93-R, loaded mags and a shoulder rig. He slipped on the rig as he moved into the crew cabin to join Benin. The Russian undercover cop opened his weary eyes as he became aware of Bolan's presence.

"Thanks for the loan of the gun," he said, passing the Desert Eagle back.

"You feel well enough to talk?"

"I'm not at my best but as long as I can sit here, why not?"

"Can you identify anyone involved in this alliance?"

"How long do you have?"

"I'm listening."

"The man in charge of the Afghan operation is Razak Khan. Last I heard—before they jumped me—he was out of the country. It seems he's on a visit to Moscow to discuss arrangements for future shipments of heroin. The shipping is to be handled by Trechenko. Did Valentine tell you about him?"

"We already had a run-in with Trechenko's crew—his enforcer, a guy named Kirov. Now the *late* Kirov."

Benin smiled. "Not all bad news, then."

Bolan told the Russian cop what had happened since his first meeting with Seminov in Paris and their involvement with Trechenko's people in Moscow.

"This connection with the American DEA team," Bolan asked. "Any thoughts?"

"What I can tell you is that Khan did have a visitor a week or so back. I didn't get to see him. But I did hear him speak, and he had an American accent. I couldn't place it. The only thing I can tell you is he had a jokey way of saying money when it came up in the conversation. I remember Khan getting annoyed each time he did it. He didn't think the American was taking the matter seriously enough. This American told him to remember who was smoothing the way for them, so he should stop pushing him around."

"So how did this American speak?"

"He kept saying *mo-ne-y.* Sort of stretching the word."

Bolan knew exactly what Benin meant. He had heard the exact same inflection himself back in Moscow when he had been speaking with the DEA team.

Specifically when he had been talking to Asa Randal.

Jamaica

"WHO WAS THAT?"

Trechenko's man, Oleg, replaced the handset, glancing around with an uncomfortable expression on his broad face.

"A call from home."

"About?"

"The Afghan outpost has been hit. Leveled to the ground. The latest shipment destroyed."

Trechenko was silent for a moment. "What about Benin?"

"He was taken away after the attack. Alive."

"First Kirov gets himself killed. Now this. What the fuck is happening, Oleg?"

Oleg shook his shaved head. He was a big man, his

powerful body hard and toned under the dark suit and white shirt. Right now he was wishing he was anywhere but here.

It became very quiet in the room. The only sound came from the TV set and even that was down to a whisper.

Oleg remained where he was. He stayed silent, too, not wanting to add fuel to Trechenko's anger. He knew his employer was angry because he wasn't saying a word. It was Trechenko's way. Before he exploded into one of his rages he became silent. Motionless except for his eyes. They showed his feelings, betraying what was going on beneath the surface. The calm before the violent storm.

"I can do without this. I came here to finalize the deal with Marley. How the fuck can I tell him we have the best organization available when all this is happening?"

Oleg cleared his throat. He had sensed a reluctance to anger in Trechenko's voice. Something was tempering his rage. He was thinking with his head instead of his heart, and considering the odds. Oleg decided it was time for him to speak up and take the opportunity to advance his own position.

Trechenko turned his head and eyed the formidable figure. Oleg was one of his best. Always obedient. Ever present and good at his job. Now it appeared he had something to say.

"Oleg?"

"Give me a team of my choosing, boss, and I'll handle this. We can deal with it so you can make your deal. If Marley gets curious, we tell him it's a local problem and we're taking care of it. Show him we won't stand for this kind of thing."

It was the longest speech Oleg had ever made. Apart from that it was the best thing Trechenko had heard all day. He stood and crossed over to where Oleg stood. He placed his hands on Oleg's wide shoulders and gripped him hard.

"Are you sure you want to take this on?"

Oleg nodded.

"Very well. Pick your team. Take the plane back to Moscow and find out what's happening. I'll call and tell Vashti you have my go-ahead. He'll give you anything you want. Money. Weapons. Vehicles. I don't care what this costs. I just want it settled. This has to be the work of Seminov and that damn American. I want them dead. And the OCD team, as well. The same goes for anyone who is tied to them. Wipe them out. It's time we started to make things happen. I have to handle these damn Colombians to keep this deal going with Marley. Time to clean house at home so we don't have problems there."

"Leave it to me."

"Oleg, don't forget Benin. Wherever they have him, get to him. Kill that little bastard."

Oleg crossed to the door, pausing. "I won't let you down. If I do, it will be because I'm dead myself."

As soon as Oleg had gone, Trechenko picked up the phone and punched in a number that would connect him to his man in Moscow.

"Vashti? Oleg is on his way back. Give him anything he wants. Cash money. Guns. Cars. Any backup he needs. Yes, he has my approval. He has something to do that won't wait. Good. Yes, I heard. It's why Oleg is coming back."

Trechenko put down the phone and crossed to the bar that stood in the corner of the spacious lounge. He spent a little time pouring himself a drink and lighting up one of the large Cuban cigars he enjoyed so much.

He had sampled Marley's generosity a number of times before. If the supply deal went as it should, Trechenko anticipated making regular visits to the Caribbean island. As much as he loved Moscow, the long, cold winters depressed him. Once the supply trail was set up he realized he could easily run it from somewhere far away from the dull Russian environment. All he needed was a telephone and a computer system.

What was the point in making all his money if he couldn't enjoy it?

Trechenko turned his thoughts to the other pressing matter: the Colombian interference in his plans to make his Caribbean connection. He was aware of their fearsome reputation when it came to dealing with challenges to their supremacy in the drug-trafficking monopoly. He accepted they weren't amateurs, as they had proved when they took out the team he had sent in to cripple Salazar's dock facility. Trechenko was still smarting over that, but the occurrence made no difference to his plans. The only nagging thought was how Salazar had known the Russians were coming. Had someone informed him? If so, who? It was another matter Trechenko needed to look into. Salazar was in for a surprise if he thought Trechenko was going to roll over and die. He would hit back hard if they made any further overtures. The Colombian would find that Trechenko had plenty to throw at him.

The war was far from over.

CHAPTER FIVE

Moscow

The battered van, its dry springs creaking as it turned the corner, came to a stop close to the outside wall of the building that housed the OCD unit. The rattling engine died as the driver switched it off. He pushed open his door and climbed out, pulling his thick topcoat around him as he leaned inside the van, fiddling with something for a moment before he closed the driver's door and locked it. He turned up the collar of his coat, hunching his shoulders against the chill, and shuffled away from the van, ignoring the pedestrians moving by him. He made his way across to the far side of the street. He took his time, attracting little attention as he moved through the morning crowds. He finally vanished from sight down a narrow side alley between buildings on the far side of the street. What no one else saw was the dark-colored Saab that was parked at the curb close to where he emerged at the far end of the alley. The van driver climbed in, pulling the Saab's rear door shut. The car eased away from the curb and merged intro traffic.

Exactly six minutes after the driver had walked away from it, the parked van erupted in a powerful explosion that totally destroyed it and the OCD building. The van had contained enough plastic explosives to turn the building into a pile of shattered bricks and twisted steel. The initial blast was accompanied by a ball of flame that ripped through the structure and engulfed most of the ground and first floors. The rumble of the explosion merged with the tumbling piles of brick and stone as the building caved in on itself. Fractured gas pipes threw streams of fire into the already burning mass. Electric cables crackled and hissed as they brushed against metal. Escaping water was turned to steam by the heat. The building that had stood for almost three-quarters of a century was destroyed in minutes.

The blast radius was wide enough to engulf a number of pedestrians on the street. Seven people died and at least a dozen others received serious injuries. Flying debris and glass accounted for a number of additional casualties.

Twenty minutes after the bomb blast, a car on the outskirts of the city was wrecked in a blast that killed all three occupants. By the time emergency services reached the blazing remains of the car, the three men inside the vehicle had been burned beyond recognition.

Valentine Seminov heard about the explosion less

than five minutes after it happened. He was on his way to his office when a message came through on his cell phone. He listened to the report in stunned silence, then closed the connection and sat back in his seat. His driver, glancing in the rearview mirror, saw the expression on his superior's face.

"Commander? Is something wrong?"

"Our building has been destroyed. From what I have just been told it sounds like a bomb."

"Our people?"

"Too early to count casualties. Yorgi, get us there as quickly as possible. I don't care how many speeding violations you make."

The driver nodded. He flicked on the siren, switched on all his lights and rammed his foot hard against the gas pedal.

By the time Seminov reached the site, there were already two fire trucks in attendance. Firefighters were playing high-pressure jets of water at the burning pile of rubble. The local police were in attendance, and an ambulance screeched to a halt seconds after Seminov got out of his car. Uniformed police officers barred his way until Seminov showed them his ID.

"Sorry, Commander," a young patrolman said. "Do you have any idea how many people might have been inside?"

Seminov shook his head. "I was on my way in when I heard. As to numbers, it could be anything from six to a dozen. The nature of our work means we come and go all the time. This time of day it's likely the whole team was there."

One of the firefighters joined them. Seminov identified himself.

"Any idea how it happened?"

The firefighter pointed to the crushed and flattened mass of metal partially buried at the base of the building.

"From the way the explosion went I'd say that was your source. Most likely a vehicle packed with high explosives parked close to the base for maximum damage."

"Have you found any survivors?"

"No. But as soon as it's safe we'll search. We have dead pedestrians out here, and a lot of walking wounded. Whatever the explosive was it had a lot of energy. What a mess."

"Listen, there could be some Americans in there. A team was here working with us. There were three of them in the group. I'll call their hotel to see how many were supposed to be in the department this morning."

Seminov speed-dialed the DEA's hotel. He asked to be put through to Reckard's room. The desk clerk informed him that Martin Reckard and his team had left the hotel together more than an hour ago. Seminov thanked him and entered Reckard's cell phone number. The call was rejected. He tried the numbers of all the other DEA people and received the same response.

Call rejected.

Seminov looked at the phone in his hand.

Had the entire DEA team been in the department building? He hoped not.

Moving away from the activity, Seminov dialed the number that would connect him to Mike Belasko's hotel room. He hoped the American was able to receive his call. Belasko had returned from his Afghanistan trip the night before, along with Benin. The undercover man had been taken to a hospital to have his injuries seen to and had been kept in overnight. Belasko had gone to his hotel. Seminov had planned to meet him there for a briefing that morning.

BOLAN HEARD his room phone as he came out of the bathroom. He picked it up and heard Seminov's greeting. There was something in the Russian's tone that warned Bolan he wasn't about to receive good news.

"Valentine? What's wrong?"

"We have been hit. A powerful explosion has destroyed the OCD building."

"Casualties?"

"Too early to tell. No one can get inside the wreckage yet. But the explosion has killed a number of pedestrians who were passing at the time. Others have been injured. One other thing. Reckard and his team had left the hotel an hour before the explosion. They were most likely on their way to the building, so they could have been inside when the explosion took place. I've tried all their cell phone numbers. No one answered."

"Valentine, think. Who would do this? Getting hold of a van load of high explosives can't be easy even in Moscow."

"This sounds like the kind of thing Trechenko would do. It has all the signs of a Mob hit."

"So where would Trechenko get the explosives?"

"I'll tell you when I pick you up."

Seminov arrived within a half hour. As Bolan joined him in the rear of the car, the Russian cop was giving orders to his driver. The car moved off as soon as Bolan had settled himself.

"Where are we heading?"

"You will see. Something else has happened. I had a call a few minutes ago about another bomb explosion on the city outskirts. A car bomb. There were three men inside. No identification yet, but I do have confirmation that the DEA car was not in the vicinity of the OCD building."

SEMINOV'S CAR SPED through the city streets. Rain had started to fall now, the tires throwing up silver spray as it hit wide puddles. Bolan noticed the landscape changing as they headed out of the city center. Buildings started to become shabbier, and they moved into an industrial area. Seminov spoke to his driver, then turned to Bolan.

"This man we are going to see is well-known to the OCD. It has never been proved, but we suspect him of being involved with the Mafia. And, which is interesting, information has been picked up more than once that Belnikov has done deals with ex-military trading in black-market ordnance. Weapons and explosives. A supplier of all things illegal, our Sasha Belnikov. A familiar problem, though. He has connections. Always the best lawyer money can buy, and there is some higher protection looking after him, as well. You understand?"

Bolan understood only too well.

His past was littered with the shadows of men who were *connected,* who used the law to shield them from prosecution while they carried on with their particular trade. They lied and cheated and murdered and maimed, and got away with it because they had influence. That was until they came under Bolan's scrutiny. His way of dealing with them was direct and final. He revoked their license to operate and paid them off in kind. Here, now, in the Russian capital, Mack Bolan's style of retribution was about to be meted out.

Seminov's car rolled to a halt at the side of a service road. The driver cut the engine and they sat staring out through the rain-streaked windows. Across the road was one of the industrial plants. Beyond metal fencing lay a large scrap metal yard. Towering above rusting piles of metal were a couple of crane arms. One had a huge circular electromagnet suspended by its steel cables, the other a steel-jawed grab.

"This is run by Sasha Belnikov," Seminov said. "The man is an animal. Believe me, I am not being flippant. Belnikov is a vicious individual. Be warned. Do not allow this man any advantage, and never turn your back on him."

"I'll remember that."

Seminov leaned forward and spoke to his driver.

"Yorgi, call central dispatch. Tell them I need some standby backup. A couple of cars out here now. Fully armed teams. No excuses. After what happened this morning I am in a less than charitable mood. You stay in the car and wait here. Keep your distance but be ready to come if I signal."

Yorgi picked up the handset and began to make contact.

"I suppose it would be naive of me to imagine you coming out unarmed, Belasko?"

"It would, Valentine."

"Then shall I introduce you to one of Moscow's undesirables?"

"Why not?"

Seminov opened his door and stepped out of the car, followed by Bolan. Both men turned up the collars of their coats against the rain as they crossed the road and approached the open gates of the scrap yard.

"In the U.S., most yards like this have large, hungry dogs on chains waiting for unwelcome visitors."

"Sasha has his own mad dog. This one has two legs. There, he's coming to ask us in from the rain."

The large man coming across the yard had to have been over six feet. Bolan's first impression had the guy as wide as he was tall. Despite the rain, the massive figure was clad in dark trousers and a thin T-shirt, already plastered to his impressive torso. He wore massive combat boots, and Bolan was sure he felt the ground tremble underfoot each time the big man took a step.

"His name is Gregin."

"You think he'll stay and sit if I call him?"

"Uh-uh."

Gregin blocked their way. He had a rounded, heavy-boned face; his skull was completely bald. He studied Bolan and Seminov with eyes that were too small for his face.

Seminov spoke to him. Surprisingly Gregin's reply was delivered in a soft, literate tone, and Bolan could follow most of what was being said.

"He says that Belnikov will be pleased to see us," Seminov said, glancing at Bolan. "He knows we're here."

"No one knew we were coming until a couple of minutes ago," Bolan said. "Valentine, there are two options. Yorgi either called it in as you ordered and someone at central is on Belnikov's payroll and tipped him off…"

"Or?"

"Or Yorgi called Belnikov from the car."

Seminov drew a deep breath. He glanced over his shoulder, muttering under his breath.

"Somehow I don't think we'll be getting that backup."

"Oh?"

Bolan glanced back and saw that Yorgi had moved the car across the road. Now it was straddling the gate and Yorgi himself was out of the vehicle, reaching for something out of the open trunk.

"This gets better by the damn minute, Valentine," Bolan said.

Yorgi straightened, cradling an SMG in his arms. He stepped around the rear of the car and walked in through the gates.

Seminov called out to him. The reply he got made the Russian cop bellow in anger. Yorgi raised the SMG, the muzzle swinging in Seminov's direction.

Bolan dropped to a semicrouch, his hand already under his leather coat, sliding the Beretta 93-R free. His finger pushed the selector to 3-round-burst mode. He tracked in on Yorgi, the pistol in a two-handed grip. He stroked the trigger and placed the triburst into Yorgi's chest, over the heart. The 9 mm slugs cored in hard and fast. Yorgi was spun around, the SMG firing as his finger twitched against the trigger. Bolan's second burst caught him between the shoulders, pitching him face-down on the wet, muddy ground where he lay in a shuddering sprawl.

With Yorgi down Bolan turned back to face Gregin.

There was a rush of sound, and Gregin's huge bulk slammed into Bolan. The sheer weight behind it drove the Executioner backward. He almost lost his footing. Before he could bring the Beretta back on line, Gregin punched him across the side of his head. The blow put Bolan on his back. For a few seconds he was out, dazed, the world spinning. He had the presence of mind to roll, his scrambled senses warning him that Gregin was still around. He heard a grunt of annoyance, felt the thump as Gregin's huge boot slammed against the ground. Bolan blinked his eyes, shook his head to dispel the mush that seemed to have taken over from his brain. He twisted again, getting his legs under him and started to push upright.

The double crash of shots penetrated the mist and cleared Bolan's head. Half upright he looked around and saw Gregin flat on the ground. One side of his large, bald skull had gone. In its place was a bloody wound that exposed shattered bone and brain matter. Gregin was kicking slightly, his massive boots scraping furrows in the soggy mud.

Seminov was standing just beyond the downed man, his Stechkin pistol in his hand. He glanced at Bolan.

"Are you badly hurt?"

"Nothing a few headache pills wouldn't cure."

"Belnikov."

They made for the single door that allowed entry into the workshop. Bolan kicked it open. The metal door came off one hinge as it swung in. Seminov barged through, Bolan covering his back.

The interior was as untidy as the yard itself. It was a cluttered mess of metal scrap and processing machines. The floor underfoot was nothing more than hard-packed earth.

On the right of where they had entered was an office. Bolan spotted a couple of dark shapes close by. They were moving away from the office, into the open, and they were armed.

"Valentine! On your right," Bolan yelled.

One of the armed men opened fire. Seminov cried out and fell.

Bolan returned fire, the Beretta spitting out its triburst. His shots were close enough to make the shooter pull back. Bolan flicked the selector switch to single shot. He dropped behind a thick metal drum and scanned the area where he had seen the two armed men. They had pulled into cover now.

Bolan heard Seminov groan. "You hurt?"

"Only my dignity. I tripped and fell."

"Well, stay down. We have a pair of shooters over by the offices."

"Let them show themselves."

Autofire erupted, twin bursts hammering at the cover Bolan had taken. As the shooting died, the soldier heard rapid footsteps as someone broke from his own cover. He peered around the edge of the drum, caught sight of a dark shape cutting across the floor of the workshop.

Seminov's pistol thundered twice. The running man grunted and pitched facedown onto the floor, his weapon clattering as it spilled from his hands.

Using the distraction, Bolan moved to the far right, circling the obstructing piles of metal and closed rapidly in on the office. He heard a man's voice call out in Russian to his companion. There was no reply. The man called again. This time Bolan was able to pinpoint the man's position. He dropped low under a low beam and as he came out the other side he saw the second shooter.

The man was hunched over, peering in the direction his partner had gone. Bolan raised the Beretta and stroked the trigger, the single 9 mm slug catching the man in the side of the head. He went down without a sound.

Bolan remained where he was, listening and waiting. When he was satisfied he backtracked until he was standing beside the metal drum he had earlier used as cover.

"Valentine?"

"I'm here."

Seminov's voice came from close by. Bolan turned and saw the Russian cop crouched in the shadows only a few feet away. He was trying to remove an oily mark on his coat.

"Is Moscow like this all the time?" Bolan asked.

"Strangely, only since you showed up."

They checked out the workshop. Seminov's man was down with two bullets lodged in his upper chest. By the time they reached him he had lost a great deal of blood. He was conscious, but only just.

"Belnikov," Seminov said.

"He doesn't look so mean now."

Seminov shrugged. He knelt beside the wounded man, reaching out to pick up the SMG the man had dropped. Belnikov stared at him with eyes still capable of an intense ferocity. He mumbled something that made Seminov shrug. The Russian cop turned to Bolan, who had heard the exchange.

"He says we are dead men. We might have stopped him but we won't stop the alliance."

"Alliance? That's a fancy word for a bunch of low-life drug pushers. My Russian isn't great. Tell him something for me, Valentine. Tell him Trechenko and Marley are the ones going down. Afghanistan was only the start."

Bolan turned away and crossed to the office. He picked up the SMG Belnikov's partner had dropped. Carrying it in his left hand, he continued on into the large, open room that comprised the office for Belnikov's scrap business.

It was untidy. There was only one desk, with a large, battered leather swivel chair behind it. The top of the desk was covered in paperwork, files, empty bottles, mugs stained from oily hands. There were two telephones, and in one corner a computer workstation that had seen better days. The floor space of the office was almost a scrap heap itself. There were metal scraps, tool chests and bulging filing cabinets. The walls were covered with technical charts, out-of-date calendars and dozens of foldouts of naked women, many of them in extreme pornographic poses.

Bolan stood just inside the door, wondering where to start. He had a couple of problems to overcome. The first was that he couldn't read Russian. Secondly, he wasn't absolutely certain what he was looking for.

If Belnikov was responsible for supplying the explosives used in the two bomb blasts, would he keep the stuff lying around in his office? It was more likely it was stored somewhere on site.

Bolan moved through the office, crossing to the desk. He placed the SMG on the desk while he sifted through the papers piled there. Nothing made much sense. He turned away and saw Seminov standing at the door.

"He's dead."

"He say anything?"

"Nothing I want to repeat. He just kept telling me we couldn't win. Mean to the last."

Bolan paced the office, the floor creaking as he moved about. He glanced back at Seminov and saw the Russian peering at the office floor.

"What?"

"Walk back toward me."

Bolan did so and paused himself. His footsteps had altered in tone. The creak of wood was replaced by a duller, solid sound. Seminov joined him and they kicked aside the scattered rubbish littering the floor. Bolan went on his knees, brushing at the dirt. He spotted the faint line where dust had sifted down through a thin gap, followed it around until he could see the square shape of a false section of the wooden floor. Bolan stood and searched the office until he located a heavy screwdriver. He pushed the tip of the blade into the gap, feeling the wood give. Putting on more pressure, Bolan worked at the gap until the wood splintered and he was able to prize away a wedge. Beneath the wood was a metal plate. Using the screwdriver blade again, Bolan eased the plate up until there was enough space for him and Seminov to grasp the edge of the plate and raise it. The metal swung upward on concealed hinges to expose concrete steps leading to a basement area. When the plate had reached a certain point lights clicked on below.

"Very thoughtful," Seminov said.

Bolan went down the steps and stood surveying Belnikov's explosives store. He saw blocks of plastique, fuses and detonators. The amount of explosives was frightening. Farther along the basement Bolan saw wooden cases that held Uzis, Kalashnikovs, handguns. Boxes of grenades. Rocket launchers.

"Valentine, there's enough explosives here to demolish half of Moscow."

"I'll make this call myself," Seminov said as Bolan climbed out of the basement.

Bolan was about to reply when he turned and looked up at the office's single window, set just below ceiling level. He held up a hand for Seminov to stay silent.

The faint sound came again. A whisper of movement. No more than a scrape of boot leather against metal.

"Is there a back way out of here?" Bolan asked.

"On the far side of the workshop. Why?"

"We're not alone, Valentine."

They moved out of the office and into the semidark of the sprawling workshop. Seminov led the way, Bolan on his heels. They weaved in and out of the piled metal, having to change course a couple of times when their path was blocked by some obstruction. They had reached over the halfway mark when a booming voice, amplified by electronics, filled the area.

"For your benefit, Belasko, this is in English," the accented voice said. "Both of you should give up now. While you are still able. Surrender, and I will see to it your deaths are quick. Painless I cannot guarantee because I have never experienced death myself. But carry on this resistance and you will not die happy."

"And I thought Russians had no sense of humor," Bolan said. "You know this joker?"

"No."

Now they could hear the thump of heavy boots on the hard earth floor of the workshop. The rattle of weapons.

Seminov put a hand on Bolan's shoulder. He pointed to a narrow opening, a door that would allow them to exit the building. The door was ajar. Seminov began to move toward it. Bolan caught his sleeve and held him back, pointing with the Beretta. Seminov followed the trajectory.

Just inside the door were wet footprints, turned to the left.

Bolan tapped Seminov on the shoulder, indicating he move back. As the Russian followed his suggestion, the soldier made a wide loop to the left himself, staying behind a high stack of metal bins. He would have preferred to take his time, knowing that there were others coming up on their rear. Right now there was little room for finesse.

The end of the stack loomed. Bolan rounded the last bin and saw the dark-clad figure waiting by the workshop wall. The man was wielding a Kalashnikov, trained on the partly open door.

Bolan raised the 93-R and put a single slug into the man's skull, the impact rapping his head against the corrugated-steel wall. The would-be assassin fell to his knees, then toppled to the ground. Bolan snatched up the guy's discarded Kalashnikov, noting that there was a taped double mag in place.

"Valentine," he said as he reached the door. Seminov stepped into view. "Let's go," Bolan said.

They slipped out through the door, moving to the right, Seminov in the lead because he seemed to have knowledge of the scrap yard from previous visits. They had barely reached the front end of the workshop when a raised voice reached them. Someone began to yell orders.

"This way," the Russian said.

He splashed his way through puddles and small rivulets of streaming water. The rain was coming down harder now, bouncing off the piled metal and creating a fine mist as it bounced off hard surfaces.

An autoweapon opened up, coming in from their far right. Bullets whined and clanged off metal. Others kicked up muddy geysers. All the shots fell well short of Bolan and Seminov.

More gunfire came from somewhere closer. Bolan felt the slugs pound the earth no more than a few feet from him.

The soldier stopped short, turning at the waist, and brought up the Kalashnikov. His target stood atop a metal tank, outlined against the rainy backdrop, and brought the muzzle on-line, gaining target acquisition and held for a heartbeat before he touched the trigger once, twice and a final time. His target stepped back, faltering, then appeared to deflate before dropping onto the tank and sliding to the ground.

"Valentine, watch yourself," Bolan yelled as another figure rose from cover.

The Russian cop spotted the potential shooter in the same instant; they fired together. The enemy gunman was blown off his feet. The stricken man crashed to the ground, partially submerged in an oily puddle.

As they hurried past the downed shooter, Seminov snatched up the guy's Kalashnikov. They reached the end of the stack of scrap metal. Peering around the pile, Bolan saw the distant entrance to the scrap yard. Seminov's car had been moved away from the gate and replaced by a dark-colored BMW. The car was standing just inside the entrance, facing the workshop, the engine idling. Vapor trickled from the exhaust, and the driver's door was open.

"Why don't they hold up a banner and invite us to try?" Seminov asked. He glanced at Bolan. The American didn't reply. Seminov could see him checking out the distance to the car.

"I know what you are thinking and I don't like it," Seminov said, disapproval in his voice. "You know it is crazy."

"We either make a run for it, or stay behind and fight off however many are behind us."

Seminov sighed. "You are right. Unfortunately."

"Head for the car. I'll provide interference."

Seminov shook his head at the insanity of the idea. He checked the Kalashnikov, stepped from cover and ran.

"Let's go."

They moved out together, skirting the workshop, angling in toward every patch of shadow they saw. The falling rain contributed in a way to providing extra cover. Their pursuers seemed to have momentarily missed them. Bolan knew it wouldn't last for long.

He was right.

They were partway across the open stretch of ground when armed men burst out of the workshop, guns up and tracking in.

"Valentine, keep moving," Bolan called.

The Executioner turned, his own weapon already up and ready. He touched the trigger, felt the Kalashnikov pull as it jacked out hard bursts of 7.62 mm slugs. His accurate fire caught the enemy on the run, spinning them off balance, bloody flesh and fragments of clothing bursting from the wound points. Hampered by their falling comrades the men following on were forced to change direction, losing their momentum, though only for seconds. It was enough to allow Bolan a second round of bursts, this time targeting the rear line. His shots hit hard, the AK's shots punching home with deadly effect. He kept up the offensive fire, pushing those still upright back inside the door. His fire ceased only for as long as it took to eject his spent mag and snap in the taped backup. He cocked the rifle, bringing it back into target acquisition as a single man chanced a look around the frame of the door. Bolan's snap shots took away the left side of his face in a minifragment of time and briefly filled the space around the guy with a fine red mist and bloody chunks of flesh and bone.

Seminov had almost reached the BMW when he spotted a figure leaning over the trunk, broad, with a heavy set to his shoulders and short neck. Seminov was sure he knew the man. He dismissed the thought instantly because there were far more important things to be concerned with.

He had seen the man jerk upright at the sound of Bolan's AK. Now the man raised himself to his full height, bringing his own weapon into view as he took a step around the rear of the car. It was obvious he hadn't seen Seminov yet because of the rain and the gloom. The Russian cop didn't allow that to hold him back. He brought up his own weapon and caught the man in his sights. He fired twice, aiming for the shoulder. He heard the man grunt as the bullets punched into him, then he went down, falling partway back behind the BMW.

Seminov rushed in quickly, not wanting to allow the man time to recover and go for his gun again. He had no reason to be concerned. Rounding the rear of the car, he saw the man flat on his back, his left shoulder and arm glistening with blood where Bolan's shots had hit. The man's gun lay feet away. The Russian cop bent and picked it up, throwing it into the distance after removing the twin mags. He crouched beside the wounded man and frisked him, finding a Makarov pistol, which he tucked into his coat pocket.

"Pushkin," Seminov said, recognizing his man. "Last time I saw you I suggested it was time you retired from this business. It appears you ignored my advice."

Seminov caught hold of Pushkin's coat and hauled him to his feet, ignoring the moans of agony. Pushkin's left arm hung loosely at his side. Seminov slammed him against the side of the BMW, reaching to open the rear door.

"Get inside."

Pushkin stared at him. His face was sickly white from shock. Blood was pulsing from the wounds in his shoulder and arm.

"You go to hell—"

Seminov lashed out with his free hand and clouted Pushkin across the back of his head.

"Inside now or I'll kill you where you stand."

Bolan appeared beside the BMW.

"Let's go," he said, glancing at Pushkin.

"We have a prisoner," Seminov replied and manhandled the moaning Pushkin into the rear seat, then climbed in beside him.

Bolan had settled himself in the driver's seat. He pulled his door shut and placed the Kalashnikov beside him. He released the brake and put the vehicle into reverse. He trod down on the gas pedal, sending the BMW into a tire-spinning surge. He held the bucking wheel as the heavy car went through the gateway, then swung the wheel, bringing the BMW in a half circle, slamming on the brakes once he was clear. Changing gears, Bolan sent the car forward along the road, away from the scrap yard.

Behind them a volley of autofire sounded. A few stray bullets clanged against the BMW's trunk.

"Straight on to the junction. Turn left, then first right," Seminov told him.

In the rear of the BMW Seminov had his pistol trained on Pushkin. He made no concessions to the fact the man was wounded and bleeding.

"This is Pushkin. Ex-military. Now he's a working man. He'll do anything if the money is right and as long as he can use his gun and hurt people. What we have here, Belasko, is scum. He's known to have associated with Trechenko. We have his criminal record in our OCD files."

Pushkin recovered enough to stare at Seminov.

"Not any more, you bastard. Not since we blew everything away."

Seminov prodded Pushkin's wounded arm hard with the muzzle of his pistol. The man groaned.

"I never fail to be amazed at the stupidity of the criminal mind."

"You can't prove anything."

"I heard, as well," Bolan said.

Pushkin gave a harsh laugh. "Who gives a shit what some American thinks?"

"Be interesting to find out who paid for today's exercise."

Seminov nodded.

"We can try to find out."

There was a pause.

"Mike?"

"Be fast getting that information, or let it hang."

"Why?"

"Because we have two cars on our tail, coming up damn fast."

Seminov turned to look out the rear window. "Pushkin's partners come to take him home."

Bolan hunched forward over the wheel, his foot keeping the gas pedal hard down.

"Not this trip. Nobody goes home today."

CHAPTER SIX

The road ahead was poorly maintained, full of ruts and potholes. Bolan had the BMW's headlights on full, the powerful beams lancing through the rainy mist. He could feel the big car rocking as it bounced over the uneven surface. He hung on to the wheel, managing to keep the vehicle on a straight course.

"Valentine, where does this bring us?"

"When we leave the industrial area it is only a minor road. There is nothing out there."

Bolan kept a check on the chase cars. They were moving up fast. Sooner or later they were going to get close enough for someone to open fire. He glanced right and left, but saw no avenue of escape. The industrial plants flashing by were starting to fade away, and almost before he knew it they were speeding along a straight road that was paralleled on both sides by open land, with only the occasional tree breaking the monotony.

CIRCLE OF DECEPTION   127

"Do you recall me saying I thought you were crazy?" Seminov said. "I think it is catching."

"You want to take the fight to them? Just what I was going to suggest."

Seminov made sure all their weapons were fully loaded. He passed back Bolan's Kalashnikov and Beretta. The Executioner was also carrying his Desert Eagle, holstered on his hip under his leather jacket.

"How are we going to do this?" Seminov asked.

"Plain and simple. Do what we can to disable those cars. And deal with the occupants."

"I don't want to ask how you intend to disable them."

Bolan's demonstration was simple and direct. He touched the brake, bringing the BMW's speed down at an alarming rate. Glancing back, Seminov saw one of the chase cars swerve violently as it almost rammed into the rear of the BMW. As it drew alongside, Bolan swung the wheel and trod on the gas pedal again, sending the heavy car into the side of the chase car. Metal impacted, sparks flying back in streams. The chase car lurched away from the BMW. It hit the edge of the road, tires squealing.

The car began to bounce wildly as it ran over the rough ground edging the road, the driver starting to lose control. Seminov felt himself thrown across the rear seat as Bolan swung the BMW back on track. He had barely regained his balance when the vehicle swerved again. Bolan had hauled the wheel around full circle, tapping the brakes and causing the car to fishtail. It went into a side skid, shuddering under the strain. Tires burned against the wet surface of the road. Bolan was working the wheel, alternately touching brakes and accelerator, throwing the BMW around until he had it facing in the other direction. As the car righted itself, Seminov looked over Bolan's shoulder and saw the second chase car. It was no more than twenty feet from them, slowing but still moving.

"You ready?"

Seminov grunted, sucking breath into his battered lungs. He felt the BMW slide then lurch to a rocking full stop. When he looked again Bolan had gone, his door wide open.

THE KALASHNIKOV WAS up and firing as Bolan reached the front of the BMW. He directed his aim at the advancing chase car. His first burst walked across the hood and into the windshield. The glass shattered, blown back into the faces of the two men in the front seats. They fell back, clutching bloody hands to their lacerated flesh. Bolan's follow-up burst punched into their throats and heads. He saw one of the rear passenger doors kick open, a heavily built, bald figure rolling out onto the ground. The soldier dropped the muzzle of the AK and caught the guy as he tried to regain his balance. The shots ripped away the lower part of the guy's left arm and hand, taking off three fingers. The injured gunner pushed away from the door, cradling his own weapon under his right arm as he tried to return fire. Bolan's Kalashnikov laid fire into the rear-door window, blowing the glass away before the 7.62 mm slugs hit the target in the chest and spun him away, blood streaming from his riddled body as he fell facedown on the road, twitching in fading agony and then into death.

Behind Bolan, the chase car he had sideswiped came to a sudden halt as it struck a hidden depression in the ground. The car rose, then dropped heavily. The front end lodged against the ground and the car stopped. The windshield shattered as the driver was thrown forward, the force taking him halfway across the crumpled hood, his head bloody and torn.

Seminov was up to the vehicle before the driver's body stopped moving. He laid a heavy burst of autofire into the car, angling the muzzle of the AK so it fired down through the rear-door window. The guy in the rear was flung across the width of the car, his body twisted against the far door, his body riddled with bullets. Moving closer, Seminov checked the interior. There had only been two gunners in the car.

Bolan closed in on the vehicle he had taken on. The two front passengers were dead, as was the man who had tried to escape via the rear door.

"Recognize any of them?" Bolan asked when Seminov joined him.

The cop viewed the bodies. "I know both in the other car. Only one here, the one you caught trying to get out. Name is Oleg. He was one of Trechenko's men. I would have expected him to be in Jamaica with his boss.

Maybe he got promoted. The two in the front are new to me. Extra soldiers hired for the job, perhaps. All the other known ones are associates of Trechenko."

Seminov went through the pockets of the dead men while Bolan returned to the BMW. He was standing watch over Pushkin when Seminov came back. The OCD man had a cell phone in his hand.

"Anything?"

Seminov didn't answer. He walked by Bolan and leaned in to drag the moaning Pushkin to the edge of the rear seat.

"Listen to me, you Georgian bastard. I want some answers, and I want them now."

Pushkin stared at him with dull eyes. Without warning, Seminov hit him. A brutal blow to the face that broke Pushkin's nose. Blood began to flow down the man's face, and he whimpered pathetically.

"Valentine, there's a better way."

"Really? Then tell me, Mike, what is the way? Maybe I should plant a bomb in the car and blow this pile of shit into little pieces, like his partners did to the OCD building. And your American friends from the DEA. Should I do that, Mike?"

Seminov was yelling now, enraged. Bolan could see that something was wrong. He grabbed Seminov by the shoulders, fingers digging in until the man was forced to respond.

"Tell me, Valentine. What is it?"

"I found this cell phone in Oleg's pocket. There were

stored numbers on it. And messages. One was from a man named Vashti. He works for Trechenko. The message was for Oleg. It was to inform him that Benin is dead. He was shot an hour ago in his hospital bed. Oleg's orders were to complete his contract on us and get back in time for a meeting tonight. The second message was to let someone else know about the meeting at Trechenko's country residence. Oleg was given a number to call."

"You recognized the number?"

"Oh, yes, I recognized the number. And it confirmed something I had discovered earlier. Why we have been having leaks from the OCD. It had nothing to do with any of my own men. No one in the OCD office. I was right when I said there was a leak. Only I was looking in the wrong direction."

"Valentine, are you going to tell me what's going on?"

"A damn conspiracy, that's what is going on, and we have been sucked into the middle. This whole mess has been rolling along right under our noses. And do you know who is up there with the damn traffickers? I'll tell you. Korsov. Commissioner Vladimir Korsov, section chief of the OCD. My own boss."

"You sure?"

"The bastard has been tracking us all along. No wonder they were waiting for us every time. They knew where we would be. Korsov knew every step we took. All he had to do was pick up a phone and set his dogs loose. You remember that telephone number we found on one of those French idiots who attacked us in Paris? I did some quiet checking on that number. I said it was a Moscow number. It belonged to a woman who has been associated with Korsov for some years. One of his mistresses. Our friend Korsov has big appetites for women, as well as money. I paid her a visit, and not a friendly one. At first she resisted but when she realized I was not fooling around she told me that Korsov has used her phone on a number of occasions to arrange things. She didn't like it, but Korsov had her scared into letting him do what he wanted. She wanted to get away from him, so I fixed it for her to leave the city."

"Can we be sure she was telling the truth? Maybe she just told you what you wanted to hear."

"Don't worry. I checked out everything she told me. And more. The phone records showed that calls had been made to Paris to a number registered to Dubois. There were also calls to Jamaica. Kingston, to be precise. An unlisted number. There were others, too. To a cell phone. I called your friend in the U.S. before I picked you up and he checked the number. It belongs to Asa Randal. The last call to him was this morning. And after the car bombing."

"Korsov can talk to the dead now," Bolan said. "If Randal is actually dead."

"One more thing. The woman heard Korsov holding conversations with a man called Marley. When I double-checked dates and times it was to the unlisted number in Kingston."

"And I'll guess we're talking Deacon Marley. Valentine, it's time to pay a house call. I'd say sometime late tonight."

Seminov used his cell phone to call the bomb squad, giving them the location of Belnikov's yard and warning them there might be resistance if any of Oleg's team had stayed behind.

THEY MADE a low-key return to Moscow, handing over Pushkin to the police. Then they drove to Bolan's hotel and collected his belongings. They had decided to go to Seminov's apartment. While the Russian made them a quick meal and hot tea, Bolan made a call to Leo Turrin, bringing him up to speed on developments. The telephone call, using the cell phone Bolan had in his luggage, took time to connect through the satcom system. Once the elaborate security clearance had been made, Turrin answered on the third ring. Bolan immediately brought him up to date on everything that had taken place.

"I want an in-depth check made on Korsov's financial background," Bolan began. "He isn't working with Trechenko out of the goodness of his heart. See if he's made any trips out of Russia."

"Somewhere like the Caribbean?"

"You catch on fast."

"I'm slow sometimes but I get there. We're looking into this car bombing of the DEA team. It's too convenient. And the timing doesn't link up. Randal can't be dead if he made that call. Doesn't make sense if Randal is our man. If he's working for Trechenko, why kill him?"

"A smoke screen. He'd know it'll take time to ID the bodies. Gives him a clear space to finalize his plan with Trechenko and then vanish. His mistake was making that call."

"Anything else I can do for you?"

"I figure if we get a result from visiting Trechenko's place tonight it might be time for me to move on."

"You feel a need for a sunnier environment?"

"Could be. It would be handy if I had backup on standby when I get there."

"I'll see to it flyboy will be on 24/7 alert, if and when you touch down."

"Thanks. Listen, the way things are working out we could have some serious security lapses in the DEA network. Run some quiet checks. Look for anything off the scale but don't rock the boat until you hear from me."

"You got it. Hey, you okay?"

"It's a little frosty out here, but I'll weather it."

They talked for a while longer, tying up Bolan's requests and to satisfy Turrin that his friend was okay.

After they had eaten, Seminov laid a number of photographs on the desk in front of Bolan. He went through them one by one, naming each individual. Bolan memorized faces and names. If things went the way they should, he was going to get up close and personal with some of those faces this very night.

ALTHOUGH TRECHENKO HAD an apartment in Moscow, his main home was well out of the city, in a secluded part of the countryside, surrounded by thick woodland. The large old house stood on the edge of a placid lake, surrounded by the forest. Some discreet checking by Seminov told them that Trechenko's man Vashti had left the city for the country residence that afternoon.

When Bolan arrived, with Seminov behind the wheel, heavy clouds had obscured the moon, plunging the landscape into near darkness. The conditions were ideal for what Bolan intended.

"I don't like the idea of you going in on your own," Seminov complained. "I'm not some raw recruit."

"No insult intended, Valentine, but I work best alone. It's what I do. And I need someone waiting to pick me up."

Seminov grumbled into the upturned collar of his thick coat. He didn't like the situation, but he was able to understand Bolan's reasoning.

"If things go wrong in there, I need someone free and clear who can tell it like it is. As long as Korsov can't link you to tonight, then we've got a chance."

"All right. So what do you want me to do?"

Bolan held up one of a pair of small transceivers from his equipment. He handed it to the Russian.

"We can keep in touch using these. Once I've gone, drive away. Get down the road and find somewhere to park, then wait until you hear from me. If all you hear is the alarm signal, get the hell back to town and call Turrin. He'll take it from there."

Seminov's expression showed he didn't favor that scenario.

"That's the worst case. I'm not intending to get caught. I want to get in there and find what I can about Trechenko and his link to Randal and whoever else they might have on their team."

Seminov watched as Bolan checked his Beretta and the Desert Eagle. His interest grew as the man went through the pockets on his combat harness.

"I can rest assured you are not going in quietly?"

Bolan looked up.

"Damn right. This is definitely a hard probe."

Bolan slipped out of the car and crossed the road, vanishing from sight in the shadows.

Seminov sat for a few moments, then started the car and drove away.

FROM WHERE he crouched in the darkness at the base of the wall fronting the property, Bolan watched the car's taillights fading in the gloom.

He spent some time checking out the area, searching the perimeter wall for any alarms. He found nothing, which didn't surprise him. Trechenko was a powerful man in his own world. He wouldn't be expecting that anyone would even dare to stand up to him, let alone invade his home. Bolan had often come across the arrogance of people like Trechenko. They believed their power rendered them invincible, immune to the normal laws of the land. That immunity had been reinforced by bringing in someone like Vladimir Korsov. The OCD section chief, supposedly working toward bringing down someone like Trechenko, was aiding the trafficker by sacrificing his own officers and using his influence and power to make himself rich.

Bolan was about to show Trechenko *and* Korsov they weren't immune.

Satisfied there wasn't anything that would announce his penetration of the grounds, Bolan scaled the rough wall and dropped lightly to the ground on the far side. He was surrounded by a tangle of untended undergrowth and trees growing in close formation. It helped him move across the property's frontage with comparative ease. Bolan moved slowly, pausing often to check his position and the possibility of patrolling guards. Trechenko might believe he was secure; Bolan was equally convinced he would have some internal protection.

Concealed behind a thick tree trunk Bolan assessed the large, stone, two-story house. The main entrance door, with a jutting porch flanked by carved headstones, had an armed hardman on duty. The guy was big, clad in dark clothing. His head was bare, pale hair cropped close to his heavy skull. His set features had the strong bone structure of the Slavic nation. He carried a gleaming SMG in his gloved hands.

Bolan freed the 93-R, setting it for single shot, then sat back and waited. His vigil was short as a second armed hardman came into view from his right. This one could have been a twin of the first if he hadn't been shorter in stature. The pair stood for a time, making conversation. The first man handed his companion a cigarette. They lit up and continued talking.

Bolan remained still. A lesser man might have taken his chance and made a move toward the house, but Bolan hadn't lived through as many missions as he had by being so reckless. He took his time. His reward came a minute or so later, when a third patrolling hardman came into sight from the soldier's left. He joined the first pair and they traded words for a few moments before parting company. The door man resumed his position while the other two backtracked, scanning the house and the immediate area.

Bolan made his move, staying well in the shadows of the trees as he paralleled the guy moving away to the left. The lights coming from inside the house illuminated the hardman as he paced his area. When he reached the extreme end of the house he paused, taking a transceiver from his jacket and speaking into it. After completing his conversation, he replaced the transceiver, then turned and began to move in the general direction of the tree line where Bolan crouched in concealment. The Executioner drew deeper into the shadows, putting the Beretta away. He opened one of the pockets in his blacksuit and took out a thin steel garrote, curling his fingers around the hardwood grips.

The approaching hardman made no attempt to conceal himself. Bolan could see and hear him coming closer. He flattened against a broad tree trunk and let the unsuspecting man walk by. Bolan slid around the tree and stepped up behind his quarry. He flipped the wire loop over the man's head, snapping the loop tight as it settled. The wire sank into unresisting flesh as Bolan increased the pressure. The hardman threw up his hands, his weapon falling to the ground at his feet. His fingers clawed uselessly at the wire. He was unable to get a grip because the wire had already sliced into his flesh, blood starting to bubble up around the loop. Bolan pushed his right knee into the small of the man's back, putting pressure on the spine as he yanked, bending the guy over his knee. As his air was cut off the hardman struggled, panic setting in. All that did was to speed the process. Harsh sounds came from his lips. He thrashed about, sheer terror washing over him, but the inevitable outcome had been signaled the moment Bolan applied the first pressure to the garrote, and it was over in a short time.

The Executioner lowered the dead man to the ground. He removed the garrote and put it away. Crouching beside the corpse, he checked its pockets and found the transceiver. He switched it off. The dropped SMG, an Uzi, provided Bolan with additional firepower. He located an extra magazine in a pouch clipped to the corpse's belt and slipped it into one of his blacksuit pockets.

Bolan headed back toward the house, checking that the door guard was still in place. He waited until he spotted the roving hardman, watched him round the end of the house, and sprinted from the trees, across the lawn and the drive, letting himself be swallowed by the shadows cast by the bulk of the house itself.

He could hear the hardman ahead of him. Bolan fell in behind the guy, tracking him like a second shadow.

A living, deadly shadow.

Bolan caught a glimpse of the man as he stopped to light another cigarette. He picked up the smell of tobacco. The hardman had taken time out to enjoy his smoke. It became his last.

Bolan struck from behind, coming in hard and fast. He reached over the guard's head, jamming the metal of the Uzi against the guy's throat, pulling him down to the ground. The cold metal of the SMG was pulled tight against the guard's flesh. As the man struggled Bolan flipped him over, facedown on the ground. He slammed a knee into the guy's back, holding him down as he pulled up with the Uzi. The hardman tried to scream, but all that came out was a bloody croak. Bolan increased the pressure, felt something give and heard a slight snapping sound. His victim went slack, body weight pulling him to the ground.

For the second time Bolan disabled a transceiver. And as before, he armed himself with another Uzi, taking the extra magazine for this one, as well. He slung the second Uzi from his shoulder and took a walk along the end wall of the house until he found a likely window.

Bolan peered through the glass and saw a dark room.

He checked out the window. Wood frame, sash type. He tried to raise the window; it was secure. Bolan used the butt of the Uzi to break the glass, then pulled the remainder from the frame one piece at a time, clearing it before swinging in over the sill and dropping to the carpeted floor inside. He crouched in the dark, ears straining to pick up any sound that might indicate he had been heard.

Nothing.

No sound from alarms, either.

Bolan figured he had just about had his share of good luck for one evening. He crossed the room to the door, turning the handle slowly. He cracked the door and stood to the side as he checked the exterior of the room.

A wide, tiled hall stretched toward the front of the house. Directly across from him was a wide wooden staircase leading to the upper floor. Lights were lit, illuminating the hall. Bolan heard sound from the far side of the hall, beyond the staircase. A dark-suited man appeared, pushing a wooden cart loaded with food and drink. Bolan eased through the door and flattened against the wall. He watched the man guide the food cart to a set of double doors, which were opened after the man knocked. Bolan caught a glimpse of a brightly lit room, indistinct figures moving around. He waited until the servant reappeared, taking the food cart back the way he had come.

Bolan checked the Uzi, then moved silently down the long hall in the direction of the double doors. As he got close, he could hear voices from inside the room. He could identify one. There was no way of telling how many others were in there.

At the doors Bolan reached for the handle, easing it until he felt the door free itself from the catch. Bolan let go of the handle, took hold of the Uzi and kicked the doors wide open. As they swung open, he stepped inside the room, moving to put his back to the inside wall, and covered the room's occupants with the Uzi.

The room fell quiet. It was broken by the chink of an ice cube in a glass. One of the doors Bolan had kicked open swung on a dry hinge.

"Enough of you understand English," Bolan said. "Someone close those doors."

Bolan wasn't surprised when Asa Randal moved into view. He crossed to the doors and pushed them shut.

"Put the bolt across, Randal."

The renegade DEA agent did as he was instructed.

"I knew you were more than you told us," he said.

"Coming from you that could almost be funny."

"Go to hell."

"I've been there. And you know what, Randal, you'll feel right at home."

"Belasko, do you think you're going to get out of here alive?"

"Like you managed to survive the car bomb that killed your team? If you can, so can I."

Bolan checked out the other occupants of the room. Behind a large desk at the far end of the room was the man Bolan knew as Vashti. Trechenko's second in command. Slender, thin faced, with a neat little goatee beard, Vashti looked like a bookkeeper. According to Seminov, the man dealt with Trechenko's finances. He stood now, staring at the weapon in Bolan's hands, reaching up to nervously adjust the steel-framed spectacles he wore. Bolan saw no threat from the man. Vashti might be deeply involved in a death-dealing business, but he was the kind who would never soil his own hands.

That description didn't apply to Vladimir Korsov, Seminov's superior in the OCD. He oozed open hostility. Bolan could recognize it in his eyes, even the curl of his lips. Korsov's arms hung at his sides. His hands were clenched into heavy fists, knuckles white from the pressure. Bolan wasn't surprised when he was the first to speak.

"Your countryman is correct. Just because you have chanced on us all gathered here does not mean you will profit from it."

"That's your game, isn't it, Korsov? Profit. It's what you people do. Make money. Export death and rake in the profit. Betray everyone around you. Kill anyone who gets in your way."

"Christ, Belasko, you'd think we invented the damn game," Randal said. "This has been going on so long no one can recall the start date."

"That's your justification? I'm damn sure Reckard and Tanberg will rest easy knowing that."

"The hell with you, Belasko. They had their chance.

Do you know how much I offered them to come in on this deal? Jesus, they just got all righteous about it. Left me no choice."

"So you took them for a ride? Planted a corpse to represent you and blew them away."

Randal grinned suddenly. "You don't know how easy it was to get hold of a body. That's where having friends like Vladimir helps."

"And Benin?"

The mention of Benin's name brought a reaction from one of the other men in the room.

Razak Khan. Seminov's information, to go with the photo, was that Khan was the chief trafficker from Afghanistan. It was his outpost and men Bolan had eliminated during his rescue of Benin.

The Afghan was a big man, running to fat under his Western clothing. He wore a suit that had to have come from one of the expensive salons in either London or Paris. His size didn't stop him from lunging at Bolan, huge hands reaching for the American's throat.

Randal yelled a warning, which was ignored by the Afghan.

Bolan sidestepped, using the solid weight of the Uzi to hit Khan alongside the head as he lumbered by. Khan grunted, tried to regain his balance, and Bolan hit him a second time. The trafficker went down on his knees, blood streaming down the side of his face and staining the collar of his white shirt and his suit.

Bolan pulled back, tracking the Uzi on the four men before him.

The final man who made up the group made his move. A solid Afghan, clad in black, Khan's bodyguard, had used his boss's move to go for the weapon he wore under his leather jacket.

Bolan caught the move in the corner of his eye, saw the bulky autopistol the bodyguard was sliding into view.

The muzzle of the Uzi swung around, Bolan's finger already on the trigger.

The bodyguard's pistol, free and clear, angled in Bolan's direction.

The burst of 9 mm rounds took the Afghan in the chest, coring through flesh and bone, the slugs tearing into his pumping heart. The guy went back without uttering a sound, colliding with a chair, and hit the floor with a solid thump.

"Randal, do something."

The high sound came from Vashti. He was pulling back from the desk, into the corner of the room, his thin hands moving about in front of his face as if he were warding off invisible blows.

Bolan remained calm, turning his Uzi back on Randal and Korsov. They were the ones who still posed threats. He knew the whole thing was going off the rails. Too much happening too soon. He had expected the probe to go hard, but he would have preferred to have stayed in full control. Bolan was a pragmatist, however, long taught in the tradition of best-laid plans going awry, and the only option was to try to stay on top when that did happen.

Fate had decreed otherwise.

No matter what Bolan might have expected, the actual events came out of left field, taking both him and his company by surprise.

The transceiver Bolan was carrying signaled an incoming call. Bolan took it out with his left hand.

"What?"

Seminov's voice sounded strained, his breathing fast. His message was simple and direct.

"Get out of there, Mike. Visitors on the way. Not friendly."

There was the sound of a shot. A second. Seminov groaned.

"Get out…"

The final warning came too late.

The windows to the room blew in under heavy shotgun fire. A hard force burst in, vaulting over the sills, fanning out across the room, weapons up and ready.

From elsewhere in the house Bolan heard a commotion. Shouting, the crash of doors and then the heavy boom of shotgun fire.

Bolan saw Vashti cowering in the corner, one arm extended as a shotgun was aimed in his direction. There was no hesitation, no explanation. The shooter triggered the weapon repeatedly, the close-range blasts literally shredding Vashti's body to bloody tatters. A final shot tore his head apart, leaving bloody debris on the wall behind him.

Razak Khan, still on his knees, was executed from behind, six blasts from the autoshotgun that opened his spine and blew out his organs before a seventh took off the back of his skull.

Aware of his own demise, Vladimir Korsov went for the gun holstered at his hip. He managed only to touch the grips before he was gunned down in as bloody a fashion as Vashti and Khan.

As the renegade cop fell to the floor in a gory sprawl, Mack Bolan leveled his Uzi and turned it on the closest shooter as the man tracked his weapon on the Executioner. He put a burst into the guy's body, knocking him to his knees, and was about to take out another when someone yelled out loud.

"Leave him. This one's mine."

Bolan knew the voice. He didn't have to second-guess. It was Asa Randal.

The cold, hard muzzle of a pistol was pushed against the side of Bolan's head. The gun was in Randal's hand. The DEA agent waved the shooters in, and Bolan was disarmed. Randal stepped back, keeping his weapon trained on the Executioner.

"Hey, Belasko, I bet you're wondering what the hell is going on, huh?"

"Whatever it is, you're doing a lot of jumping around. Who is it this time?"

"The guys I've been working for before I even came to Russia. We were trying to figure how we could get this Afghan-Russian-Jamaican alliance out of our hair.

Then I got offered this assignment here in Moscow, and it all fell into place. Like a dream, Belasko. The best wet dream I ever had."

"The Colombians?"

Randal laughed. "Yeah. Give the man a cigar."

Randal moved to the doors and unbolted them. They swung open to allow three more armed men to enter the room.

"This one comes with us," Randal said, indicating Bolan. "Belasko, I'm buying you a ticket to meet the head honcho. All the way to Colombia. You're a prize, pal, and I'm going to make the most of you."

Bolan's hands were cuffed behind his back with plastic strips and he was led out of the house. More bodies lay in the hall, resting in pools of blood that were spreading across the tiled floor. The front door was wide open. The man who had been guarding the front of the house lay on his back, throat cut. There were two 4×4s parked and waiting. Bolan was pushed in the direction of one, Randal close behind.

"It was handy, you dealing with the other guards," he said. "Your buddy Seminov took the hard way out," Randal said coolly.

He waved his gun in the direction of a body lying in the drive. In the half light Bolan recognized Seminov. Dark patches of blood were forming under the Russian's body.

Bolan was pushed into one of the 4×4s. Doors slammed, and the vehicles rolled away from Trechenko's house. As they turned onto the road, a series of heavy explosions sounded behind them. The house was engulfed by flames and thick smoke.

"He wasn't going to need it much longer, anyway," Randal said from the front seat. He turned to smile at Bolan. "Ain't life a bitch, Belasko? Ain't life a fucking bitch?"

CHAPTER SEVEN

Colombia

The second morning of Bolan's enforced stay at the dockside apartment he had visitors. He was on the balcony of his room, looking out across the bright water of the bay when he heard the sound of an approaching helicopter. He watched it fly in and settle on the concrete pad directly below his room. Four men climbed out, crossing the pad and moving to the building, where they vanished from his sight. He studied the chopper. If he got the chance, it might be his way out. He looked down at the stainless-steel manacle around his left ankle, which was connected to a long steel cable that was in turn secured to a plate bolted to the floor. It allowed him full access to the room and the attached bathroom.

Bolan had spent a long time inspecting the manacle and the cable before accepting there was no way he could free himself without the key. Once that was established he took the opportunity to relax and wait for whatever his captors had in store for him. Nothing had happened until this morning. With the arrival of the helicopter and its passengers, perhaps things would change.

Bolan sat down in one of the comfortable leather loungers, facing the door, and listened to the footsteps nearing his room.

Asa Randal entered the room first, moving to let Hermano Salazar come in next. Behind Salazar were two armed bodyguards, carrying Heckler & Koch MP-5s. They positioned themselves where they could see everyone in the room. One of them closed the door.

"So is there anything you need?" Randal asked.

Bolan rubbed his chin, feeling the thick stubble. "A shave and shower, but it's not desperate."

"Good job, pal, 'cause it ain't about to happen."

Randal appeared to be enjoying himself, grinning as he spoke.

"Does it do tricks, as well?" Bolan asked, glancing at Salazar. "Or haven't you got that far with him yet, Salazar?"

Randal lunged at Bolan, looping a wild swing that clipped the warrior's left cheek.

"Asa," Salazar snapped. "Leave it."

Randal drew back, breathing hard. His face was set, flushed with anger because he knew Bolan had seen the control Salazar had over the rogue DEA agent. Bolan's reference to a trained pet hadn't been far from the target. Here Salazar was master and Randal nothing more than an obedient servant.

Salazar turned his attention to his prisoner. He saw the American reach up to touch the bruise forming on his cheek. Apart from that Belasko remained calm, almost relaxed. In that brief appraisal he knew that Belasko was the better man. In a physical confrontation Randal wouldn't be able to stand up to the man. There was something about him that impressed the Colombian. A quiet self-assurance, stemming from inner control and pure confidence in himself. Belasko was one of that rare breed who had no need to broadcast his strength of character or his innate skills. He would only exhibit them during a time when they were required. At all other times he would appear calm, in control, and he would never show fear.

Salazar envied the man his qualities.

"You and I understand each other, I believe," he said. "We are on different sides, and that will never be resolved. That I understand and respect. What I would like to know is who you really work for. Your appearance in Moscow had little or nothing to do with a Justice Department review of the DEA. You proved this yourself by your actions against Trechenko's people and your visit to Afghanistan."

Salazar paused. Bolan was watching him closely, his gaze fixed on the Colombian. Despite himself Salazar felt a degree of unease. The American's scrutiny had that effect on him. Almost as if the man were seeing inside his skull and dissecting his thoughts.

"I should thank you for what you did there. Destroying Razak Khan's base. A stroke of luck for me. I understand that was not your prime motive for what you did. Even so."

Randal gave a sigh of frustration, turning away to stare out of the window.

"Your American friend cannot see the irony in the situation."

"And I don't like the allusion to him being my friend." Bolan said. "Tell me something, Salazar. Do *you* trust him? The man has changed sides more times than he has a right to. He doesn't care who suffers. He even arranged the deaths of his DEA partners. I'll take a stab at the reason only because it's so obvious. Randal wants money out of all this. Right? It's the only reason he's in the game, and that means he can't be trusted."

"Are you telling me this because you care what happens to me?"

It was Bolan's turn to smile.

"Hell, no, I hope he cuts your throat one night. I'm just curious why someone who considers himself to be smart would let himself be fooled by a dirtball like Randal."

"Asa, this one is very smart. He has seen through you already. What should I do with such a man? Kill him? Or perhaps offer him your position?"

Randal turned from the window, pulling a pistol from under his jacket. He jacked back the slide, letting it return with a solid click.

"Let me blow his fucking brains out here and now. He's starting to get on my nerves."

"Of course. Exactly what he wants. To make you angry. He is playing with you, Asa, and it is working. Now put away the gun."

Randal did as he was told, making no more protest. He remained unsettled, glaring at Bolan. His actions reinforced the soldier's feelings about the man. He was totally under Salazar's control. The Colombian had him just where he wanted him. As long as Salazar held the purse strings, dangling the promise of more money under Randal's nose, the renegade DEA man would do exactly what he was told. There was another facet to the situation. Randal's greed, his disregard of friends and colleagues, placed him out on a limb. He had cut his ties to the DEA and to anyone who might have had regard for him. All that remained was Salazar's financial input, plus the inescapable truth that Salazar held Randal's life in his hands. If Randal went too far, or made the Colombian angry, a mere snap of the fingers would sign the man's death warrant. Randal's betrayal of everything he had once represented had left him totally vulnerable.

"Will you talk to me, Belasko? Tell me what I feel I should know about you and the people you work for? Tell me here in the comfort of this room. The alternative is not very pleasant. I am sure you realize that. An intelligent man like yourself would not want to put himself through such an ordeal."

"It looks like I'm going to have to disappoint you, Salazar. Maybe I'm not as smart as you give me credit for."

Salazar thrust his hands deep into the pockets of his immaculate trousers.

"So be it, my friend. We will talk again, but not in such comfortable surroundings."

Bolan stood up, facing the Colombian.

"It had a nice view until you brought that into the room," he said, nodding in Randal's direction.

Randal turned on his heel, jabbing a finger at Bolan as he crossed the room to face him.

"We'll see how lippy you are after they work on you."

"I guess we will," Bolan said.

And then he hit Randal in the nose, a single blow, hard and without mercy. Blood spurted onto the floor and Randal staggered back, cupping a hand to his face. He moaned, too much in pain to even think about going for his gun again.

Bolan stepped back, holding up both hands to show he intended no further aggression. Out the corner of his eye he saw Salazar watching with interest, a faint smile on his lips. The Colombian instructed his bodyguards. One moved to Randal, first relieving him of his weapon before escorting him from the room. Salazar took Randal's gun and held it on Bolan as the second bodyguard stepped behind the American and bent to unlock the manacle around his ankle.

"I understand your motives," Salazar said, "but it will only increase his anger against you." The Colombian held Bolan's gaze. "I sense that making another enemy does not upset you."

"It goes with the territory."

"Later then, Belasko. I will talk to you again." Salazar left the room.

The armed bodyguard motioned for Bolan to walk ahead of him. When they stepped out of the room and walked along the passage Bolan saw two more armed men waiting at the head of the stairs. His escort led him to the ground floor, out across a tiled inner courtyard, to a heavy wooden door. As they crossed the courtyard, Bolan made a visual sweep of his surroundings, noting the ornate archway that led to the open quayside. By his estimation of the setup, the helicopter pad would be to the right of the arch.

One of the guards opened the wooden door and Bolan was pushed inside, down a steep flight of steps that brought them to a basement area. A short passage ended at another door. Bolan felt the prod of a gun barrel in the small of his back. One of the guards went ahead and pushed open the door, and the soldier was taken inside. He had time to register the door banging shut behind him before something struck him across the back of the skull and he fell to his knees.

Washington, D.C.

"I DON'T GIVE a damn about protocol, deniability or the last chorus of *Oklahoma*. I just want to know where he is, Hal. I sent the guy on this mission, and now he's vanished."

Hal Brognola, seated across from Turrin, knew just how the man was feeling. He had lost count of the times

Bolan had vanished out in the field. Sometimes for a few hours, more often for days, and as Turrin was experiencing, it was a frustrating time.

"Leo, I've got Aaron's team doing everything they can. They're checking all their contacts to see if there are any pieces of information coming down the wire. Up to the time I left the Farm we didn't have a sniff."

"All we have for certain is this mess at Trechenko's house outside Moscow. Place razed to the ground. Trechenko's staff dead. Trechenko's accountant dead. An Afghan called Razak Khan dead. From what we got via Moscow he was the local drug lord who ran the poppy fields supplying Trechenko. Now here's one to make you think. Also found dead was Commissioner Vladimir Korsov, section chief of the OCD. In effect, Valentine Seminov's boss. What the hell was he doing inside the house alongside the bad guys?"

Brognola didn't say anything, but his expression spoke volumes. The information coming out of Moscow was sketchy, so hard facts were spare at the moment. The big Fed had his own theories, but he was keeping them to himself until he felt certain he could voice them with accuracy.

And that might not happen until Valentine Seminov was able to speak.

The OCD cop was alive, still recovering from the operation to remove two bullets from his chest. It had been touch-and-go since he had been found, but the Russian was resilient.

"DEA is still trying to figure out the bombing of

their team's car," Turrin added. "They're waiting to hear from the Russians over identification of the bodies. Same with the members of the OCD personnel from the building. I spoke with a local police chief over there. The bomb made one hell of a mess of everything."

"This whole thing has gotten screwed up. Everybody's running around hog wild."

"One thing we haven't mentioned, Hal. The Colombians. We know there's bad feelings between them and the Russia-Jamaica alliance. Maybe this hit was another round in the war."

"It's worth considering. I'll have Aaron run some deeper checks on that thread."

"Mack could probably bring us up to date on the whole damn mess. If we knew where he was."

Colombia

THE ROOM WAS BUILT from stone. A powerful, bright light, set in the ceiling, threw stark white illumination into every corner. To Bolan's right a metal bench was bolted to the wall and floor. Laid out on its surface was a collection of metal knives and probes, rubber and metal tubing. On the wall facing him a pair of metal clamps were fixed at a position that suggested they were for securing a man's wrists above head height. It didn't take a great deal of imagination to work out their purpose.

The room held the chill of fear. It was a noticeable presence. Echoes of others who had been brought here on Salazar's instruction. Bolan wondered if any of them had left alive.

The guards behind Bolan caught his arms and hauled him to his feet, pushing him into the center of the room.

The guard facing Bolan turned, crossed to the bench and laid down his MP-5. He picked up a length of solid rubber tubing. As he turned back to face Bolan, he began to slash the air with the tube. Behind the soldier one of the other guards made a sound that might have been a laugh.

The man with the rubber tube closed in on his victim. He lashed out with the tube. Bolan stepped back, and it missed him by inches. Some unseen person grunted in annoyance, then the butt of his SMG thudded against Bolan's ribs. The blow was followed by more blows, pushing Bolan forward, and this time when the rubber tube was swung he couldn't avoid it. The hard impact, across his lower torso, drew a gasp from his lips. The blows came fast then, burning welts across his body. Ribs and chest, more behind from the weapons of the other two guards. Another slash from the tube caught him across the left cheek and the corner of his mouth. Another on the right, just above his eye. Blood ran hot and wet down his face. Bolan could taste it in his mouth. He dropped to his knees, shielding his head with both arms as the attack continued.

He knew this was just a softening-up process before they locked him in the clamps fixed to the wall. If they got that far, he'd be finished. He needed to make his break now, before he became too weak.

Down on the floor Bolan let his tormentors get in

close, absorbing the punishment until he made his move. When he did, it was with a supreme effort.

He let himself fall prone on the floor, turning on his back. For a brief second he was clear, under the blows. Bolan made a scything leg sweep that took one guard off his feet. The guy went down hard, unprepared, slamming bodily to the stone floor. The back of his skull cracked against the floor with a solid thud. Bolan kicked out hard with the sole of his boot, slamming it into the downed man's face, turning it into a crushed, bloody mask. The soldier rolled clear, in the direction of the other armed guard. He saw the guy bringing his weapon to bear, fumbling for the safety. The Executioner powered up off the floor and slammed bodily into the man, driving him backward. Bolan slammed his right palm in under the guard's chin and drove the back of his head into the wall behind him. He used every ounce of strength, his energy getting its power from the burning sting of the blows that had been inflicted on him. Three times in rapid succession Bolan rammed the guard's skull against the unyielding stone until it turned to soft mush. He felt the man slip from his grasp, a deadweight, and turned away, searching for the third man.

The pipe-wielding guard had already crossed the room, abandoning his torture instrument as he reached for the SMG he had left on the bench.

Bolan slammed into the guy and they slid along the edge of the bench, crashing against the far wall. The soldier got his right arm around his adversary's neck and he hugged the guy close, increasing the tension in his arm. The guard struggled against the choking pressure. Bolan increased it, feeling the crunch of bone and cartilage. The guard's heels drummed against the hard floor, his body twisting in desperation. All he did was speed his death. Bolan dragged him to the floor, maintaining his grip until the guard became still.

Pushing to his feet, the Executioner picked up the MP-5 from the bench. He armed himself with the mags from the weapons of the other two guards. One of them had a Beretta 92 tucked in his belt. Bolan took that, as well.

He moved to the door and eased it open. Finding the passage clear, he raced up the steps and cracked the outer door. The open courtyard was deserted. Bolan hugged the wall and made his way to the exit that led out to the inner courtyard. He recalled what he had seen on his way to the basement room.

The inner courtyard was clear. Bolan didn't hesitate. He sprinted for the archway and the dockside beyond. As he moved through the archway, he could see the blue water of the harbor in front of him. On the far side he could make out figures working around the warehouses.

A flicker of movement caught Bolan's eye, and he turned in time to face an armed guard rounding the corner of the archway. The Colombian, dressed in light tan shirt and trousers, had an MP-5 slung from one shoulder. When he saw Bolan he moved to bring the weapon into play. The soldier struck first, driving the body of his own weapon into the guard's face, feeling it cave in under the savage blow. The guard fell back against the wall, blood streaming from his crushed nose and torn lips. He was too dazed to offer any resistance. Bolan used the SMG again, delivering crippling blows to the man's throat. The guard went down, gagging harshly, hugging his ruined throat.

Bolan stepped around him, peering out across the dockside. The Bell 430 was still on the pad, the rotors spinning as the pilot made preflight checks. Bolan's timing couldn't have been better. If the chopper was being readied for takeoff, he wasn't going to get a better chance.

The soldier checked the H&K, making certain it was locked and loaded. He broke from cover and ran across the dock, making it to the chopper without challenge. Reaching up, he yanked open the passenger door and climbed inside.

The pilot glanced around, eyes widening when he saw the blacksuited, disheveled figure. He saw the battered, bloody face, the ice-blue eyes that were fixed on him, and if he never learned anything else that day he understood it wouldn't be wise to argue with this man. The presence of the MP-5 pointing at him reinforced that realization.

"You understand English?"

"Enough," the pilot said.

"Then get this bird off the ground. *Now.*"

The pilot gave a quick nod and reached for the controls. He powered up the twin turbines. The already warmed engines responded, the rotors blurring as they accelerated. The pilot knew his aircraft well. He needed to because the urgency in Bolan's order told him he needed to get the chopper off the ground as fast as was possible.

"Do it," Bolan snapped, pulling the seat's safety belt around him.

"We need—"

"No. *You* need to get this in the air faster than you've ever done it before. Your life depends on it. Understand?"

The pilot nodded.

Bolan saw armed men moving into view. He opened the passenger door and leaned out, triggering the MP-5. His first burst stalled the armed guards. His second put one down with 9 mm slugs coring into his upper legs. The others scattered. Bolan fired again, hit a second man in the side, dropping him to his knees.

The helicopter began to lift slowly. The pilot, wincing at the chatter of Bolan's weapon, realized his own life *was* at risk if return fire damaged the chopper. He countered the lack of height by banking the chopper away from the dock and out across the harbor, out of range of the armed guards. As the helicopter swooped away from the facility, it skimmed low over the water until the pilot was able to gain altitude.

"Can I ask something?"

Bolan looked across at the pilot. "What?"

"Where are we going?"

"That's going to depend on what you tell me next."

The pilot's puzzled expression almost drew a smile from Bolan.

"Are you going to cooperate?"

The pilot nodded.

"Show me where we are on your map."

Bolan examined the location, then checked out distances.

"This thing got full tanks?"

"Oh, yes. *Señor Salazar* insists I keep it fully fueled at all times."

Bolan nodded and showed the pilot where he wanted to go.

Panama City.

THE DRUG LORD'S rage paralyzed everyone in earshot. His voice reverberated around the open lounge of his private apartment within the dock facility.

"I pay you idiots to prevent this kind of thing from happening. I pay you vast amounts of money. Provide any luxury you require. We live like kings. Have the best of everything. And now it could all be at risk because you morons were unable to contain one man. One man. Three of my men are dead, two more wounded and this Belasko has stolen my fucking helicopter."

Salazar looked at every man in the room. They stood in uncomfortable silence, not daring to say a word in case it further enraged their boss.

"Don't any of you understand what his escape means? He could go to any of the enforcement agencies and give them details of this place. We could have them marching in here at any time."

"But…he saw nothing of the operation," one man said. "What can he tell them?"

"He works for the American Justice Department. He will have contacts in high places. He knows that Randal has not only deserted the DEA, but has killed two of his own partners. It isn't going to take them long to make a connection."

"Then we should remove all the cocaine. Clear the warehouse and take the shipment somewhere for safety until things quiet down."

This from the same man.

Salazar rounded on him, silent for a moment. He jabbed a finger at the man.

"Then you are responsible, Georgio. See to it. Use as many of the men as you need. Empty the storage warehouse. Replace it with bags of ground coffee. We have plenty to spare."

Georgio began to give orders. The grouped men moved instantly. It gave them the opportunity to get away from Salazar while he was in his angry mood. The drug lord was left with just a couple of his lieutenants.

"Barco, I want you to locate the helicopter. Put out the word. As far as you need to go. The usual rewards. I want that American. I want his tongue on a plate."

One of Salazar's men was standing close by a window. He heard a car outside and checked it out.

"Randal is back," he announced.

"Bring him here, then leave us alone," Salazar said.

RANDAL ENTERED the room cautiously, unsure of his reception. He had been told what had happened on his return from the local medical center where Salazar's influence had got him instant treatment on his broken nose. He saw that he was alone with Salazar.

"Come in, Asa. Do you think I am going to shoot you?"

Randal bobbed his head, wincing at the surge of pain it created. Despite the treatment and the covering over his nose, any undue movement hurt.

"The thought had crossed my mind."

"Sit down. You look terrible."

As well as his bandaged nose, Randal's face was marked by darkening patches beneath his eyes.

"Can I get you anything?"

"No. I can't have alcohol until the drugs wear off."

"Asa, things are not going too well. It's good that we hit Trechenko's home and removed some of his people. But he is still alive and so is that Jamaican—Deacon Marley. I have a feeling this feud is not over yet. They are proving to be as stubborn as I am, and with this damn Belasko on the loose I can see more problems looming."

"What can I do to help? Just let me know."

"Your faked death has unfortunately been discovered, so you'll have to stay away from any of your former colleagues. But when the fuss over all this has died down I will still need your input. Your knowledge of DEA workings will be invaluable. They can't completely restructure the organization, so much of what you know will still be valid. As long as you stay with me you will be secure. And so will your money."

Randal kept a respectful silence. He didn't want to say a thing that might jeopardize that promise.

"I believe it is time we took the fight to Deacon Marley and that upstart Russian, Trechenko," Salazar said. "And showed those amateur cops in Kingston how we do things the Colombian way."

U.S. Embassy, Panama City

"A SHORT AND NOT very sweet visit," Bolan said in answer to Leo Turrin's question.

"Dammit, Mack, you have a habit of moving around faster than the proverbial speeding bullet. Superman would hand in his cape if he had to go up against you."

"Bring me up to speed."

"Your vacation in Afghanistan upset the locals. Whatever you did got them so riled they've been burning out Khan's poppy fields and giving his followers all kinds of hell. It's like a local civil war up there. This local boss man, Jahangar Arik, is kicking up a hell of a fuss."

"He's a good man and needs all the help we can give him."

"When our people contacted him and asked if he wanted anything, one of the most important seemed to be a supply of magazines for a Beretta 93-R."

Turrin couldn't understand why Bolan found that funny.

"I'll explain when I have more time, Leo."

"The other good news is that Seminov is recovering."

"He's alive?"

"Hell, yes."

"Last time I saw him he was bleeding all over Trechenko's driveway. I didn't think he'd survived."

"I guess you had other things to think about."

"Some."

"That check into Korsov's finances paid off. He had a few million bucks salted away in offshore accounts. The son of a bitch sold out his own people to work for Trechenko."

"Isn't going to be any use to him now."

"Next stop Jamaica?"

"Like I said, I'm going to see this all the way, Leo. You wanted the house cleaning."

"How do you want to play this?"

"Quiet until I need it otherwise. Could do with some local help if it's available."

"I'll talk to the Jamaican authorities. See if they're feeling in a helpful mood. We have some contacts. They're as pissed at this alliance as we are."

"Don't forget Jack and the Lady. I might need a fast way out if things hot up."

This time it was Turrin's turn to chuckle.

"I say something funny, Leo?"

"Some things go together. You know what I mean. Coffee and doughnuts. You and things getting hot. Always go together."

Bolan smiled. "Say good-night, Leo."

"Good night Leo."

CHAPTER EIGHT

Jamaica

The marks on Bolan's face were still vivid enough to draw attention to him. He tried to keep out of the crowds as much as possible, but short of wearing a face mask it was difficult.

The cabdriver bringing him into Kingston from the airport kept staring into his rearview mirror.

"You want a face like this?" Bolan asked.

"No, man."

"Then keep your eyes on the road. It's how I got these. Not watching where I was driving."

"They look sore, man."

"Not as much as they were."

"You here on vacation?"

"Why not?"

Bolan wasn't in a talkative mood. He was still sore from the punishment he'd received during his short stay in Salazar's underground cell. The Colombian guards had taken their job seriously. Their attack had left some heavy bruising on Bolan's upper body. He was thankful he'd managed to end it before it had gone too far. Since his escape he hadn't had much opportunity to rest as much as he would have liked. Once he had talked with Turrin, things had moved with surprising speed.

His stay at the U.S. Embassy in Panama City had lasted for two impatient days. In that time Turrin made arrangements in Washington, which resulted in a courier boarding a flight to Panama. Bolan's brief meeting with the courier had him accepting a sealed package that contained a U.S. passport and credit card in the name of John McCall. There was also cash money and a new cell phone. Eventually he was driven to Tocumen International Airport, where he boarded a commercial flight across the Caribbean for a touchdown in Jamaica. On arrival he walked out of the airport and hailed a cab to take him to Kingston, to the hotel where a room had been booked for him.

"Any messages for me?" Bolan asked at the desk as he signed in.

"Just one," the pretty Jamaican woman said. She handed Bolan a sealed envelope, trying to avoid looking at his face.

"Automobile accident," Bolan said, wondering why he felt he needed to explain.

He collected his key and took the elevator up to his floor. In his room he dumped his single bag on the floor and opened the envelope. Inside was a slip of paper with a telephone number written on it. He reached for the room phone, then changed his mind and took the cell phone from his pocket. He tapped in the number and heard it connect.

"Can I help you?"

The voice was cool, calm and British.

"McCall. Our mutual friend in Washington suggested you might be able to help."

There was a pause.

"Okay. Take a cab and ask to be dropped outside the *Gleaner* building on North Street. Wait at the entrance. I'll pick you up in thirty minutes."

The line went dead.

Bolan called the desk and asked for a cab. When he reached the foyer he checked around for a souvenir store and went inside. He chose a pair of aviator sunglasses from a rack, paid for them and stepped outside the hotel wearing them.

His cab was waiting. He climbed in and gave the driver the address, then sat back for the ride, which turned out to be shorter than he had anticipated. Bolan paid the driver and took up his position close to the entrance to the *Gleaner* building. He was standing outside the offices of the *Daily Gleaner,* Jamaica's oldest newspaper, founded back in 1834.

His contact was on time. An old British Hillman Minx, circa the late sixties rolled to a stop at the curb. The driver leaned his head out of the window. He was tanned and his blond hair was thick, falling over his eyes. He wore a light suit and shirt.

"No bloody mistake," he said in a British accent. "You have to be McCall. Can't be two of you wandering around Kingston with a face like that. Get in."

Bolan walked around to the passenger side of the car and climbed in.

"Rollie Benson," the man said as Bolan settled in the passenger seat. "Her Majesty's Customs and Excise."

Benson eased back into the traffic, weaving in and out of the flow. He drove with the ease of someone who knew the local terrain. Nothing was said as the Briton took the car down through the city streets and brought them to a spot where they could look out across Kingston Harbor. Benson set the brake and cut the motor.

"What can I do to help, Mr. McCall?"

Bolan stared out across the water. Sunlight rippled on the surface. He ran a hand through his hair, gathering his thoughts.

"I guess my people talked to yours and you got the short straw?"

Benson chuckled. "Something like that. Not that I mind. Things have been a little slow around here lately. I could do with a change in my routine."

"Did you get any kind of background on why I'm here?"

"Not a great deal. As I understand it, you've been involved in some kind of undercover work. To do with a tie-up between our local drug boss, Marley, and the Russian Mob?"

"Little more than involved. I could do with some local detail on Deacon Marley. His operation. Anything you can give me."

"I'm your man if that's the case," Benson said. He tapped his fingers against the steering wheel. "Tell me to mind my own business if I'm out of line, but I get the feeling you're here for more than just a sneaky look at the bloke."

"You could say that. Does it create a problem?"

Benson shook his head. "Mr. McCall, I've been out here for almost eighteen months. Surveillance. Trying to get the goods on Marley and his bloody outfit. We work with the Jamaicans, and they're doing a cracking job. But we're up against it every way we turn. This Deacon Marley runs a tight ship. His people are loyal to the point of being bloody fanatics. Too scared to open their mouths because Marley would have their throats cut and their tongues nailed to the floor if he found out. We know he's supplying drugs bound for the U.K. and your country, as well. We're aware of this tie-up with the Russian Mafia but have no hard evidence. Marley is laughing at us. His legal people fend off any and all we throw at him. There has been a great deal of violence lately. Two Jamaican undercover men have been found dead. Tortured before they were killed. I knew both of them."

"And you wish you could do something about Marley? Take the law into your own hands and end it?"

"It's the only wish I have for Christmas," Benson said.

"They say if you wish hard enough things *can* happen."

"Look, McCall, just ask and I'll give you whatever you need."

"I might hold you to that. And the name is John."

Benson drove through Kingston, out onto the open road. He parked across from an industrial unit.

"Grande Café is the trade name for Marley's coffee business. That's the home office and distribution center. His plantation is in the Blue Mountain range up country. It's where he has his main home."

"What other enterprises is Marley involved in?"

"Money lending. Very suspect. I believe you call it loan sharking. He runs a car-rental business. Freight haulage. Couple of nightclubs. Discos. Escort services. With the emphasis on the special services. Busy man, our Deacon Marley."

"I need to know if there's somewhere he'd have for guests. Out-of-town guests. Someone like Fedor Trechenko."

"You mean Trechenko's here?"

"I'm pretty certain. I know he left Moscow shortly after I became involved with some of his local boys. He hadn't returned when I left. If he's heard what happened back home, I'm guessing he's decided to hang around here for a while."

"And what did happen back home?"

"A less than social call from some of Hermano Salazar's boys. They did some demolition on Trechenko's country residence."

"Salazar isn't going to sit back and let the Russians tie up with Marley and muscle in on his operation."

"Exactly. As long as that pair keep up their opposition Salazar is going to bite back hard."

"You think they will?"

"One thing I've learned about drug traffickers is they're all greedy for more. Nothing is ever enough. They see a chance, they go for it and they keep on going. It's a circle they all get locked into. The problem is they're all deceiving themselves into believing *they* will win in the end. If innocents get hurt or killed along the way, they won't give a damn."

"I get the feeling you've been there before."

"A few times." Bolan studied the Marley building. "Rollie, I need as much detailed information as you can get me on Marley's businesses. Time to rattle his cage and watch him jump."

Benson started the car and they moved off.

"Will do. I'll send it over to your hotel. Any other place you need to visit?"

"Yeah. I'd like to introduce you to a couple of friends of mine."

Dragon Slayer

BENSON WAS IMPRESSED by the combat chopper. He walked around *Dragon Slayer,* stopping every so often to examine a particular section, then moved on again.

"You sure this guy isn't related to McCarter?"

Bolan smiled. "What makes you ask that?"

"Look at him, Sarge. He's got the same crazy look in his eyes. I think all those Brits are the same."

"Jack, if they are, I wouldn't be sorry to have a dozen of them backing me."

"That's because you're as crazy as they are. I mean, have you seen what you look like? Jesus, Sarge, those Colombians could have killed you."

"It wasn't as if I had any choice, Jack."

"Hell, I guess not. You sure you're okay?"

"I'm fine."

"Yeah."

They were inside a medium-size hangar situated in the commercial-aviation section of Kingston airport. Grimaldi had flown *Dragon Slayer* in himself, the chopper secured in the cargo hold of a Lockheed Martin C-130 transport from a charter company through Leo Turrin's contacts. The C-130 was parked out on the apron, the crew taking an unexpected break in Kingston until Grimaldi needed them for the return trip.

"I need a map of the island," Bolan said.

"Figured that one myself."

Grimaldi produced a large sheet map of Jamaica. He spread it out flat on a workbench, using tools to hold down the edges. Bolan called Benson across. The Briton examined the map and pointed out various locations where Deacon Marley owned properties. He ringed each one with a pen.

"And this is his house up in the mountains. Old plantation land. It stood empty for a long time, then Marley bought it and had the place renovated. Started up the coffee growing again. Story goes he spent a lot of money on the house. One thing he isn't short of."

"It's how he got it that bothers me," Bolan said.

"If Trechenko is here on the island, that's where he'll be. Marley had a wing built on with a number of luxury apartments included. Thinking about it, I figure that's definitely where Trechenko will be. Close at hand. This bloke throws parties to end all parties. Guest list like a Hollywood premier. They fly in, come in their luxury yachts. Marley has a big rep throughout the Caribbean."

"Don't people know what he does for a living?" Grimaldi asked.

"It's never been proved. That's the snag. Marley plays the big man. Uses his reputation to attract. There are always those who like to play the danger game. They get their buzz from mingling with Marley's kind. The glamour it attracts. They have too much money and time on their hands. Life gets dull for them, so rubbing shoulders with a suspected drug dealer is exciting."

"And some of them will actually be customers," Bolan said.

"Too bloody right," Benson agreed.

Bolan glanced at his watch. He wasn't going to start anything until dark. During the next hours he could gather his equipment, then return to his hotel and catch some rest.

"Jack, open up. I need some tools for tonight."

"Maybe you don't want me seeing too much," Benson said. "I can take a walk."

"Ask Jack nicely—he'll give you a tour of the chopper," Bolan suggested.

"No problem," Grimaldi said. "Only thing is I'll have to kill you once you've seen inside."

"What the hell. I'll take a chance."

Bolan found his gear stowed in the crew cabin of *Dragon Slayer*. There was a large leather carryall for him to transfer clothing and weapons. Blacksuit and boots, Beretta 93-R, Desert Eagle and an Uzi. Loaded mags for each weapon. A sheathed knife. There were also incendiary devices with detonator-timers attached. Bolan took a dozen of these. He considered taking some of the plastic-explosive packages but reconsidered. Most of the targets he was going for were in Kingston itself, and Bolan wanted to hurt Deacon Marley, not innocent citizens. He packed the bag and closed the zip.

"That is some bloody marvelous machine," Benson said, climbing out of *Dragon Slayer*.

"She'll do," Grimaldi told him.

"I'll be getting back to you," Bolan said. "Stay close."

Benson drove Bolan back to his hotel.

"Should I be asking what you'll be doing next?"

"Not really. Just be ready to catch any fallout."

The Briton smiled. "You have my number. If you need anything just call."

"I could use a car for tonight. Something inconspicuous."

"I'll figure something out. When I bring your information I'll leave it in the hotel parking lot. Round the back. Keys will be in the package."

Bolan stepped out of the Hillman and took his carryall.

"Thanks for your help, Rollie."

BACK IN HIS ROOM Bolan stowed his carryall in the wardrobe. He stripped off his clothes and got under the shower. He turned up the temperature as hot as he could stand and had a long soak, letting the water stream over his bruised body. He let his thoughts drift. Bolan admitted he was tired, ready for a break. At the same time he knew there would be no letup until he had completed this particular offensive. There was a lot of credence in the old saying about the enemy never sleeping. They were always out there, in different forms, but ever present. And he couldn't afford to let them gain the advantage. If he did, they would devour him, swarm all over him and tear him limb from limb. He had to keep his guard up, maintain his watch and give them no quarter.

Bolan lifted his head as he caught the sound of the telephone ringing. He turned off the shower and grabbed a towel as he headed for the bedroom.

"McCall."

"Rollie Benson. I just received a call. I thought you should know about it in case it infringes on your business."

"Go on."

"One of the Jamaican drug cops, name of Bob Jackson, left a message saying he'd spotted a team of Colombians in town, led by a character called Santana. I know the bloke. Bad reputation. Likes to cut up people with a knife. Had three, maybe four people with him. They have a big seagoing motor launch out in the harbor. The *Caliente*."

"Another round about to start. Have you managed to speak to Jackson?"

"No. I tried to get him back on his cell phone but I'm not getting a reply."

"Keep trying him."

"Will do. Listen, I'll have your transport sorted in the next hour. And I'll leave a photo of Jackson in the package I drop off at the hotel."

"That's great."

Bolan replaced the phone. He dried himself, then pulled on a pair of shorts and a T-shirt. He stretched out on the bed and closed his eyes. Rest was in order before the coming night's work.

AT EIGHT O'CLOCK that evening Bolan made his way down to the desk and asked if a package had been left for him. As promised, Benson had delivered. Bolan took the envelope back to his room. He broke the seal and spread the contents across the bed.

Benson had sent him a street map of Kingston, ringing the locations of Marley's business establishments. A couple of printed sheets gave a breakdown of the suspicions Benson's people had over what Marley was getting up to. The Briton had included photographs of Marley, his principal lieutenants and also one of Bob Jackson, the undercover cop. As a bonus there was a shot of the man Benson had called Santana. The Colombian, lean and dark, was in a group, laughing at something said. Bolan was quick to spot that the humor didn't reach the man's piercing eyes. They were cold and empty. Like the eyes of a shark.

There was also a car key, with a label taped to it, giving the make and registration number.

Bolan laid out the photographs and studied them as he dressed for his night's work. Blacksuit first, then he filled the pockets with extra mags for his weapons, added a Ka-bar sheathed knife. He checked both his pistols and the Uzi, loading each weapon and making sure they were all set on safety until needed. He checked the incendiary packs, as well. These all went into a small carryall. Satisfied with his equipment, Bolan pulled a pair of light slacks and a shirt over the snug-fitting blacksuit. He slipped on his boots.

He took the printed data sheets Benson had sent along and read through them, absorbing any of the information he thought useful. He placed the papers, along with the photographs, in the large carryall, closed the zip and locked the bag away in the wardrobe, placing the key beneath the room phone.

It was close to nine when Bolan pulled on his leather jacket and left the room, making his way down to the lobby. It was quiet, with only the desk clerk behind the desk. She had her back to Bolan, slipping messages into room slots. He walked out of the hotel and followed the signs to the rear parking lot.

The car Benson had provided stood in a line with others belonging to hotel guests. It was an older Ford sedan, dark gray in color. Bolan unlocked it, climbed in and stowed his carryall on the passenger seat.

When he started the car, the engine purred into life. Bolan took a moment to check out the street map Benson had provided, then rolled out of the parking lot. The Ford handled well. He could feel the power under the hood. When he tried the brakes they were in as good a shape as the engine.

Twenty minutes later he reached the coffee plant. Bolan drove by and chose a quiet spot a couple of hundred feet farther along to park in the deep shadows of a stand of trees. He stepped out of the car, then slipped off his jacket, shirt and pants. He placed them in the Ford's trunk, along with the carryall once he had donned his weapons and combat vest. A small backpack took the incendiary charges. Bolan slipped the straps over his shoulders, locked down the car and pocketed the key.

He waited in the shadows, checking his surroundings. Being an industrial area, there was little activity at this time of night. Bolan chose his moment and sprinted along the edge of the dusty road, then across to the perimeter fence of the coffee plant. He dropped into a shallow ditch that ran parallel with the base of the fence, spending silent minutes observing the enclosed freight yard and the administration building. Farther back was the plant building itself, separated from the administration building. A number of haulage trucks bearing the name of the company were parked for the night.

The fence surrounding the yard had seen better days. The loose chain-link fencing offered little resistance when Bolan lifted the bottom edge. He was able to wriggle under with ease, moving quickly to crawl beneath one of the parked trucks, where he spent more observation time, scanning the layout and watching out for any patrolling night watchman or armed guards. Marley might have reason to maintain an armed presence at his premises.

Bolan's patience was rewarded after five minutes when he spotted a pair of men moving across the yard. There was enough light for him to see they were a long way off from being watchmen. No uniforms. Expensive casual clothing and M-16s slung from their shoulders. Bolan watched them stroll by, deep in conversation. Their presence seemed a little extreme for a coffee plant, he decided, unless Marley was packing something other than beans. The only other explanation was that the price of coffee had gone through the roof, and Bolan didn't believe that for a second.

There could be another reason. A simple explanation. Marley was making sure he was well protected against any further attacks from Hermano Salazar and his Colombians, which, coming on the news that there did appear to be a Colombian team on the island, would be a sensible precaution.

Bolan followed the armed sentries as they made their way to the front gates of the yard, checking they were secure. The pair separated then, one making his way across to the far side of the area, while the other cut back in the direction of the admin building.

Staying in the shadows, Bolan trailed the second man as he checked the main doors, then took a walk around to the far side of the building, where the wall stood parallel with the outer fence.

The guard made his way along the narrow concrete path edging the building. Bolan followed, closing quickly. He had only a couple of feet to go when the man stopped, raising his head to listen, then turned unexpectedly. He saw Bolan, registering surprise, then hostility. The M-16 slid from his shoulder, his finger going for the trigger.

Bolan stepped forward, not away from the man, jabbing the muzzle of his Uzi into his adversary's face. The hard muzzle ring caught the guy under his left eye, gouging the flesh as Bolan put on the pressure. Blood began to run from the gash. The Jamaican gasped in shock, his hesitation giving the Executioner the advantage, which he took without pause. Driving in, Bolan slammed the Uzi against the side of the guard's skull. He hit repeatedly, driving the guard against the side wall, the Uzi thudding against the man's head and face. Up close Bolan drove his right knee into the Jamaican's groin, hard. The man moaned, clutching at his vulnerable flesh, resistance evaporating with the onrush of burning pain engulfing his lower body.

Bolan drove a booted foot against the guard's left knee, pushing his limb back against the joint. The guy lost the use of his leg, slumping with his back to the wall, and Bolan let go of the Uzi, snatching the M-16 from the guard's hands. He reversed the rifle and swung it clublike, the buttstock cracking against the Jamaican's skull, pitching him facedown onto the ground.

Bolan tossed aside the M-16, brought his Uzi back into play and moved on. He reached the far side of the admin building and crouched in the darkness, surveying the way before him. It was no more than twenty feet across a near empty parking lot to the production plant. Satisfied he had an open run, Bolan took off for the building. He had covered the distance save for the last few feet when the door set in the wall swung open. A tall, lean Jamaican, armed with an M-16, stood framed in the opening. He barely managed to register any surprise before Bolan's powerful form struck him head-on, knocking him back through the door.

The gunner gave a startled cry as he went backward down the steep concrete steps inside the doorway. He lost his balance and fell hard, rolling and twisting as he crashed to the bottom of the steps, coming to rest against the door there.

Bolan just barely held himself back, throwing out his arms to keep himself from imitating the Jamaican. Regaining his balance, he pulled the outer door closed, then went down the steps himself, stepping over the unconscious guard. Bolan picked up the M-16 and took it with him as he eased open the basement door and stepped through.

He found himself in a dimly lit corridor, featureless, the concrete walls cold to the touch. Halfway along the hall Bolan saw another door. He reached it and pushed through.

He heard laughter, music coming from a radio.

Canvas sacks were stacked against one wall of a wide, low-ceilinged room. About a dozen people were busy scooping powder from canvas sacks on top of wooden tables, weighing the amounts on scales before transferring the powder to smaller plastic bags. Most of them were wearing dust masks. Others took the sacks and sealed them with rolls of wide tape.

Bolan stood against the inner wall, unseen, surveying the activity in Deacon Marley's drug-distribution center.

He might have stood there for longer if someone hadn't glanced up and seen him. A yell brought the attention of an armed man leaning against one of the tables, chatting to one of the packers, a Jamaican woman clad in a thin cotton dress, who was eyeing him with obvious interest.

The guard pushed away from the table, turning his M-16 toward Bolan.

Bolan hit the guard with a burst from his own acquired M-16. The Jamaican gave a stunned cry, falling back across the table, scattering the plastic bags and knocking a set of scales to the floor. His dying reflex jerked his finger against the M-16's trigger, sending a burst of fire into the concrete floor. Bolan covered the packers with his weapon. There didn't appear to be any other armed guards.

"Everybody outside. *Now.* Stay and you can end up like him. The choice is yours."

The packing crew moved in concert. They dropped what they were doing and ran for the door, stepping wide as they passed Bolan. He could hear them running along the passage and clattering up the concrete steps.

Once the last packer had exited Bolan moved, planting half a dozen of the incendiary devices around the room. He set the timers for two minutes, giving himself time to get clear. He left the room and headed back along the passage, up the stairs and out the exit door.

As he ducked to the side he heard the familiar sound of an M-16. The 5.56 mm slugs took chunks out of the concrete wall over his head as Bolan dropped and rolled, coming up on one knee. He set his own rifle against a shoulder and returned fire as he saw armed figures converging on his position. Bolan's long familiarity with the M-16 paid off as one of the attackers went down hard. He caught a second in the shoulder, the 5.56 mm slugs ravaging flesh and bone in a microsecond of searing pain. The wounded man went down howling, clutching at his torn, bloody shoulder.

Bolan drifted back into the shadows where high grass and foliage bounded the perimeter fence. He used it to retreat back the way he had come in.

Partway along the side of the admin building Bolan took out another incendiary pack. He smashed a window with the butt of the M-16, set the detonator on the pack for thirty seconds and dropped it inside the window.

Autofire crackled behind him.

Bolan's silent, blacksuited form flattened against the ground.

He heard the dull detonations as his planted devices went off in the drug-packing room. The combined power from the six packs would have turned the room into a white-hot inferno.

As Bolan moved on again, the pack he had planted through the broken window detonated. A flare of incandescent fire threw its glare through the window as the room inside was consumed.

Bolan reached the freight yard, taking the chance to skirt the area and lose himself in among the parked vehicles. He had three packages left and set them under the trucks, giving himself twenty seconds to get clear, then activated the devices. He pulled back, searching the surrounding gloom as he headed back for the place where he gained entry to the compound.

There was no challenge as Bolan dropped to the ground and crawled under the wire. As he gained his feet, the trio of devices detonated. The fierce heat spread quickly, licking at the undersides of the vehicles and eating at the bodywork. Bolan was already on the far side of the road when the fuel tank of one truck blew. The swell of flame reached out to ignite other vehicles. A second tank went, adding more hungry coils of scorching fire and smoke.

Bolan unlocked the Ford's trunk. He slipped off his harness and dropped it in the trunk, adding his weapons. He pulled on his outer clothing, closed the trunk and climbed in behind the wheel of the car. Firing up the engine, Bolan drove slowly away. Behind him the yard of Deacon Marley's coffee plant was brightly illuminated by the fiery conflagration that engulfed his trucks. Flames were also starting to show from inside the administration building. Bolan saw this through his rearview mirror as he cruised along the road, taking himself back the way he had come, a thin smile on his lips.

Round one was complete.

And the night wasn't over yet.

BOLAN'S NEXT TARGET was the car-rental service Deacon Marley ran. It was away from Kingston center, which suited Bolan. There was no way he could do anything about the nightclubs because they were still open, even in the early hours, and he couldn't do anything that might be potentially harmful to the public at large.

The rental company was along a strip that competed with other rental businesses. The Marley establishment consisted of a small office, with nine rental vehicles parked out front. They were all late-model American cars, gleaming under the security lights.

Bolan drove by and parked around the first corner he came to. He opened the trunk and took out the last two of the incendiary devices, which he tucked under his jacket. He grabbed the Beretta and pushed it under his belt at the back.

The soldier walked slowly along the street. There was little traffic and no pedestrians. As he drew level with Marley's enterprise, Bolan glanced in through the large glass frontage. The office was deserted. There was only a low security light inside. He turned quickly and walked up the side of the office, to the rear. He crouched and set one of the devices for a five-minute countdown. The other he set for five-and-a-half minutes. Activating the incendiary device, Bolan slid it under the raised base of the office. He stood, moving back past the office and down to the street. As he walked by the end vehicle, he activated the second device and bent to slip it under the car.

Bolan returned to where he had left the Ford, climbed in and turned it around. He rolled onto the street and drove away, glancing at the clock on the dashboard. He drove to a safe distance and watched the countdown, leaving the Ford's engine running.

The moment the devices blew, creating a ball of flame that brought temporary daylight to the area, Bolan drove away. Behind him Marley's car-rental parking lot became an instant disaster area. Six out of the nine cars were totally destroyed as the heat and destruction from one car set off its neighbor. For at least three minutes there was a constant series of explosions as gas tanks blew. The surviving cars, though intact, suffered from extensive bodywork scorching, the paint blistering and cracking. Windshields and door glass shattered from the high temperature; rubber tires burst and melted.

Bolan drove back into Kingston center, following the signs for the harbor. He parked and stood beside the car, checking out the boats. He saw the *Caliente*. An impressive oceangoing motor launch. It was at anchor, riding the swells. Lights blazed in the large cabin section and Bolan could make out figures moving about on deck. He stayed for a few minutes, then took out his cell phone and called Benson. The phone rang for a time before it was answered.

"Did I wake you?"

"Actually, you bloody well did," Benson said. He sounded half-asleep. "I suppose you're going to tell me you had nothing to do with the occurrence at the Grande Café plant."

"Oh? Has something happened?"

"It seems they had the biggest fireworks display since the last Kingston Carnival."

"The Marley car rental seems to have had a similar accident."

"Good God, what next?"

"Enough for one night. Rollie, I'm at the harbor,

looking at the *Caliente*. Have you heard anything else from Jackson?"

"No. To be honest, I'm starting to get a little worried. Bob's no slouch when it comes to staying in touch. He might have walked into something he couldn't handle with this crew of Salazar's."

"Where would I be most likely to find him?"

"Be faster if I showed you."

"I'll wait here at the harbor for you. Hey, don't bother to shave. Just get here."

BENSON'S CAR ROLLED to a stop, beside Bolan. The Briton climbed out and joined him.

"I've been ringing around while I drove. I checked out every contact of Jackson's I could think of."

They climbed into the Ford.

"Any results?"

"No. But I got a feeling some of them were playing dumb, as if they knew what I was after and they daren't say."

"Who would be most likely to give us the truth?"

"The only one I can think of would be Bob's girl-friend. Mary Angelus."

"We'll start there," Bolan said.

CHAPTER NINE

Bolan put his foot down hard once they cleared Kingston's city limits. They were on the coast road, heading east. Mary Angelus had a beachside bungalow a few miles out. Benson filled the American in with details of Jackson's girlfriend. She worked as a freelance photographer, selling her pictures to the *Daily Gleaner* and tourist publications. According to Benson, the woman was a talented photographer who had presented her work at a number of exhibitions around the Caribbean.

"Does she understand Jackson's work?" Bolan asked. "I mean his working against the drug traffickers could put her at risk."

"Bob told her the nature of his job when he first met her. He tried to put her off, in fact, but Mary is a stubborn young woman. She told him their friendship was more important than any possible threat, and if he walked away she threatened to stalk him. She has a sense of humor, too."

"She might need it."

It was starting to show light ahead of them. Bolan glanced at his watch. They were driving into the dawn.

"Around the next bend," Benson said, "there's a side road on your right. The bungalow is only a few hundred yards along."

Bolan spotted the turn. He slowed the Ford and took it off the main road. Driving along the narrow road for a few yards, he then swung it into the trees and lush shrubbery that edged each side of the track. Bolan cut the engine.

"Are you armed?" he asked the Briton.

Benson nodded. He opened his jacket to show a shoulder rig that held a SIG-Sauer P-226.

"Courtesy of Her Majesty's Customs purchasing department. And no, I haven't had to use it yet."

"If you pull it," Bolan said, "remember the other guy isn't going to wait while you show him your entry warrant."

"That hits the spot."

"*Hitting* and *spot*, Rollie. Not the best choice of words you ever made."

Bolan opened his door and climbed out, Benson following. He stayed close behind the American as they worked their way through the shadows, aware of the daylight filtering in through the trees.

The low outline of the bungalow took shape ahead of them. Beyond it the Caribbean rolled up against the white strip of beach.

Bolan held up his free hand. The 93-R had appeared in his right. He signaled Benson to join him.

Two cars were parked near the bungalow.

"Recognize either of them?"

Benson nodded.

"The blue Renault is Bob's. I don't know who owns the Toyota." The Toyota was a black SUV. Benson took a closer look. The vehicle had local plates. "Could be a rental."

"What about Mary?"

"She has a red sports job. Loves the thing and won't drive anything else."

"Doesn't look like she's at home."

As Bolan spoke, there was a disturbance from inside the bungalow. It sounded to Bolan as if someone had knocked something over.

"Keep your eyes open. Watch that front door."

He moved out then, staying low as he approached the bungalow. He ignored the front, rounding the side of the house and crouch-walked to the rear.

There was more sound from inside the bungalow. Bolan heard someone moaning. He picked up the pace, only pausing to check the beach side of the building. He peered through the railings of the veranda that ran the length of the bungalow. There was a porch door about two-thirds of the way along. No one in sight. No guard. Bolan guessed they were all inside, enjoying whatever was happening.

He vaulted over the veranda railing and flattened

against the board wall, leaning to his right so he could see inside.

Three men, two with MP-5s. The third loomed above a fourth man, who was hunched over in a chair. The third man had something in his hand that caught the light as it curved in at the man in the chair. Bolan saw the gleam of blood, saw the seated man jerk back, mouth opening in a cry of pain.

Bolan flicked off the Beretta's safety. He ducked below the window and went for the porch door, took a step back to give himself room, then raised his right foot and drove it at the door. The wood frame splintered around the lock, and the door flew inward, Bolan following.

It was an open-plan room; a bright, pleasant room that had been temporarily turned into a torture chamber. Furniture had been thrown around. Ornaments smashed on the floor.

The man in the chair, wrists bound to the arms, looked as if he had been cut to ribbons. His face was a bloody mask, chest slashed and raw.

His torturer, who turned to look over his shoulder as Bolan crashed into the room, was the Colombian named Santana. In his right hand he held an old-fashioned open razor. Droplets of blood sprayed back from the blade as he jerked his hand.

He yelled something to his pair of hardmen, and they broke out of their moment of hesitation to turn the SMGs they wielded on the intruder.

Bolan had dropped to a crouch, the Beretta in a two-fisted grip. His first triburst took its target high in the chest, the 9 mm slugs driving the breath from the man's lungs, kicking him backward. The Colombian gunner's weapon triggered harmlessly into the ceiling, bringing down a shower of plaster and dust. The Beretta tracked in on the second hardman, Bolan firing even as the Colombian triggered his own weapon. The SMG crackled briefly. Bolan felt the burn of slugs as they chopped through his jacket and clothing to tear at his side. As he reacted to the bullets' impact, Bolan saw his own target stumble back, bloody wounds opening in his neck. The Colombian clapped his left hand over the ragged wounds, pulling his SMG back on line as he struggled to regain his balance. Bolan's second burst caught him in the chest, the follow-up taking out his lower jaw in a bloody burst. The Colombian tumbled to the floor, the MP-5 bouncing from his hand.

Santana spun away from his bound victim, bending to snatch up the fallen SMG. He scooped it off the floor and began to straighten, bringing the muzzle to bear on Bolan as the American pushed upright.

The front door crashed inward under the impact of a heavy kick. Santana's expression changed as he continued to raise the SMG.

Rollie Benson, framed in the open door, leveled his P-226. He pulled the trigger and fired three fast shots that caught Santana in the right shoulder, blowing out chunks of flesh and splintered bone. Bolan's Beretta coughed out its own burst, the 9 mm rounds coring in through Santana's left thigh, shattering the bone. The impact knocked his leg from beneath him and dumped him facedown onto the floor.

Bolan stepped across to where Santana lay moaning, blood pulsing in steady streams from a severed artery in his thigh. The back of Santana's shirt was soaked, as well, the raw exit wounds exposing torn flesh and ragged bone ends. Bolan kicked the MP-5 clear of the Colombian's clawing left hand. He bent and picked up the razor Santana had dropped.

Crossing to the bloodied figure, Bolan severed the thin cord that bound him to the arms of the chair.

Benson came up behind Bolan, staring with undisguised shock at the Jamaican in the chair.

"Oh, Christ…it's Bob."

"You'd better call it in," Bolan said. "Get medical help out here."

"No."

The plea came from Bob Jackson, pushed through his slashed and bloody lips with effort.

"You need help, Bob," Benson said.

Jackson raised one hand, blood dribbling from his fingers.

"You listen. Never mind about me. Go help Mary… he sent a crew after her. She…went to the…"

The effort seemed to weary him. Jackson stared up at Bolan and Benson, his eyes pleading from the depths of his ravaged, bloody face.

"Where did she go?" Bolan asked.

"The cabin."

"I know where he means," Benson said.

"How many of them?" Bolan asked.

"Four. They kill her…she got something they want. I took it from their boat. Damn fool I. Not clever 'cause they saw me. Jesus, go to Mary. I let her down…told them about the cabin…couldn't help…"

"Doesn't matter," Benson said. "You couldn't…"

"Rollie, I need you again," Bolan snapped.

"We can't just leave him," Benson insisted.

Bolan reached over and took Benson's cell phone from the Briton's pocket and handed it to him.

"You can call *and* walk to the car, can't you?"

"Do it, man," Jackson pleaded. "Don't worry about me. I'm not the one who matters. You go get Mary safe. Make sure Santana's people don't get to hurt her."

Behind Bolan the sound of someone moving across the floor reached his ears. He turned and saw Santana crawling across the floor in the direction of the door. He left a glistening red trail behind him.

"Give me that razor," Jackson whispered.

Bolan placed the bloody razor in Jackson's hand. The Jamaican cop gripped it hard, making a failed attempt at stopping his trembling.

"Now I got *my* chance."

"You sure?"

"No problem. Now get away from here and find Mary. Do this for me, Rollie."

Bolan turned and went out through the front door,

Benson trailing behind, the cell phone already pressed to his ear. Bolan could feel the warm creep of blood from the painful tears in his side. There wasn't much he could do about them right now. If they had been serious, he would have felt the effect by now. He closed his mind to the burn.

They were in the car, just moving off when a high, shrill scream reached them from inside the house. It rose higher, then cut off into a sobbing whimper. Bolan kept driving. There was no need to go back inside the house. Something instinctively told him the scream had come from Santana. Bob Jackson was having his moment of retribution.

Benson was giving the location of the house, telling the police to get an ambulance to it, informing them that one of their officers was in need of urgent attention. He cut off the call before too many questions could be fired at him. Benson gave Bolan his route, telling him it would take them a couple of hours to reach the weekend cabin in the foothills of the Blue Mountains. Bolan put his foot down, hoping they would arrive in time to prevent a repeat of what had happened to Bob Jackson.

MARY ANGELUS STEPPED out of the shower, picking up a large towel. She dried herself as she made her way to the cabin's small bedroom. Bright sunlight flooded the room from the window overlooking the sweep of foliage sloping away from the rear of the house. The cabin lay in thickly timbered terrain, the heavy grass and ferns creating a deep layer of lush greenery that spread in every direction.

Angelus finished drying herself and reached for the clothes on the bed. Once she was dressed she made her way through to the compact kitchen. She turned on the electric hot plate and placed a kettle of water on it. While it boiled she stepped outside and stood in the calm of the day, letting her thoughts drift. She would have been the first to admit to being nervous. The sudden change in her circumstances was upsetting. But Angelus wasn't a woman to be frightened that easily. It wasn't foolishness on her part, simply a reasoning that she couldn't control what had happened or what might happen in the future. That was out of her immediate control. But that didn't mean she had to go scurrying around in the dark, afraid to do or say anything for fear of reprisals. Her life was important to her and so was Bob Jackson's. She understood his work, knew it was important, and she would stick with him no matter what.

Her thoughts centered on Bob Jackson, wondering where he was and why she hadn't heard from him. Things had happened at a frantic pace since he had turned up at the bungalow the night before. She had known immediately that he had a problem. For the first time since she had found out what he did for a living, Jackson had seemed concerned. It was a side to him she found a little disturbing. He had a look in his eyes that told her he needed help.

When he explained what had been happening she

surprised herself by telling him she would help, and she made it clear there would be no arguing the point.

Jackson had a laptop with him, wrapped in a piece of cloth. He had given her the computer, asking her to take it to the cabin in the Blue Mountains and wait for him there. She recalled his words, and the urgent tone of his voice.

"Go there, Mary. Stay there. I need to do things. Wait for me. If you don't hear from me by noon tomorrow, take this to police headquarters in Kingston. Ask for Captain Wallace. No one else. Give this to him."

"What is it?"

"Could be the break we need to pin something on these Colombians. Mary, just do this. And just one thing. Don't call me. No excuses. Trust me."

She had packed a few of her belongings into a carry-all, including the laptop, and had driven away from the bungalow in her red Triumph sports car. It was late enough that Angelus encountered no traffic the entire journey. She arrived at the cabin in the early morning, parking the car and taking her bag inside.

She had tried to sleep, but it eluded her. On more than one occasion she had picked up her cell phone, desperate to speak to Jackson. Then she recalled his insistence on her not phoning. In the end she did drift off into a restless sleep, waking at first light. She had fallen asleep in one of the armchairs and she felt stiff.

She checked her cell phone. No messages. Again the temptation to call Jackson was strong. She resisted once more.

Angelus had gone outside to the concrete bunker that housed the small generator that provided power for the cabin. She started it, securing the door, and went back inside. She checked the water level in the storage tank that stood on a wooden platform by the cabin door. The level was high, so she would be able to have a shower. She took a pair of faded jeans from her carryall, underwear and T-shirts and laid them out on the bed, wandering through to the shower unit built into one corner of the cabin.

Now refreshed and dressed, Angelus made herself a mug of strong black coffee and took it back outside, sitting on the porch, her back to the cabin wall.

THE DRIVER of the Toyota 4×4, identical in make and model to the one that was still parked outside Mary Angelus's bungalow, could feel sweat trickling down the side of his face. The sun had only just started to push its way skyward so the temperature was still on the cool scale. The Colombian's sweat had nothing to do with the heat of the day. It was there because the man was nervous. He was nervous because he had just gotten lost for the second time, and that wasn't going down well with the team boss.

Julio Gomez, running the team, was fast losing his patience with the driver. They were wasting precious time. Gomez wanted to reach the cabin before any third party interfered. The loss of the laptop was something Gomez couldn't survive. The information contained in the computer would cause ripples that could reach as far as the United States, and it had been Gomez's total responsibility. He had held off informing Hermano Salazar because the boss would have immediately ordered Gomez's head on a plate. And knowing Salazar as he did, it wouldn't have been an idle threat. The narco baron was well known for his direct and brutal punishment. So it was natural that Gomez feared for his life.

"Enrico, get us back on track now, or I will put you out of your misery myself."

Enrico, the driver, nodded.

"It is difficult," he said. "I do not know this place and there are no signs."

Gomez refused to admit the fact, even though he was not so certain himself where they were. There was no road as such, just narrow dirt tracks that wound through the foothills, and one looked much like another.

"We should have brought that Jamaican cop with us," one of the team said.

"I didn't notice you interfering with Santana," Gomez said.

"Did I say I was crazy? Do you remember when Guzman interrupted Santana? He still carries the scar on his cheek."

"Shut up," Gomez yelled. He pointed through the windshield. "Enrico. There is the fork in the trail. With the big rock on the left. The cop said when we reach that we take the left trail and stay on it. Do it. Do it, pronto."

From the rear of the car a voice murmured, "I thought he said take the right fork."

Gomez stared into the rearview mirror. "I hear you, Baptise. Do you want to get out and fucking walk?"

Baptise shrugged.

The 4×4 topped the slight hump at the fork and started down a long, uneven stretch of the trail.

They drove for another ten minutes before Enrico braked the vehicle.

"There," he said.

Gomez climbed out of the 4×4 and felt the cooling breeze coming down off the higher peaks of the Blue Mountains. It felt good against his skin. From where he stood he could see the isolated cabin. There was a red sports car parked beside it. Gomez felt his panic easing. He turned and nodded at Enrico, then got back in the SUV.

"Go," he said.

MARY ANGELUS HEARD the soft sound of the approaching SUV. The clear air of the mountain slopes magnified sound well. A stranger wouldn't notice the phenomenon, but a native of the area could use the sound-traveling qualities to become aware of visitors in advance.

The woman pushed to her feet and went inside the cabin, peering through the window that let her see the trail leading to the cabin. What she did see alarmed her instantly. It was unusual to see vehicles up here. The narrow trails were primarily there to be used by those who knew the foothills. They were well off the normal tourist routes.

Angelus reached for her cell phone and switched it on, waiting impatiently as it picked up the signal. She needed to talk to the policeman, Wallace, now. The phone rang, startling her and she pressed the receive button.

"Mary?"

She didn't recognize the voice immediately.

"Mary. It's Rollie Benson."

She almost cried out in relief.

"You okay, love?"

"I don't know. I mean, no. I'm at the cabin, Rollie."

"Yes. We're on our way to you now. Not far off. Bob sent us."

"There's someone here. In a 4×4. I can see them, Rollie. They're coming to the cabin. They have guns, Rollie…they have guns."

"Can you get out before they reach you?"

THERE WAS no answer. Benson could hear background sounds. Frantic movement.

"Mary. Come on, love, talk to me."

Bolan pushed down hard on the gas pedal. According to Benson, they were almost at the cabin. The Briton's knowledge of the most direct route to the cabin had allowed them to make good time, but from the conversation with Mary Angelus, it seemed likely they might still be too late.

The Ford bounced over deep ruts in the dusty trail, sliding until Bolan regained control. He swung it around a sharp twist in the trail, up a sharp slope. As they bounced over the top Bolan saw the black SUV parked across the track, doors open. He hit the brakes and brought the Ford to a slithering stop inches from the SUV's rear end.

The urgent crackle of autofire reached Bolan as he went down the grassy slope in the direction of the cabin, Benson close behind him.

Four men were ahead of them, fanning out as they moved around the cabin to intercept the figure of a young woman in jeans and a T-shirt who was running away from the cabin in the opposite direction.

"It's Mary," Benson called out.

His voice reached one of the woman's pursuers. The man turned, bringing up the MP-5 he had cradled in his hands.

Bolan fired first, his Beretta spitting out a triburst that took the Colombian gunner high in the chest. The gunner twisted in pain, toppling backward. He struggled to rise, and Bolan hit him with a second burst, dropping him on his back.

GOMEZ TURNED as he heard the rattle of gunfire, and saw his man going down as Bolan triggered the 93-R. Even in that busy moment he recognized the shooter as the American who had escaped from Salazar's Colombian stronghold.

"Baptise, get that fucking bitch," he yelled. "Enrico, with me."

Enrico nodded, turning to target the American. Bolan triggered a burst that took Enrico in the head, driving him to the ground.

Gomez braced himself against the side of the cabin, bringing up his own MP-5. He fired at the American, shaking his head as the volley of 9 mm rounds cut to the right. He forgot to compensate for the way the SMG pulled off target. He made to fire again, then had to pull back as the American returned fire, his burst chunking into the plank wall close by his head. Wood splinters exploded from the wall of the cabin, some of them biting into the side of his face, tearing at his flesh. Gomez brushed at the splinters but only succeeded in aggravating the wound. The slivers of wood were like barbs, pulling at his flesh. The pain brought tears to his eyes and Gomez retreated, angry at his own inability to handle his weapon correctly. He stumbled over a jutting stone, banging against the side of the cabin. He looked up and saw the American getting closer. Gomez swore angrily. He jerked the MP-5 toward his adversary, his finger pulling back on the trigger too early. The volley had no target. The American had vanished.

"Over here," Gomez heard someone say.

As he turned, he felt something coring into his chest. The triburst dropped Gomez to his knees, a deep pain starting to engulf his upper body. He slumped back against the cabin wall, head falling on his chest. He saw that the front of his shirt was bloody.

Gomez looked up and saw the American was standing over him, the muzzle of his pistol aimed at Gomez's head. The Colombian looked beyond the gun muzzle, saw the eyes behind it. They were the coldest he had ever seen, and the last thing he ever saw.

"Game over," Bolan said and blew the top of Gomez's skull away.

ROLLIE BENSON ROUNDED the edge of the cabin. Ahead of him he could see the Colombian—Baptise—chasing after Mary Angelus. The Briton wanted to call out to the woman, but he realized that might put her off her stride. Instead he brought up his P-226 and fired at the Colombian. His shot missed by inches, plowing into the ground just ahead of the man. The Colombian stopped, turning to face Benson, and triggered his MP-5. The volley kicked up earth around Benson until Baptise tightened the pattern. His second volley stitched a burning line up Benson's right leg, from midcalf to halfway up his thigh. The numbing effect kicked Benson off his feet. He managed to stay on his knees as Baptise turned away and tracked the MP-5 in on Angelus's running figure.

"No!" Benson screamed.

Baptise pulled the trigger. His burst caught Mary Angelus between her shoulders, the impact throwing her off her feet. She hit the ground in a loose sprawl, her body jerking as Baptise fired again, the stream of 9 mm slugs impacting against her flesh.

Benson gripped his P-226 in both hands and began

to fire as Baptise turned away from the woman, his upper body coming around to face the Briton. He had used one round from the 15-round magazine. Now he emptied the contents into Baptise, firing one round after another and following the Colombian's twisting bloody form as he went down. The SIG's slide locked back after the final shot. Benson was still trying to pull the trigger when Bolan reached him.

"It's empty, Rollie."

Bolan saw the bloody mess in the Briton's leg. He reached into Benson's pocket and took out his cell phone. He checked the stored numbers until he found one logged in as "Office." Bolan tapped the call button and listened to the ring. A woman answered.

'I'm calling for Rollie Benson. He's been injured in a shooting incident. He needs medical attention ASAP. His location is the cabin owned by Bob Jackson, Kingston police officer. Get help up here fast. A young woman has also been shot. Mary Angelus."

"Can you—?" the woman began.

Bolan cut the contact. He made his way to where Mary Angelus lay, bending over the still form. There was nothing he could do for her. She was already dead. The Colombian's fire had been devastating. Bolan gently turned the body over. Exit wounds had only added to the damage done. Bolan was glad that her eyes were closed. He wouldn't have wanted to be confronted by her accusing gaze.

He stood and returned to where Benson had let himself fall back. Bolan examined the Briton's wounded leg. The 9 mm slugs had gouged and torn the flesh, the raw pulp sodden with blood. Benson stared up at the American.

"Mary?"

"She didn't make it, Rollie. Sorry."

Benson shook his head. His face was sickly white from shock and pain.

"What the hell is wrong with these bastards? Why someone like Mary?"

"They decided she was a threat. They only have one answer to threats, Rollie. They eliminate them."

CHAPTER TEN

"Get everyone out on the streets. I want to know who did this. Find out. No one sleeps until I get answers. You hear I? Earn your damn money. Make this happen."

Deacon Marley cut off the cell phone. He stood for a moment, staring about him, his face angry. His grip on the cell phone increased until the plastic creaked. He could feel the anger boiling inside him, rising until it threatened to cut off his breathing. He turned suddenly and crossed the room, pushing open the French windows so he could step out onto the balcony. He leaned against the railing edging the balcony and sucked cool mountain air into his lungs. In the distance he could see the Blue Mountain peaks, the soft white clouds hanging in ragged clumps above them. Below him lush tended grounds surrounded the sprawling house. Deep greenery splashed with brilliant flower colors. He remained where he was until the inner rage began to subside.

He tried not to think about the destruction of the drug-packing room at the coffee plant. The amount of heroin stored there had been huge. He didn't even want to think about how much money he had lost. Added to that was the administration building and his truck fleet. A great deal of money. Small compared to what he earned from his drug business, but enough to cause him concern. He hadn't forgotten about the rental agency, either. His fleet of near new cars gone. The ones that hadn't been totally destroyed would need extensive repair.

What hurt him most was the total disregard for his power. Marley was top dog in the drug community. No one defied him. Or hit at him in such a personal way. When he found those responsible he would make them suffer.

Marley called one of his men and told him to fetch Trechenko. It was time they finally hammered out the details of the alliance. All problems considered, the near future was going to be a busy and interesting one. There was too much at stake to back away now.

What smarted was the fact that the disruptions had happened at all. Marley was going to put out an all-island contract on Hermano Salazar's people.

Marley could only see the strikes against his property as another act of destruction by Salazar. The Colombian was doing his best to wipe out the partnership between Marley and Trechenko. It would never happen as far as Marley was concerned. This was his turf. Not the Colombians'. It was time for their grip on the drug business to be broken. They had become too big, refusing to allow anyone else to move into areas they considered their own exclusive domain.

Marley saw the market as open, there for anyone with the balls to challenge the Colombians. When he considered the money to be made from the U.S. market, Marley could almost feel himself drooling. The amounts were staggering. So large they could lose their meaning in terms of realizing just how much there was.

FEDOR TRECHENKO MADE his way from the apartment to the main house, his mind full of the things that had been happening over the past few days. He had managed to keep most of the disasters from Marley, not wanting the Jamaican to look on their merger as a total waste of his time. As far as Trechenko was concerned, he would recover. He had no other option. He accepted that his organization had, between Belasko and the Colombians, taken a battering. But he was far from defeated. Already there was rebuilding in Moscow. Trechenko's force was regrouping, and he had sent orders for a team to be assembled and flown out to Jamaica. It was both a way of providing protection for himself, and also of showing Marley that his Russian partner had the means to carry the fight forward.

The news of the deaths of Vladimir Korsov and Razak Khan during the attack on his house had been a blow. Losing Vashti he regretted more than anything. The man had been an important part of his Moscow operation. The disappearance of Asa Randal had been a surprise. After his faked death in the car bombing, Randal's kidnapping had left Trechenko without his contact to the American DEA. If Salazar had the American in his hands, Randal wouldn't be having a pleasant time. If he was still alive.

The only pluses to have come Trechenko's way had been the death of Benin, the OCD undercover man. Despite the efforts of Belasko to rescue the man, Trechenko's people had gotten to him in the hospital and dealt with him. And the Colombians who had carried out the attack on his house had also shot Valentine Seminov. Arguably not a complete victory there because the cop was still alive.

And what about Belasko himself?

He seemed to have vanished. Since his clash with Oleg's team at Belnikov's yard and after, Belasko had disappeared. The man had become a dangerous nuisance. Now with his apparent vanishing act, he still had the ability to annoy Trechenko.

Trechenko walked the length of the tiled veranda that connected the apartments to the main house. His bodyguard walked a few respectful steps behind him. If he had any regret this particular day it was the loss of Oleg. A pity. Oleg had been faithful and trustworthy. Fired by his own ambition, he had put himself on the line for Trechenko. For that he was grateful, but Oleg's death, wasted though it was, only proved to Trechenko that it was something that could happen to any of them, at any given moment.

There were two of Marley's own protection squad at the entrance to his personal suite of rooms. They stood aside to let Trechenko enter. The Russian's bodyguard remained outside with them.

"You heard about the hit against the coffee plant? And the car rental?"

Trechenko nodded as he joined Marley. They sat facing each other in deep leather armchairs.

"No more screwin' around," Marley said. "I want that Colombian fuck to know who he's dealing with. We join forces, we got something to hammer that shit with. Tell I now. Deal?"

Trechenko nodded.

"Deal."

Marley stood and crossed to the bar at the far end of the room. He blended a couple glasses of liquor, adding ice and lemon juice.

"Celebrate, man. This is a good day."

He handed Trechenko his drink and returned to his seat.

"There's a team of shooters flying in right now. If Salazar wants a war, he can have one."

"Good. I have the word out to spot any of Salazar's people. We give him something to think about."

There was a tap on the door.

"Come."

One of Marley's Jamaicans crossed to stand beside the drug lord's chair.

"Tell me, man."

The man spoke in a rapid local patois that left Trechenko struggling to understand. Marley listened in silence until the man had finished.

"Okay, get back to the streets. Pass the word. I want to know all about this."

After his man had gone Marley sat playing with the drink in his hand.

"Deacon?"

"It's like this. A cop is in the Kingston hospital. He was with the drug squad. Pretty bad cut up. Be lucky if he lives. He was found at a beach house belonging to a local woman. Also there were three Colombians. All shot. Not by the cop. But he took a razor to one of the Colombians and chopped him pretty bad. They're all dead. Couple of hours later there was a gun battle in the foothills. Somebody call the cops. When they got there they found the girl who owned the beach house dead and four more Colombians. Dead, too. There was also a British customs agent there. Wounded but alive."

Marley leaned back, staring at the far wall. Trechenko sipped his drink.

"You think the British agent shot them?"

"We'll find out. I have my people checking. I know about this Brit. He been on the island for a while. He working with the Kingston cops. They're all trying to get me. But they're not smart."

"You think this customs agent has a partner?"

Marley leaned forward, eyes searching Trechenko's face.

"You know somethin', man. Spill it."

"I had trouble back in Moscow. The Americans sent in some investigator from their Justice Department. He was supposed to be monitoring the DEA team working with the OCD. He wasn't. He was some kind of independent operator. Caused me some problems."

"What kind problems?"

"He teamed up with some Afghans and they hit Razak Khan's distribution center in the mountains. Took it out."

Marley nodded slowly.

"Looks like we both got caned."

"So we turn this thing around and do some hitting ourselves. Or we quit and take up something less stressful."

Marley laughed. "Now that I like. So when your boys coming in?"

"Later today. And I can send for more if we need them."

"We get them up here. Make them feel at home and then send them to work."

Trechenko felt a little better after his confession. He had held back some of the detail, not wanting Marley to have to absorb all the bad news in one session. Once they had their hit teams out in the field, dealing with Salazar, there would be too much going on to worry about Trechenko's setbacks.

"You think this American might be on the island?"

"Maybe."

"I have my boys check out this, too."

"The Afghans will organize another shipment and get it to us."

"That's no problem," Marley said. "I have a reserve shipment ready to move out, man. This boy thinks ahead. I'll go make arrangements."

WHEN THE TELEPHONE rang Marley's man answered. He listened to his instructions, put down the phone and crossed the warehouse office. Opening the door, he yelled to his team that it was time to load the shipment. He called in his foreman.

"Get the load ready. And don't forget the other stuff."

The additional cargo was a large consignment of weapons for shipment to the U.S. This was on top of the drug shipment, a secondary source of income devised by Marley himself, in conjunction with a couple of brokers who had a need to push the arms into America as part of their own agenda.

Yassar Hajhi and Razzi Munar had approached Marley, via a discreet contact. They had offered the Jamaican a good deal. All he had to do was ship the weapons cache along with his heroin. Marley had the contacts and the ability to smuggle his cargo into the U.S. on a regular basis, which suited Hajhi and Munar. They were conducting their own business, as part of their ongoing struggle to create dissident agitation within the U.S., and the money they offered Marley had been too much to turn down.

Drugs and weapons. It all meant the same thing to Deacon Marley. Profit. He understood the concept of business. Supply and demand. The addition of a cargo of extra crates meant little difference to his own operation. The cash money that Hajhi and Munar had come up with had been a gift Marley would have been foolish to refuse. He didn't give a damn what the guns were used for.

THE CARGO SHIP at the dock rode the swell that was starting to grow. The loading crew noticed the imperceptible buildup, but carried on with their work. They were used to the changes in the weather. It was part of their lives. The Caribbean was prone to unexpected weather conditions, and the people lived with it.

Throughout the morning the climate change continued. By early afternoon the swell had become stronger. A wind had blown in from the sea, swaying the trees and tugging at the men as they continued to load the ship.

The first rain came in midafternoon. A few drops at first, pushed by the increasing wind. A heavy fall hit around three o'clock. Sweeping in off the Caribbean, the rain drove across the dock area, bouncing off the ground and slapping against the warehouses. In the next hour the force of both wind and rain had increased to the extent that concerns were being raised. The water inside the dock area was becoming rough, and the cargo ship was straining at its moorings.

Marley's man at the docks called his employer and informed him it was going to be difficult to get the cargo ship under way. They discussed the situation and decided that it would be wiser to keep the ship in dock until the weather eased off.

Radio reports warned of incoming high winds and rain. There would be little relief from the extreme weather for at least the next eight hours. Storm warnings went out across the island.

The loading crews were stood down. The men were sent home until conditions improved. Only Marley's armed crew remained at the dock.

As the torrential downpour increased, along with the heightening gale-force winds, nothing moved on the deserted dock—until a flitting shadow eased along the fronts of the warehouses; a tall, dark-haired figure clad in a form-fitting blacksuit and rigged for war.

Mack Bolan was bringing the battle to the enemy.

And in no mood for compromise or mercy.

BOLAN'S INITIAL meeting with Captain Simon Wallace, head of the Kingston drug unit, had been decidedly frosty until the Jamaican spoke to Leo Turrin over the phone. Bolan had called Turrin to let him know what was happening, and the man from Justice had requested to speak with Wallace. That conversation went a long way to easing the situation.

Wallace had been brought up to speed with the incidents at Mary Angelus's bungalow and the cabin in the Blue Mountain foothills. Police units had moved in to seal off both crime scenes. The Jamaican cop, shocked at the brutality of the incidents, had taken his frustration out on the quiet American, though he had tempered his anger due to Rollie Benson's intervention. The British agent, even though still in severe pain from his leg wounds, had insisted on seeing Wallace, and had explained in great detail what had happened, pointing out that if Bolan hadn't been on hand to administer emergency aid and call in the incident report, Benson wouldn't have survived.

"I'm still not too happy with all this, McCall. This is Jamaica, not Tombstone."

"You have a problem here, Captain Wallace, not of my making. I got involved because I walked into it. I only have regrets because your undercover men got badly hurt and a young woman died simply through being caught up in this mess. Bob Jackson and Rollie Benson were doing their jobs. I was doing mine. Maybe if you people stopped worrying about the damn regulations and played these people by their own rules this might have been avoided."

Wallace stood up and crossed his office to close the door. He didn't speak until he was behind his desk again.

"I was about to throw the book at you, McCall. Until I spoke to Benson and your Mr. Turrin. But you know what—off the record—I'd like to give you a bloody medal." He ran a big hand through his hair. "Direct action is my dream. Being able to go for these traffickers is what I want to do. We all know the bastards are guilty. I'm chained to the wall by procedure. Rule of law. Legal restraints. And we have the problem of paid informers.

Marley's people on the streets. Buying and selling information almost before the print is dry on the paper. How can I compete with a man who will hand out thousands of dollars for a piece of information? What can I offer to an out-of-work man who can earn himself a small fortune for a few minutes' work?"

"Nobody ever said being on the right side was going to be easy."

The Jamaican smiled. "Well at least we agree on something."

"This alliance between Marley and Trechenko is going to bring you a damn sight more trouble," Bolan said. "Hermano Salazar isn't going to sit back and let it happen without a fight. And that means the battle ground is going to be here in Jamaica. Gang war. It's never pretty because these people are fighting to gain control of a multimillion-dollar business. They aren't concerned who gets caught up in it. Who gets hurt. There have been too many good people hurt already in this. We have to take the fight to them, and do it before they regroup. Hit them on their own ground where civilians aren't going to be caught in the cross fire."

"I get the feeling you've already been doing that. The coffee plant? Marley's car rental?"

Bolan stayed silent. Wallace was no fool. The cop was chewing over what he already knew, and his acceptance that Bolan was some kind of loose cannon only opened the way to further off-the-wall action against the traffickers.

"Let's accept those incidents as read. Marley has other outlets. Were they on the agenda?"

"Other things got in the way. Bob Jackson and Mary Angelus were priority."

"I have information on a shipment of heroin," Wallace said. "This came to me from one of *my* informers. Marley doesn't have it all his own way. The word is that Marley has a cargo being readied for sailing out of his dock. By the time I get all the necessary documentation for a raid, if I even could, the stuff will be on its way."

"All I need is the location. Then you forget you even mentioned it."

"As this comes from an unofficial source there's no record," Wallace said. "That's how it will stay. If you take this on, McCall, I can't offer you any backup."

"Understood."

"How's your side? Are you fit for action?"

Wallace was referring to the bullet gouges Bolan had sustained during the firefight at Mary Angelus's bungalow. Bolan had been attended to at the hospital where Benson had been airlifted. Bolan's injury was slight compared to the damage to the Briton's leg. Bolan had received concerned looks when the discolored bruising on his body had been discovered. He had explained it happened during the course of his work.

"I'm fine," he told the cop.

Wallace had broken off to glance around as sudden gusts of wind rattled his office window. He got up to check it out.

"Looks as if we could be in for a storm."

"Handy for cover," Bolan commented. "How about you give me some detail on this hypothetical shipment, Captain."

BOLAN HAD LEFT his car in an alley between a couple of disused warehouses. He went EVA and approached Marley's dock area, the torrential downpour soaking him within minutes. The soldier didn't concern himself with that. He was grateful for the storm. It helped to cover his approach. The wind-driven rain was literally bouncing off the street, which was awash.

Bolan gained entry to the dock by the simple maneuver of going over the fence that enclosed it. He scaled the fence and dropped onto a metal container parked close to the perimeter. From the shadows at the base of the container he was able to scan the dock, the poorly maintained warehouses and the scattering of boxes and old machinery that littered the area. Marley's dock area wouldn't have won any prizes for tidiness. Bolan guessed this was a deliberate attempt at distracting interested parties.

He crossed to the main warehouse complex, hugging the wall. Through the mist created by the downpour Bolan could see the cargo ship moored at the dock. The vessel was riding the powerful swell, rolling from side to side as the water surged violently.

The cargo ship was an old rust bucket. Her paint was stained and flaking. Bolan studied her for a time, searching the deck area for any sign of crew or guards. He saw nothing. If there was anyone on board, they would probably be under cover. This would be his best chance to board the ship.

His observation had shown him stacks of large wood crates lined along the dock, parallel with the ship. The crates would provide him with cover for access to the ship itself.

Bolan checked his Uzi was secured by its strap, then moved out quickly, angling across the open area between the warehouse and the crates. This was where he would be most exposed. It couldn't be avoided. There was no other way to reach the crates. He felt a moment of relief when he was able to slip in among the crates and work his way along the dock until he was level with the cargo ship.

Drawing level with an open cargo hatch in the side of the ship, Bolan spent more time surveying the area. He could see through the open hatch into the hold. No one appeared to be in the immediate vicinity.

He worked his way to the front of the crates, checking in both directions along the dock, then turned his attention back to the open hatch, watching the rise and fall of the moored ship. There was only a gap of a couple of feet between the dock edge and the hatch, but the rise and fall of the vessel added to the possibility of missed footing. Bolan unlimbered the Uzi, holding it close to his chest as he leaned out, then took long strides across the wet dock, reached the extreme edge and pushed out for the open hatch. His right foot landed firm, his left slipped on the wet hatch opening and he would have fallen if he hadn't thrown out his left hand and caught hold of the hatch frame, hauling himself inside.

Bolan stepped deeper into the gloom of the hold, feeling the roll of the vessel as the heavy swell lifted her.

He turned to start checking out the cargo and sensed movement to his right.

Bolan twisted, eyes searching the shadows, and saw a bulky figure lunging at him, the gleaming blade of a fire ax keening the air as it swept down at his skull.

CHAPTER ELEVEN

Bolan ducked and the blade skimmed the top of his hair, then clanged against the hatch frame. As the man leaned in toward him, Bolan reacted out of pure instinct, letting the Uzi hang by its strap as he punched hard into the ax man's paunchy gut. The soldier hit hard with his right fist, heard the man grunt as the blow caught him off guard. Reaching up with his left hand, Bolan slammed his palm under the guy's chin, pushing his head up and back, then swung his right again, this time to connect with the man's jaw. The blow landed hard, delivered with all of Bolan's concentrated strength, and it spun the guy back across the hold. Bolan followed, not allowing the man time to recover. He caught hold of a flailing arm and swung the guy face first into the metal bulkhead. Bone snapped and flesh split. The guy slithered to the deck, his face awash with blood.

Bolan moved into the hold, inspecting the cargo. He

found sacks of coffee beans. He slipped out his knife and cut open a number of the sacks. There was nothing on the top layer but when he got to the lower sacks he found tightly packed plastic packs of white powder pushed deep inside the sacks of coffee beans. He cut open one of the packs and tasted the powder.

Heroin.

He moved around the hold, checking out the rest of the cargo. He located more stacks of coffee bean sacks, again with the lower layers containing packs of heroin.

Bolan was about to move on when something caught his eye—the edge of a box that looked somehow familiar. He pushed the sacks out of the way until he could get a grip on the box and drag it out. He recognized the Cyrillic lettering—it was Russian—and the designation was for weapons. Bolan snapped open the catches and threw the lid back. Nestling in the box were a dozen Kalashnikov AK-47s. He hauled away more of the sacks, uncovering up to a couple of dozen boxes. There were also a large number of ammunition boxes—5.45 mm.

Bolan was trying to make sense of the find even as he set one of the incendiary devices against the ammunition boxes. He placed a couple more where they would directly attack the sacks holding the heroin. He set the timers for two minutes, turned and headed for the open cargo hatch.

He braced himself on the deck frame and saw that the distance between the ship and the dock had widened. The vessel was tight on her mooring ropes, sucked away from the side of the dock. Bolan braced himself as the ship rose, then fell again. The storm had increased in its ferocity even during the short time he had been on board the ship. The vessel wallowed in a trough, the dock feet above Bolan. He slid his Uzi so that it hung down his back and waited for the ship to rise as the water changed direction.

When it happened Bolan was almost caught by the sudden surge. The ship rose, the motion almost throwing him through the cargo hatch. He braced himself against the hatch, gauging his move so he jumped at the right moment. His leap threw him toward the dock, but the ship sank from beneath his feet at the critical moment. Bolan found himself below the dock level. He threw out his arms and gripped the edge of the dock, hanging by his hands for agonizing seconds, aware of the ship's threatening bulk behind him.

The rising howl of the wind and the crash of the sea against the dockside made him realize he needed to move quickly. He began to haul himself up the side of the dock, straining every muscle.

Behind him the cargo ship dipped, then began to rise, this time swinging in toward the dock. Bolan could sense the massive deadweight of its bulk closing in on him.

The threat of being crushed added impetus to his scramble to get clear. He swung one leg over the top of the dock wall, rolled and pulled his other leg out of harm's way.

Bolan rolled across the dock, feeling the impact as

the ship hit the dock. He heard the rolling rumble as the edge of the shattered dock wall broke apart and heard, too, the protest of buckling metal.

Pushing hard against the line of packing cases, Bolan mentally counted down the remaining seconds of the timers. He was close in his estimation. The incendiary devices blew with muffled thumps. The open hatch was filled with blinding light and fire. Bolan felt the rush of heat as the incendiary devices began to burn.

He gathered his feet under him and pushed away from the side of the ship, remembering the ammunition boxes in the hold. The incendiary devices would generate heat powerful enough to detonate the ammunition quickly. The stored munitions began to blow before Bolan reached the end of the dock, the crackle and repeated explosions trailing his moves.

Ahead of him people began to rush out of the warehouse, weapons in plain sight. They hesitated, staring in the direction of the cargo ship as more flame and smoke billowed out of the hold, and Bolan might have made it if one of the Jamaicans hadn't turned in his direction. The guy set up a warning shout and turned his SMG on Bolan's running figure. The volley blew stone chips against the back of the soldier's legs as he kept moving.

The traffickers took up the pursuit, firing on the run, which saved Bolan's life. He felt the impact of bullets on the concrete around him, heard the vicious snap of more bullets striking the edge of the warehouse, blowing chunks out of the wall as he ducked behind its cover.

Bolan let his pursuers get close before he stepped back around the corner of the warehouse and burned off half a clip from the Uzi, his shots catching the traffickers as they closed in on him. Bolan put three down for good, his shots coring into them with deadly effect. The Executioner turned sideways as one guy came at him, screaming wildly, firing his weapon with total disregard for target acquisition. The American warrior's 9 mm slugs took away half of the yelling guy's face and silenced him in a moment of blinding pain. The last two traffickers hauled back, aware they had pushed into action too quickly, realizing they were in the open and totally exposed. Bolan switched the Uzi's muzzle to encompass them both as he stitched a bloody pattern across their bodies. They hit the ground, jerking in agony until the soldier's final burst stilled them for good.

Bolan pulled back and reloaded, cocking the Uzi before he moved off toward the fence. He climbed up on the container and went over the fence, head down against the driving rain as he returned to his car. He slid behind the wheel and started the engine, moving off to make the return trip to Jack Grimaldi to replenish his ordnance and establish his next target.

"IT HAS TO BE him," Trechenko said. "The American. He must be some paid killer working for the U.S. government. I think this Justice Department thing was just a cover."

Deacon Marley stood at the window of the office

above the dock warehouse. He hadn't moved for ten minutes, had simply stood motionless, staring down at the still-smoking cargo ship. Things had gone from bad to disastrous. His backup shipment destroyed; the cache of weapons reduced to scrap; his ship listing in the water, being dragged back and forth on its mooring ropes by the stormy sea. It was almost as if the whole damn world had conspired against him at the moment.

To top it off, his street informers had spotted more Colombians in Kingston. They were splashing money around and buying favors from anyone they could. The damn mothers were laughing in his face. In his own fucking town.

"Fedor, have your people arrived yet?"

The Russian nodded. "I got the word a little while ago. They are on the way to your place right now."

"This time we make the rules. I want every Colombian and their fuckin' informers spotted and dealt with. We been sitting back and they walk all over us. No more. You hear? *No more.*"

"I NEED TO MOVE farther out. See if I can clear the storm area. We're taking a battering here, Señor Salazar."

The Captain of the *Caliente* gripped the edge of the desk with his free hand as he listened to Salazar's reply. The motor vessel was pitching badly as it pushed head-on into the rising storm. He was doing his best to maintain a safe course through the heavy seas, his course taking him away from Jamaica.

"Yes. All the men are ashore. Perez has taken charge now that Gomez is dead. They are looking for the American, Belasko, and the missing computer. I understand, Señor Salazar."

The captain put down the telephone. He looked out through the control cabin, watching the waves that were surging all around the motor vessel.

"Keep a steady course," he instructed the helmsman. "Always into the storm. The *Caliente* can take it. Just do not allow her to broadside."

The captain had faith in the boat and his crew. They were skilled, and this wasn't the first time the Caribbean had turned its hard face against them. In truth he was happier to be out here facing the storm than back in Jamaica having to handle Deacon Marley and the lone American who kept showing up at the most inappropriate times.

"JUST GIVE THE WORD," Grimaldi said, "and we're out of here."

Bolan finished reloading the Uzi and moved to check his extra ammunition. He was in the crew cabin of *Dragon Slayer,* his equipment spread around him.

"Jack, don't do this just because of me. It's bad out there. I'm not going to put you and the lady at risk."

"You let me decide that, Sarge."

Grimaldi was standing outside the combat chopper, leaning against the open hatch. Bolan knew he was chafing to get into action. To push the game to the limit.

"This weather gives us the best chance to cut Deacon Marley down. We take out that place of his up in the hills, he's going to be hurting. And if Trechenko is there, as well, we can cut the odds pretty thin."

Bolan completed his check of loaded magazines for his Uzi, Beretta and Desert Eagle, then slung the Uzi and holstered his pistols. Next he sheathed his knife and clipped a number of fragmentation grenades to the vest.

There was quiet determination in Bolan's actions. The business of a pure professional. Jack Grimaldi had seen it many times before, and admired the detached way his old friend went about these tasks. He made no show of handling his deadly weapons, showed no relish in his upcoming combat. There was no joy in what he had to do, only a genuine sadness that he was forced to maintain his self-imposed role. Bolan did what he did because the death dealers he faced understood only one thing—fierce and relentless opposition to their unchanging stance.

Grimaldi had walked with Bolan through many of his campaigns, had fought beside him and hauled him out of fire zones, and he would carry on doing it as long as he was able. His personal loyalty to Bolan was undiminished. Never spoken because there was no need to put it into words.

And this night, if Bolan wanted to carry forward his war against Deacon Marley, Grimaldi and *Dragon Slayer* would be there down to the final countdown.

"I'll take your word, Jack."

"Then let's do it."

It was early evening. The day was prematurely dark, due to the prevailing storm conditions. The heavy wind and the unceasing rain had cast a twilight mood over the island. Visibility was reduced, and the lowering cloud formations promised a continuation of the bad weather.

As far as Mack Bolan was concerned, the conditions were just right for an unannounced strike at Deacon Marley's residence.

GRIMALDI RAN his preflight check, receiving positive responses on all his indicators. Satisfied that *Dragon Slayer* was fully operational, he turned to his secondary checks and ran through his weapons systems. HE and HS missiles. Three Stinger air-to-air. All stored in the stub-wing missile pods. The 30 mm chain gun responded to his activation test, swiveling on its underslung pod.

"Locked and loaded, Sarge," Grimaldi called over his shoulder.

"Patch me through to Stony Man, Jack."

Grimaldi used the satcom link to make a connection to the Farm, where Aaron Kurtzman had been analyzing the data from the laptop Bolan had recovered. The computer had been connected via an electronic link in *Dragon Slayer.* Kurtzman had accessed the data banks, including the hard-drive memory, downloading all of the stored information. His initial report had told Bolan that all the data was in Spanish and Kurtzman would need a rapid translation before he could make any sense of it.

"My Spanish isn't that good," Kurtzman had said. "I'll get our people on it. Let you have what I find."

"Keep Leo up to speed," Bolan told him.

"Will do."

Barbara Price answered the call.

"Hey, big guy, how's the Caribbean?"

"It could be better."

"Weather got you socked in?"

"Not enough to cancel."

"You guys take care."

"Has Aaron come up with anything?"

"You'll love this," Price said. "The database only showed Salazar's contacts from Jamaica, through Florida and all the way to Mexico. It was like the guy's address book. There were even pickup and drop-off points."

"No surprise why they were frantic to get it back. Salazar won't be too happy about that falling into our hands."

"Aaron has sent Leo relevant information so they can move on some of the people and shut down Salazar's pipeline. There was a bonus, too. A couple more DEA names appeared. Minor players, but it looks like they might have been greasing the way for Salazar's Mexican end. Leo is taking charge of that himself. Something about needing to get out of the office and get some exercise."

"Tell him to watch his back."

"Will do. Hey, same for you."

"Keep a candle burning for us."

"I ordered an extralarge box."

THE HATCHES SEALED shut. Grimaldi coasted *Dragon Slayer* out through the open hangar doors. The wind and heavy rain struck the combat chopper, rocking it on its undercarriage wheels, but Grimaldi's firm hand on the controls kept the helicopter stable. He moved the chopper out into the open, then upped the power to the rotors, feeling the powerful turbines gathering speed.

Bolan was in the bodyform seat alongside Grimaldi. He felt the chopper turn as the Stony Man pilot took them off the ground, gaining height and setting *Dragon Slayer* on a northerly course that would take them in the direction of the Blue Mountains and Deacon Marley's isolated residence.

TRECHENKO WAS briefing his six-man team when the door to the spacious lounge burst open and Deacon Marley stepped inside.

The Jamaican stared around the room. He had a detached expression in his eyes, his dark face sheened with perspiration. He was holding a long *daito* sword in his right hand. The gleaming weapon, with its keen cutting edge, had been the sword of the Japanese samurai warriors.

One of Trechenko's men made a slight move toward one of the autoweapons resting on a coffee table close to where he was sitting. Trechenko stopped him with a quick gesture.

"Deacon, what's wrong?"

"You do not know?"

Marley moved farther into the room, raising his sword in the direction of the window.

"He's coming. This night. And you know him, man."

Trechenko frowned. "You mean Belasko?"

"You a religious man? No, I think not." Marley glanced at the Russian. "This island has plenty 'tings not understood. You believe, you not believe, it still happens."

"You're not making sense, Deacon. *What* is going to happen?"

Marley jabbed his sword at the assembled team.

"Show me they not here to waste time. These *soldiers*."

The Jamaican turned and left the room.

"What was that?" one Russian asked.

Trechenko failed to give him an answer. He didn't have one. Marley's behavior had been unsettling. The Jamaican had always struck him as a stable, if not dangerous man. After what he had just witnessed the Russian found himself wondering whether he really did know his new partner all that well.

MARLEY RETURNED to his office. He couldn't explain his mood. The feeling that prompted his actions had made itself known about an hour ago and Marley had tried, but failed, to resist as long as he could.

Something was warning him of trouble coming his way and Marley, born and bred on the island, found it impossible to ignore his feelings. The old superstitions, instilled in him by his long-dead grandmother, had always been there. They had made themselves known to him on other occasions, coming like ghostly shadows at the back of his mind. Whispers that only he could register. They were there now, flitting in and out of his consciousness. Warning him. Telling him to be ready for what was already approaching. There was no escaping. Destiny couldn't be avoided. It had to be faced.

On this night, disturbed by the capricious mood of nature, with the rain and wind creating a sensation of menace, Deacon Marley felt a threatening presence coming his way.

That presence would be in the physical form of a black-clad figure who would come out of the sky.

GRIMALDI'S ON-SCREEN terrain map pinpointed their current location.

"ETA two minutes," he said.

Bolan scanned the monitor. The displayed chart provided him with a precise image of Marley's residence.

The former plantation mansion, now vastly expanded from its original size, sat on the crest of a flat-topped hill, overlooking the plantation grounds and fields. These spread out across the shallow slopes of the rising ground, surrounding the house itself. To the east were the storage and holding sheds for the harvested coffee beans.

Grimaldi's approach brought them in from the southeast, along a ridge that rose almost to a level with the house itself. Once Bolan left *Dragon Slayer* he would have a quarter mile of terrain to cover, bringing him to the rear of the house.

"I still think I could drop you closer in."

"Don't worry about it, Jack. This way there won't be any chance they might spot you."

Bolan held up the compact transceiver-homing device Grimaldi had provided.

"Yeah, I know. Wait for the call, then come in making like the Seventh Cavalry."

There was a warm grin on Bolan's face as he clapped a big hand on Grimaldi's shoulder, then raised it in a farewell salute. A moment later he had gone.

CHAPTER TWELVE

Sheeting rain and the rush of the wind covered Bolan's approach. He took shelter beneath the overhang of an extended deck that jutted from the main body of the house, supported by thick timber joists embedded in the earth. He moved through the timber supports, easing the Uzi across his back, securing the strap to prevent the weapon from interfering with the upcoming climb.

His way to the open deck was by hand-over-hand climbing using the interwoven wooden timbers. The wet surface of the wood made the climb slow. Bolan determined each move with caution. Added to the slick surfaces was the constant downpour, and the wind threatened to drag him clear. Bolan estimated he had at least twenty-five feet to cover, his progress hampered by the poor light and the hostile conditions.

He had reached halfway when the buffeting wind swirled in and caught at his clothing, Bolan losing the grip of his right hand. For long seconds he hung by his single hand, struggling to regain his hold. Perversely it was the wind, changing direction again that saved him, slamming into him with a force that took his breath. He was pinned to the wooden frame, throwing out his hand to regain his grip and staying motionless until he was able to move on.

Bolan's climb progressed foot by foot. He made no attempt to finish his climb with any speed, content to simply stay the course until he reached the wooden railing edging the deck. Bolan chanced a look through a panoramic window and saw a large room, well furnished and lit by subdued lights.

Easing under the lower rail Bolan rolled across the deck, staying prone as he caught a flicker of movement on the far side. On that side of the area there was a walkway that ran along the side of the house. An armed figure, caught in the light from the room beyond the glass, moved into view.

The guard was clad in a waterproof jacket, head down as he moved out of the protection of the building into the open. Rain was bouncing across the deck, striking the panoramic window. The guard took his walk across to the extreme end of the deck area, then turned to make his slow way back to the cover provided by the building.

He was too late to react when a dark shape rose from the deck in front of him. All he saw was a black-clad form a split second before something clubbed him across the side of his head. The blow was uncompromising, dropping the guard to his knees.

Bolan struck a second time, the Uzi slamming down across the guard's skull. The guy pitched facedown on the deck. The Executioner wasted no time in stripping off the waterproof jacket and pulling it on. The fit was loose, but Bolan wasn't concerned about that. He zipped the coat over his blacksuit, shouldered the Uzi and dragged the unconscious guard into the shadows close to the house, picking up the man's dropped weapon. It was an H&K MP-5. He found a spare magazine in one of the jacket's large pockets. Bolan checked the MP-5, made sure it was operational, then moved on.

DEACON MARLEY stared in frustration at his man.

"Say again?"

"It those two guys you were shipping the weapons for. They're here. Want to see you now."

Marley pushed his chair away from his desk.

"What do they want?"

"I think they hear about the ship. Want to know about their cargo."

Marley was tempted to send the pair away. He had enough on his mind without them making a fuss. On reflection he decided it might be best to see them. He had to deal with them, so right now was as good a time as any.

"Bring them here. Ras, keep some of the boys close. Understand?"

Ras nodded. "No problem, boss."

YASSAR HAJHI and Razzi Munar were shown into Marley's office. They faced him across his desk, looking for all purposes like men come to sell him insurance.

They wore neat suits, crisp shirts and ties, expensive shoes. There was something intimidating about their appearance. Marley knew them to be hard negotiators, men who knew what they wanted and the price they were prepared to pay.

"It came to our attention there has been an incident involving your cargo ship. Extreme enough to suggest that our cargo has been damaged," Hajhi said.

"We thought it best to come and talk the matter over with you." Munar paused. "And there have been other incidents to do with your business ventures."

"These are worrying developments, Mr. Marley."

"These things happen. This is a risky business. Rivals are always out there trying to take over. This what happen now. Hit me. Hit the ship. I'm dealing with it."

"Not good enough," Hajhi said. "You contracted to deliver our weapons. Took our money. Now the weapons have been destroyed. We have a problem. Our people are expecting those weapons. We have to deliver."

"It happens. You want back your money? Okay, I give it back. No other thing I can do."

"Returning the money is not acceptable. Our principals will be most displeased at this setback."

Marley slammed his fist down on the desk. "They be displeased? What about me? Right now I'm fighting for my fuckin' life an' you make all this fuss about you guns. It not the most important thing to me right now."

"Actually it should be," Munar said softly. "Perhaps you should reconsider before it is too late."

"You threatening me now, in my own place? I think not."

"It doesn't end with us," Hajhi said. "Once it starts it never stops. Betray us and we come after you."

"Go to hell. Ras, in here."

The door swung open and three of Marley's men rushed into the office. They were all armed and moved to cover Hajhi and Munar.

"We got trouble, boss?"

Marley smiled. "They got trouble. Tellin' me I got problems. Already I offer back their money but these boys, they got aggravation."

Marley walked around his desk, casually picking up the samurai sword, sliding it from its scabbard. He let the blade trail behind him as he confronted Hajhi and Munar.

"You come to this island. Without invitation. But I listen to you. Agree to ship your merchandise. I do this even though it could make trouble for me. Now you come and bad-mouth me when the deal go wrong. Threaten me with your fuckin' vengeance."

"He do that, boss?"

Marley nodded.

"Bad mistake," Ras said softly, stepping back as he caught the merest flicker in Marley's eyes.

Marley barely seemed to move. Lamplight gleamed

against cold steel, the sword in Marley's hand whispered all too quietly.

Hajhi felt little more than an ice-cold touch against the side of his neck. There was no time for anything else. His severed head toppled to the floor, bouncing and rolling. His body remained upright for a few seconds, blood spurting from the stump of his neck, spilling down to soak his neat suit and shirt. As the corpse dropped to the floor Marley turned slightly, the sword flickering with light again. This time the razor-edged blade cut in across Munar's body, opening him up from left to right. He collapsed in a silent sprawl.

Deacon Marley stepped back, lowering his sword.

"They don't threaten me. Nobody threaten me."

The distant sound of autofire reached their ears then, coming from somewhere at the far side of the house.

"Go tell Fedor. Tell him we got our visitor. And this time he not walkin' away."

BOLAN HAD FOUND a way into the house. He met opposition almost at once. The waterproof coat fooled the Jamaican for only a short time as he walked along an upper landing, straight for the American. Bolan had kept his head down, hoping he might confuse for longer than he actually did.

The armed Jamaican peered hard at Bolan, snapping out some rapid words that defied translation.

The soldier hauled the MP-5 on line and triggered a short burst that caught the trafficker in the chest as he brought up his own weapon. The Jamaican uttered a shrill scream, the concentrated fire tearing his flesh open and kicking him backward. He fell against the railing edging the landing and went over, falling three floors to the entrance hall below.

Bolan shrugged out of the redundant waterproof coat, plucking the spare MP-5 magazine from the pocket and pushing it into a pocket in his blacksuit. There was no more use for subterfuge. His presence in Marley's house was known. From here on in it was going to be open warfare, with Bolan against the traffickers until there was one man standing.

SOUND ALERTED Bolan and he turned toward it. Three armed Jamaicans were climbing the stairs, yelling in unison. He caught them midflight, the MP-5 spitting flame, 9 mm slugs chewing into vulnerable flesh. The squirming figures crashed against the wall, blood spraying in trailing arcs as they fell back. An SMG stuttered to Bolan's right. Bullets bypassed him by inches, ripping ragged slivers of wood from the railing. The soldier launched himself belly down on the landing, pushing the MP-5 on track. He triggered a burst that blew the legs from under the shooter. The Jamaican stumbled, his shattered limbs giving way beneath him and as he fell, Bolan's next burst hit him in the head, spinning him over on his back.

On his feet again Bolan headed along the corridor. To his right double doors opened into the spacious lounge he had seen through the large picture window while he was outside. Bolan ducked in through the door, checking out the room. It was empty, so he spun on his heel to move on. Ahead of him he saw people at the head of the corridor. He flattened against the wall as the thunder of autofire filled the corridor, slugs ripping apart plaster and wood. He freed a fragmentation grenade and pulled the pin, popping the lever and holding the sphere for seconds before lobbing it along the corridor. Bolan withdrew into the protection of the open doorway. He picked up the yells of panic that preceded the solid impact of the grenade as it detonated. As the sound faded, the yells were replaced by the cries of the wounded. Bolan stepped out and saw the bodies sprawled in bloody heaps on the corridor floor. One guy still remained on his feet, leaning against the wall, his left side bloody and shredded. He still had the strength to raise his autorifle. Bolan cut him down with a single burst, then turned and made for the stairs. He went down two at a time, stepping over the bodies of the three he had already put down. Before he reached the next landing Bolan ejected the MP-5's magazine and clicked in the spare one.

He cocked the SMG, pausing at the foot of the stairs to peer around the corner of the wall. He was confronted by another corridor with doors leading off on either side. There didn't appear to be anyone on this floor as Bolan encountered no confrontation. He could hear voices below him, orders being passed back and forth, then the sound of movement on the stairs leading down from his floor. This time they were different voices. Not Jamaican. Bolan recognized Russian, which told him Trechenko *was* here.

Bolan moved to the side wall, watching until he saw a shadow fall across the landing. He spotted the muzzle of a weapon ease into view, heard the subdued whisper as the owner spoke to his partners. He was ready to confront the newcomer when a voice called out from somewhere above Bolan's head, shouting a warning. The warning was followed by the snap of autofire, slugs whacking into the wall where Bolan had been an instant before. He leaned back against the wall, raising his head to see one of Marley's Jamaicans leaning over the railing of the upper landing. Angling the MP-5, Bolan squeezed off a burst, the stream of 9 mm slugs catching the trafficker in the stomach, kicking him away from the railing in a shower of splintered wood, and the moment he'd fired Bolan twisted back in the direction of the stairs as the hesitant Russian made his play, lunging up off the last step, turning to face his target. Bolan swung up his right leg and hammered the sole of his boot into the Russian's gut, the force of the kick sending the guy back down the stairs, arms and legs windmilling before he slammed into three of his companions who were coming up behind.

Bolan followed through, raking the stairs with the H&K, stitching his bursts into the figures scattering to get away from his relentless volleys. He saw them stumbling and falling, bodies gouting red from the 9 mm hits. As another pair of armed men showed themselves, Bolan took a second grenade and tossed it into the landing below. The blast blew a hole through the floor, took out most of the railing and tossed the armed men aside, bloody and dying. As Bolan went down the stairs, he discarded the empty MP-5 and brought his Uzi into play, catching one Russian survivor on his knees and trying to bring his SMG into play. Bolan's burst from the Uzi caught the guy in the throat, knocking him back across the sagging landing. The Russian clung to the shattered timbers until his fingers weakened and he slipped from Bolan's view. Skirting the edge of the hole, the soldier pressed against the inner wall, checking out the corridor ahead, saw no immediate resistance and continued on, kicking open doors as he moved along.

TRECHENKO HAD JOINED Marley in his office as his Russian team had gone in search of the intruder. The house was filled with the rattle of autofire, and Trechenko had also heard a grenade blast.

The Russian saw the two bodies on the floor of the room and the bloody sword in the Jamaican drug lord's hand.

"They do something to upset you?"

"More like somethin' they said," Marley told him.

"Remind me never to answer you back," Trechenko said quietly.

A second grenade blast rattled the walls of the office.

Ras caught Marley's eye. "Boss?"

The Jamaican leaned against the edge of his desk. "He comin' to us. Let him."

Trechenko quietly took stock of their situation. The office was a large room, with a wide picture window looking out across the surrounding terrain, but there was only the one entrance. Trechenko didn't see the wisdom in waiting for the enemy from a position of limited exits. He reached under his jacket for the P-226 he carried in a hip holster, letting his gun hand swing out of sight behind his right hip as he stood off at the far side of the room from Marley and his three men.

THE DOUBLE DOORS caved in under Bolan's kick, swinging open to show him the large room. Across the room was a large executive desk, a tall Jamaican clad in dark clothing leaning casually against it. The man had a gleaming *daito* sword in one hand, the steel blade glistening with fresh blood. On the smooth wood floor only feet away from the Jamaican lay a pair of bloody bodies. The head of one was visible close by.

"You come see me? Deacon Marley?" the Jamaican at the desk asked. "Here I am, Belasko."

There was a cocky arrogance in the man's words that added caution to Bolan's reaction. The American eased forward slowly, his eyes scanning the setup in the room.

Behind the desk was a large picture window, and in the brief moments before he stepped across the threshold, Bolan caught the images reflected there—three armed men, off to his left and hidden by the open door, and a fourth farther across the room. The fourth man—not a Jamaican—looked unarmed, until Bolan spotted the position of his right hand, hidden partially behind his right leg.

In the split seconds Bolan absorbed the information, he created and used his plan of action.

Bolan swung the Uzi toward the left-hand door, triggered the weapon, sending the entire contents of the magazine into and through the door. The 9 mm slugs ripped through the softwood door, blowing out ragged chunks as they exited—into the bodies of Marley's three Jamaicans. The resultant fatal wounds—some caused by the splintered wood, others by the 9 mm slugs—bloodied the trio as they pierced flesh and shattered bone.

As Bolan cleared the doorway, he felt the Uzi lock on empty. He dropped the weapon, snatching the big Desert Eagle from its holster on the move.

Deacon Marley let go a scream of defiance, pushing away from the desk, the *daito* blade making a deadly arc as it slashed at the moving, black-clad figure of the American.

Bolan saw the Jamaican coming at him, aware of the threat from the shimmering blade. He brought the barrel up and fired, knowing immediately he had missed his target. The .44 bullet thudded into the wall behind Marley's desk.

The sword blade slashed in, clanging against the Desert Eagle, ripping the pistol from Bolan's fingers.

"Fedor!" Marley yelled. "Now we take him."

The man on the far side of the room stepped forward. Fedor Trechenko.

Bolan registered the name even as he dropped to the floor, sliding in under Marley's sword to slam the sole of one boot against the Jamaican's right knee. The impact cracked bone. Marley's leg collapsed and he stumbled, agony etched across his face. Bolan's second kick struck him above the waist, lifting him up and back. Marley crashed down across the desktop, rolling frantically, dropping to the floor on the far side.

As Bolan gained his feet, he pulled the Beretta clear of leather, swinging around to face Trechenko as the Russian trafficker lunged across the room, his SIG-Sauer P226 hoving into view.

Flashing images skittered across Bolan's mind—Seminov's OCD cops, the dead undercover man, Benin, DEA Agents Tanberg and Reckard, innocent bystanders killed in the explosion outside the OCD offices, all linked to Fedor Trechenko—and he stroked the 93-R's trigger.

Trechenko felt the impact in his chest, not understanding how Belasko had fired first. Then he realized he hadn't raised his P-226 more than a few inches. He lost his balance and went down on his knees, pain starting to engulf his chest. He coughed once and blood gurgled in his throat, dragged up from a punctured lung. The Russian fell back against the wall, strength draining from him as the room hazed into a distant, echoing mist.

GASPING FROM the impact, Deacon Marley lay for a disoriented moment behind his desk. He picked up the diminished sound of Bolan's Beretta. The Jamaican pushed up off the floor and used the desk to lever himself upright. He favored his right leg, clenching his teeth against the pain when he tried to put his weight on the limb. He was still gripping the sword in his right hand, his defiance still capable of filling him with wild anger.

Bolan saw the Jamaican push into view behind his desk. He tracked in with the Beretta and fired the moment he had Marley in his sights. The drug lord took the shots full in the face. The 9 mm slugs wrecked his features, driving him away from the desk, the back of his skull blown away by the exiting rounds. Bolan walked around the desk and put a second burst directly into Marley's heart, seeing the body jerk under the impact.

He turned and retrieved the Desert Eagle, crossing the office to where Fedor Trechenko lay against the far wall, bleeding heavily from his chest wound. The Russian stared up at Bolan's tall figure, seeing the very image Marley had imagined in his mind—black as death and out of the sky. It was Trechenko's final vision in the moment before Bolan lowered the Desert Eagle's muzzle.

BOLAN TOOK OUT his transceiver and contacted Grimaldi.

"Pickup time, pal."

"On my way. I'll flash my lights so you can see me."

Bolan picked up his Uzi and reloaded. He left Marley's office, moving cautiously through the levels of the house. There was no more resistance. The only people he met on the ground floor, were domestic employees who only had one thing on their minds— to get out of the place. The moment they saw Bolan's distant figure they fled in panic, ignoring the storm conditions. Bolan let them go. His quarrel wasn't with them.

Grimaldi picked him up minutes later and once they were back in the air, heading in the general direction of Kingston, Bolan called Captain Wallace.

"It might be in your interest to send some units up to Marley's place," Bolan said. "I think him and his Russian partner had some kind of falling out."

"You think so?"

"I'll let you decide, Captain."

"I think I already have. Will Mr. Marley be asking for his lawyer?"

"Mr. Marley will not be asking for his lawyer."

"We've had a busy night down here, too. Clashes between Marley's boys and some Colombians. Casualties on both sides. Some fatalities."

"The *Caliente?*"

"Out at sea somewhere. Riding out the storm, I presume. Waiting until it's safe."

Bolan completed his conversation and glanced across at Grimaldi. "Are we okay for a little side trip?"

"Small boat, large ocean?"

"I know you can do it, Jack."

"Let's smoke the sons of bitches."

THIRTY MILES out the motor vessel rode the settling swell. The storm was blowing itself out. There was still rain, but it was light compared to the previous night's downpour.

The captain stood watching the sky, a cup of coffee in his hand. He was waiting for the call that would take him back to Jamaica to pick up the team sent in to hit Deacon Marley. The sooner he had them on board and they were heading back for Colombia, the better he would feel. Too many things had gone wrong lately. The Russian-Jamaican alliance, the interference from the American agent, it had all become too involved. Though he would never voice his opinion, the captain felt Salazar should draw back for the present at least.

"Captain."

The captain turned and saw one of the crew members pointing. He picked up binoculars and focused on the black speck in the empty sky. It was moving fast, in the direction of the *Caliente*. The captain studied the object. It was a helicopter, a sleek, matte-black aircraft, with an unusual configuration—and no markings of any kind.

It sent a chill through the captain. A black helicopter that was also unidentifiable. There was something ominous in that. He didn't understand what. He simply felt an unsettling sensation as he watched the black machine, which hovered twenty feet above the waters.

"Who are they?" someone asked.

"No one to do us any good."

"Captain, we should leave."

"You think they will not follow?"

"We should set up the machine gun."

The captain took a sip from his coffee cup, turning to the speaker, and smiled in regret.

"At times like these," he said, "I wish I had taken my father's advice and become a priest."

"Do IT, Jack," Bolan said.

He felt *Dragon Slayer* shudder slightly as the HE missile sprang from the launch pod. The thin white vapor trail showed its swift path to where it met the *Caliente*. Bolan watched the motor vessel dissolve in an incandescent ball of fire, spreading wreckage across the water.

A strike for Rollie Benson, Bob Jackson and Mary Angelus.

"Back to Kingston?" Grimaldi asked.

Bolan nodded. "Time to prepare for a trip to Colombia, Jack. Unfinished business."

CHAPTER THIRTEEN

Colombia

The weather had cleared as Grimaldi took *Dragon Slayer* on a direct flight toward the Colombian coast. The combat chopper carried additional wing tanks, giving them an extra three hundred miles flying distance. Despite the extra fuel, Grimaldi was going to need to take on more for the return trip. Satellite images, relayed from Stony Man directly into the helicopter's computer guidance system, pinpointed Hermano Salazar's dock and warehouse facility. Once Grimaldi locked in the course, *Dragon Slayer* took over, finding the requested altitude and boosting up to speed. It allowed Grimaldi time to run a series of in-flight diagnostic performance checks.

PRIOR TO LEAVING Jamaica, Bolan had made contact with Turrin and they brought each other up to date with the various strands of the operation.

"Not that it makes much difference now," Turrin said, "but the Russians have informed us that two of the bodies in the car that got blown up were Tanberg and Reckard. Appears they'd been drugged so they were unconscious at the time of the blast. The third body was finally identified as a Russian dressed in Asa Randal's clothes. Drugged, as well."

"Real pleasant partner those two had."

"You said it."

"How's Valentine?"

"Last report was he's been demanding someone bring him a bottle of vodka. Says the water the hospital is giving him is slowing his progress. When he does get back to the job he'll find some big changes. Looks like his old boss, Korsov, had been running his tricks for quite a while. The man was some piece of work."

"I guess you got the details from Captain Wallace about the Marley-Trechenko partnership being dissolved?"

"Word for word. Marley's organization is taking to the hills. The man had a reputation as unstoppable. Now that he's dead the talking has started. It's payback time for a lot of people. The Kingston drug squad is uncovering stashes of drugs and money. Marley's people are being fingered. The Colombians you stranded on the island are on their own. Some arrests already. We were able to feed back some of the data from the laptop you got hold of, to Captain Wallace. It should help plug some of Salazar's Jamaican connections."

"I'm planning to cut the guy off permanently," Bolan reminded Turrin.

"I know. And don't forget ex-Agent Asa Randal."

"He has a special place in my heart, Leo."

"You heard about my upcoming vacation to Mexico?"

"I heard. No heroics, Leo. These are some nasty people."

"Hey, I've done this before, hotshot. Before you cut your teeth on a hollowpoint. But point taken. Same applies to you, pal, and say hello to Jack for me."

BOLAN PEERED through *Dragon Slayer*'s side window. Blue sky, blue ocean below. Some scrappy white clouds. It looked peaceful enough. He thought about what lay ahead. It was bound to be less than peaceful. Salazar would be harboring bad feelings against Bolan. The drug trafficker's reputation meant a great deal in the business. Salazar had to hit back at anything and anyone attempting to knock him off his throne.

"We should be able to see the coastline anytime now," Grimaldi said. "Coordinates have us on course for touchdown a couple of miles behind Salazar's hooch."

Bolan chuckled. "Some hooch, Jack."

"Call it what you like, it's still home to vermin."

TWENTY MINUTES on and the Colombian coastline flashed below them. Grimaldi had taken control of *Dragon Slayer*, and his skilled hand took the chopper in over the dense foliage. He swung in a wide arc, skimming the treetops of the remote area until he spotted a likely landing zone. His approach had brought him in well below any possible local radar surveillance. The moment Grimaldi touched down Bolan slipped out of the passenger seat and moved into the rear. He was on the ground moments later, raising a hand to Grimaldi and vanishing in the undergrowth.

Grimaldi shut down, putting the chopper in standby mode, with the proximity sensors active. The thermal waves would pick up approaching objects and send signals back to Grimaldi's monitor screen inside the control cabin.

A couple of minutes after Bolan had vacated the chopper Grimaldi picked up an incoming transmission through his comset.

"Just checking," Bolan said.

"You're through loud and clear. Got your signal on the tracking monitor. Keep on your current heading and you'll hit target okay."

"I'll keep my eyes open for any filling stations."

"Try and find one with freebies," Grimaldi said. "You know how much it costs to top this lady up."

"You and your expensive women, Jack."

"Maybe, Sarge, but this one performs to order and always takes *me* home."

CROUCHING IN THE DENSE foliage, Bolan studied the warehouses and dock built around the harbor. On the far side was the apartment complex. The sight of the

Bell 430 helicopter sitting on the concrete pad brought a slight smile to Bolan's lips. It was almost like old-home week.

He stayed in position, watching for movement around the dock area. The warehouses themselves looked deserted. Perhaps Salazar had pulled his drug operation for a period following Bolan's earlier escape, in an effort to deny any official visits the chance of finding anything. Bolan sat back and kept his vigil for another half hour, seeing nothing, and eventually decided it was time to move.

It took him only a short time to reach the rear of the warehouses. They backed directly onto the greenery, with only a single-panel corrugated-steel barrier to hold back the lush vegetation. Bolan checked the barrier for sensors. There was nothing. He climbed the barrier and dropped down on the narrow concrete path that ran around the buildings. There was a three-foot gap between the warehouses. Bolan made his way along the gap, his Uzi in his hands. Three-quarters of the distance along he spotted a narrow side door in each warehouse wall. One was open a few inches. Bolan eased it wide enough to slip through.

He pressed against the cool inner wall, breathing in the rich smell of roasted coffee beans. The warehouse was half-full of wooden pallets holding filled sacks. The big doors at the dock end of the storage shed were open, allowing sunlight to enter the warehouse.

Bolan made his way along the inner wall until he was at the entrance. Nothing. No sound, no movement…

Until Bolan picked up the tang of cigar smoke drifting in through the warehouse door. He heard a soft footfall, too, immediately outside the door and waited. He saw the shadow first, falling across the opening and then the figure of an armed guard. The guy had his MP-5 slung from its shoulder strap. He moved at a slow pace, plainly relaxed as he drew on his cigar, smoke wreathing his head.

Bolan reached out and caught hold of the guy's left arm, yanking him inside the door, spinning him and slamming him up against the inner wall. The smoking cigar dropped from the guard's lips as Bolan drew the keen blade of his Ka-bar across his throat, laying it open with a deep, wide cut. With blood starting to surge from the gash the guard was left with little to do other than attempt, vainly, to stop it.

Bolan moved back to the door and scanned the area. No alert had been raised.

Behind the Executioner the stricken guard fell facedown onto the warehouse floor, a pool of blood starting to spread out from his head.

The soldier slipped out the warehouse door and moved in the direction of the apartment complex, staying close to the warehouse frontage. He reached the far side of the dock without interruption. Across from him the Bell 430 sat on the concrete pad. Bolan made for the archway leading to the inner courtyard and paused to make another status check.

He saw the stairs leading to the upper floor where he had been held in the room overlooking the bay. On the other side of the courtyard were the steps leading to the basement room used to extract information.

The first thing Bolan noticed was the silence.

Had he walked in on an empty site?

He took the initiative and crossed the courtyard, reaching the closest door and pushing it open. The room was empty. No signs of current usage. The next three doors yielded the same. At the far end Bolan pushed open a door to reveal a superbly equipped kitchen. Gleaming tiles and steel units, but no cooking food or steaming pans.

Bolan took the stairs on the run, along the upper level. He kicked open door after door.

Nothing.

Hermano Salazar's residence appeared deserted.

He stood in the very room where he had been held captive, looking down on the dock and the warehouses, enveloped in the overwhelming silence. Had he made a wasted trip here? He expected resistance but encountered only a single guard.

Something didn't sit right.

Salazar might be away, and he might have shut down his operations for a while. But would he abandon his facility so completely, even down to leaving his helicopter on the landing pad?

Bolan stepped out of the room and checked the rest of the upper floor.

He had almost completed his checks when something caught his eye.

In one room overlooking the dock area, a window hung open, a faint breeze drifted inside, catching the thin rise of smoke from a hastily crushed cigarette butt in an ashtray. Someone being clumsy? Bolan made no sign of having spotted the smoke. He turned to leave the room, and picked up the faintest creak of wood as weight was put against it. The sound came from a door that led to the adjoining room.

He wasn't alone.

Salazar had anticipated Bolan's return and had baited a trap, allowing Bolan to walk right into the middle before closing the door. The drug trafficker's men *were* here, hidden and waiting. Only one had been unable to resist a smoke, hastily extinguishing his cigarette when it came time to hide.

Bolan backed out of the room, making no show, and as he stepped through the door he reached up and activated the transceiver, speaking softly.

"Jack?"

"Here."

"Pedal to the metal, buddy. Real fast."

Then he turned and kicked open the door to the next room. There were three of them, all armed, and clustered around the dividing door, unaware that

Bolan had stepped back outside, until he hit the door behind them.

The three turned, caught in their own trap, and tried to shoot their way out.

Bolan's Uzi stuttered, stitching the three with 9 mm hellfire. Torn bodies tumbled across the room as the Executioner turned and moved along the passage, heading for the stairs.

Someone started to shout in Spanish. Doors banged and feet slapped against the floor.

Bolan kept on along the passage, ignoring the stairs, and hit the door at the far end. By his calculation this one would open on a room that was directly over the archway leading out onto the dock area. He closed the door, slid the bolt home and crossed to the window. He was above the archway, with the curving brick formation just below his window.

Bolan slung the Uzi, pushed open the window and climbed over the sill. He had no idea how long his diversion might buy him. How long the Colombians might wonder where he was. However long, it might just allow him the chance to get down to ground level.

The overlapping rough brick and stonework provided a degree of hand- and footholds. Bolan didn't stop to consider the risk. The alternative was no better. He went down as fast as he could, slipping a couple of times and skinning the ends of his fingers. The overlapping formation of the arch took him down faster than he expected. From twenty feet up to just under eight feet in a matter of seconds. Hanging by his fingertips, then letting himself drop, Bolan struck the ground and rolled, grazing a shoulder as he landed.

From overhead he heard a man yell, the cry followed by the savage chatter of an autoweapon. Bullets chipped the concrete inches from Bolan's face, stinging his cheek.

Bolan, on one knee, unlimbered the Uzi and triggered a burst in the direction of the shooter leaning out a window, saw his bullets powder the man's face with brick dust. The man withdrew. The soldier ran to the arch and pressed against the wall. He peered around the edge and saw armed figures racing across the inner courtyard in his direction.

He swung around and stood in the archway, the Uzi tracking the bunched figures. His finger stroked the trigger, sending 9 mm death at the Colombians. Some went down while the others scattered across the courtyard, returning sporadic fire in the direction of the archway. Bolan triggered another burst.

He picked up the familiar sound of *Dragon Slayer*'s turbine engines. Over his shoulder he saw the black silhouette of the combat chopper as it rose above the warehouses. Bolan cleared the archway and made for the Bell helicopter, keying his transceiver.

"You see me, Jack?"

"Yeah."

"The archway behind me? Lay in some gunfire."

Grimaldi swung the chopper across the dock, hovering above the water, and triggered the chain gun, laying down a long burst of 30 mm fire. The howling shells ripped at the archway's brick and stone, blowing away chunks and filling the air with dust. Much of the fire went directly through the arch, impacting against walls within the courtyard.

As Grimaldi held his fire, he spotted armed figures on the upper level of the apartment complex, saw them leaning down to fire at Bolan as he headed for cover. The Stony Man pilot made a disapproving sound as he nudged up *Dragon Slayer*'s nose, then raked the upper level with more fire, the brutal power of the chain gun delivering a nonstop, lethal stream of shells that tore at the brickwork, blew out windows and chewed at steel frames. Debris fell to the dock below, dust drifting across the frontage of the building.

Bolan backed up to the Bell 430, watching for further movement. He was about to call in Grimaldi when he heard a noise on the far side of the helicopter. The soldier moved around the aircraft, his Uzi up and ready—and found himself face-to-face with the pilot who had flown him out on his previous visit.

The pilot had the cabin door open and was ready to leave. When he recognized Bolan the man simply stared.

"This cannot be happening again."

"Your lucky day," Bolan said. He motioned with the Uzi.

"Do you realize the trouble I had getting away from Panama?" The pilot shook his head. "Señor Salazar wants you dead after last time."

"I'm touched. Let's go."

"I'm in the Bell chopper on the dock," Bolan informed Grimaldi. "When we get in the air I want this place flattened. Everything. If Salazar comes home, I want him to see what it's like having your life blown away."

"Okay, Sarge."

The Bell fired up and Bolan watched the apartment in case any of Salazar's hit team showed their faces. He felt the Bell surge as the pilot upped the power. It rose, clearing the pad and angled out across the harbor, the rotors stirring the placid water.

"Take us clear," Bolan said, watching as Grimaldi brought *Dragon Slayer* into position.

Grimaldi laid HE missiles into the warehouse, the resultant explosions demolishing the buildings. As the structures collapsed, flame rising through the dust and smoke, Grimaldi swung the combat chopper on the apartment complex. He laid in more HEs, reducing the stylish building to a mass of smoking rubble. Grimaldi's final act was to swing *Dragon Slayer* out to the middle of the harbor and fire off missiles that brought the dock wall down into the water.

"That do, Sarge?"

"Affirmative."

Bolan turned to the pilot. "Salazar's airfield. How close? He has to have something nearby."

"How did…?" The pilot shrugged. "Why should I care? It's ten miles inland. South. You want me to take you there?"

"You learn fast."

The pilot swung the Bell around. "At least it's not as far as Panama City," he muttered.

"Hey, Sarge, where we going?" Grimaldi called.

"To get you that top-up." Bolan spoke to the pilot. "Does Salazar have any protection at the field?"

"Only a three-man team."

"What do they have for defense?"

"Machine gun mounted on a Jeep. It patrols the perimeter."

Bolan relayed the information to Grimaldi.

"Looks like you're going to have to fight for your supper."

"Just lead me in."

THE AIRFIELD HAD BEEN carved out of the near jungle terrain. The strip itself was a solid concrete affair long enough to receive a large commercial aircraft. The small block building that served as a control tower boasted a radar dish and radio mast. Set aside from the tower was a maintenance building and a medium-size fuel truck. Bolan spotted a number of figures in coveralls around the maintenance building. The Jeep, machine gun visible, was parked close to the control tower.

"You want me to land?"

Bolan shook his head as he sensed *Dragon Slayer* dropping below them, the chopper's nose tracking in on the Jeep. A figure in a tan shirt and pants ran from the tower building and jumped up into the rear of the vehicle, positioning himself behind the machine gun. He swung the barrel around, tilting it as *Dragon Slayer* hovered.

The thunder of the chain gun reached through to Bolan's ears as Grimaldi fired. The first shots hit the ground just short of the Jeep, then engulfed the vehicle, tearing ragged holes in the hood, through the windshield and on to pulverize the gunner into a bloody mush. The gunner's body was slammed off the back of the Jeep, barely striking the ground before the fuel tank blew in a ball of flame and smoke. Grimaldi destroyed the radar and radio setup on the roof, then held *Dragon Slayer* motionless, menacing the area with his now silent cannon. Two more men stepped out of the building, arms held above their heads. They stood waiting as Grimaldi landed.

"Now you can land," Bolan told the Colombian pilot.

Bolan climbed out of the Bell the moment it touched down, the pilot shutting down and following him as they approached the control building. Grimaldi, armed with an Uzi, came around from *Dragon Slayer* and covered the pair by the building.

"Call the maintenance crew," Bolan told the pilot. "I want the black helicopter refueled. Jack, show them what you want."

Grimaldi followed the fuel tanker as it was driven to where *Dragon Slayer* stood. With a minimum of fuss he got the maintenance crew to start pumping fuel into the auxiliary, as well as the main fuel tanks.

Bolan had the two guards walk out until they were about twenty feet away, then had them lie facedown on the ground, hands at the back of their heads. He had the pilot instruct the men that they were safe as long as they remained where they were.

"When my chopper is fueled, I'll get yours seen to," Bolan told the pilot.

The man regarded him with a puzzled expression. "Why?"

"Let's say it's in payment for what you're going to tell me next."

"Oh?"

"Salazar and the American, Randal. Where are they?"

The pilot understood the question. He also understood his own position. It was looking all the more likely that Hermano Salazar wouldn't be returning to Colombia. This American, in his quiet, unassuming way, was proving an extremely deadly threat to his employer. Salazar, who had always organized himself with professional determination, was looking decidedly on the edge. His trip out of the country, for business, might turn out to be his last.

"If I tell you?"

"*When* you tell me, that helicopter is yours to do what you wish. Go where you want. Consider this as a one-time offer."

The pilot recalled the way the American had dealt with Salazar's people back at the dock facility. The cold and clinical way he had ordered the destruction of the buildings. And the similar treatment here at the airfield. He was under no illusions. If the American decided he wasn't getting what he wanted, he wouldn't hesitate to use the same methods.

"He has gone to meet his distributor in Mexico. The American, Randal, is with him. They flew out from here in Salazar's own Gulfstream V."

"Protection squad?"

"Six of his best."

"Who and where in Mexico?"

"Ramon Huerta. He is based in Nuevo Laredo, below the border from Texas."

Nuevo Laredo, Mexico

LEO TURRIN RECEIVED a call shortly after he had booked in at his hotel. Turrin was accompanied by a younger agent from his Justice Department team, Cal Walker. The hotel, on the southern edge of town, was low-key and comfortable. Turrin had just finished unpacking and was thinking about taking five when his room phone rang.

"Señor Turrin?"

"Yes."

"Agent Morales, Mexican drug squad. I am in the bar with my partner, Agent Garcia. I thought it best we meet in a quiet place."

"I'll be down in a few minutes."

"Thank you, Señor Turrin."

Turrin broke the connection, then tapped in Cal Walker's room number. The agent picked up immediately.

"Cal. It's Leo. I just got a call from our Mexican counterparts, Morales and Garcia. They're down in the bar. I guess they want to break the ice before we get official tomorrow."

"I just got undressed to go in the shower. Give me a couple of minutes and I'll throw some clothes back on."

"Hey, relax, Cal. Go have your shower. Come on down when you're ready, okay?"

"You sure?"

"I'm sure. See you later."

Turrin pulled his jacket back on and headed for the door. He took the stairs and made his way through the thronged lobby to the bar. He checked out the place, searching for the two men he only knew from 10 photographs. He didn't find them. He wandered through the bar, easing his way past the standing drinkers, before returning to the entrance.

He decided to check at the desk, then felt the hard muzzle of a pistol as it was pushed into the base of his spine.

"Señor Turrin, we are going to walk outside. No foolishness. My orders are quite simple. If you resist, I am to kill you here and now. Make no mistake. I will do it. On the other hand, if you cooperate, you reach the car parked outside without harm. My partner is standing beside the hotel exit. In the light-colored suit. We join him. Now."

Turrin felt a hand slide over his jacket, locate his handgun and take it. Under pressure from the gun at his back he crossed the lobby, the unseen gunman close behind him.

At the door the partner in the light suit nodded. He was lean and young, a thin mustache on his upper lip.

"Good evening, Señor Turrin," he said.

Turrin walked out of the hotel and down the steps to where a dusty, dark-colored Mercedes waited. There was only the driver inside.

The young Mexican stood to one side, blocking off any escape route Turrin might take.

"Get in the back, Señor Turrin," he said.

Turrin opened the rear door and felt himself being ushered inside. The young man had already walked quickly to the other side of the car, opening the opposite rear door and sliding into the seat. The man with the gun sat next to Turrin, pulling the door shut behind him. He leaned forward to tap the waiting driver on the shoulder.

"*Vámonos.*"

The Mercedes rolled away from the hotel entrance, picking up speed as it merged with the traffic.

AN HOUR LATER the call was received in Washington that Leo Turrin had disappeared. As soon as Hal Brognola had confirmation of the authenticity of the information, he relayed it to Mack Bolan.

CHAPTER FOURTEEN

Leo Turrin was embarrassed at being taken so easily. For someone with his experience to have walked into such a setup was an awkward admission of his failure to see what was coming. From that point Turrin saw only the positive. Regrets weren't going to get him out of his current situation. It was down to him alone. And to that end Turrin analyzed his condition.

For whatever reason he had been taken alive and so far had been kept alive. Which meant his life was worth something to his kidnappers. What that worth was he didn't know yet. But there had to be a point where he would be informed—if his cooperation was required. That being the case Turrin decided it would be worthwhile trying to figure out just what his worth was.

The men who had kidnapped him weren't Mexican cops. But they had known the details of his arrival in Nuevo Laredo down to the last word. So there had to be a source for their knowledge. Again that could have been a number of sources. A leak within the Justice Department. Or the Mexican drug squad. Perhaps someone had his arm twisted and was given a choice of life or death for the information. Which only added further complications to Turrin's assumptions.

Prior knowledge of his arrival in Mexico had been well in advance of his showing up at the hotel, given that he was supposed to be meeting the genuine Morales and Garcia the morning following his kidnapping. The imposters had shown a great deal of confidence coming to his hotel. Turrin felt certain they had done this kind of thing before, which showed in their cool, unhurried manner.

The moment they had all settled in the rear of the Mercedes a black hood had been slipped over Turrin's head, shutting him off from any views of the exterior. As the car left the hotel it turned left. If Turrin had been imagining it might betray the way they were traveling, he was quickly disappointed as the car made a right, then a series of turns that left him totally unable to figure out which way they were going.

The ride lasted a good couple of hours. At some point the Mercedes left the main highway and rolled along a rutted side road, bouncing heavily on its suspension. Eventually the car came to a stop, doors were opened and Turrin was led across hard-baked earth and through a door. He was escorted across a room, through a door and a passage. Another door was opened and Turrin was pushed through. Someone snatched the hood from his head, allowing him to see for the first time since entering the Mercedes.

He was in a plain room. About twelve by twelve, with a single window that had been nailed shut and had a metal grille over the outside. The room itself was functional. Plain white walls, concrete floor. A single electric light in the ceiling, behind a wire cover. There was a small wooden table and chair and a single bed. At the far side of the room an open door revealed a toilet and wash basin. There was no window in the washroom.

Turrin had been left alone in the room, the door closed as his kidnappers left. He heard it being locked and bolted.

Left alone Turrin inspected the room inch by inch, checking for any possible avenue of escape. His eventual decision was that the only way out was through the door.

Later on the door was opened and the fake Garcia stood in the opening, an M-16 pointing at Turrin. Morales came in, carrying a tray with food and drink. No utensils. Plastic cup and plate. The tray was deposited on the table and Morales walked out, followed by Garcia. The door was secured again.

The food was palatable. Spiced and fried chicken and vegetables wrapped in a corn tortilla. The plastic cup held very hot, strong coffee. Turrin might not have preferred this introduction to Mexican cuisine, but he was in no position to be picky, and he might not get anything else for a long time, so he ate the food and drank the coffee. After an hour the tray was removed and a plastic bottle of water left behind.

Turrin's captivity ran into three days. He was fed regularly. Brief conversations took place between Turrin and his captors. In between he was left alone. He could hear movement in the room beyond his door, music coming from a radio, muted voices. Once he heard a car drive up. It stayed for a couple of hours, then left. His door opened only once other than at mealtimes, and a bundle of magazines was tossed into his cell, which was what he had dubbed his room. Turrin had checked out the magazines. A couple of auto magazines, some hunting journals and a number of copies of *TV Guide.* He spent some time going through the TV magazines, indulging in a bout of choosing an imaginary night's viewing. When he added up the programs he had chosen to watch, Turrin found he would still have a lot of time on his hands. So much for the drawing power of TV, he decided, flinging the magazines across the room.

ON THE THIRD DAY Turrin reached a decision. It was going to involve risk, but he saw no profit in just sitting it out and waiting for his captors to initiate some kind of action. If he allowed them to retain control, he would eventually be dictated to by whatever they wanted. It didn't sit right with him. Turrin wasn't the kind to stand meekly by and let others decide his fate. So he made up his mind to do something on his own behalf.

There was no way out of his cell except through the door he had come in by.

Fine so far.

When his meals were delivered Garcia stood in the door with his M-16 and Morales placed the tray on the table. The one Turrin needed to disable was Garcia. There was nothing in the room Turrin could use as a weapon, so he would have to rely on something being brought into the room.

Turrin focused on the tray, the only object he might use was the plastic cup of coffee. It was always full, and it was always extremely hot.

So there was his weapon. And his target had to be Garcia.

Turrin chose his spot: to the right of the door, which swung in to the left. Garcia always stood on the right. Turrin considered his plan of action. It was a thin chance he was taking, so thin he could almost see through it, but he had no other options.

He glanced at his watch. Coming up to noon. His meals came at the same time each day. The midday meal was exactly that—delivered at twelve.

Turrin placed himself near the table, judging the distance. Only a few feet maybe, but with an autorifle trained on him?

He heard the rattle of the bolts, the key turning and saw the handle move.

Don't screw up, Leo. You will get one shot at this. After that it might not even matter.

The door was pushed open and the lean figure of Garcia stood there, his weapon trained loosely on Turrin. Morales stepped by his partner, carrying the usual tray, which held exactly the same food Turrin received at every mealtime.

As Morales took his first step into the room, Turrin moved forward, reaching out toward the tray.

"Am I ready for that coffee," he said. "Hey, maybe you can find me a bigger cup, huh?"

He kept his tone light, allowing a smile to curl his lips. There was no reaction from either man. Turrin closed his fingers around the plastic cup, ignoring the heat that threatened to blister his skin, because that was what he needed. He lifted the cup, then turned on his heel and threw the contents into Garcia's face. His aim was true and the scalding liquid struck the Mexican full-face.

Garcia howled in pain, letting the M-16 hang from his right hand as he pawed at his burning face with his left.

In the split second it took Morales to register what had happened, Turrin swiveled and kicked out with his right foot, the toe of his shoe catching the man between the legs. The blow wasn't as on target as it should have been, but it delivered enough damage to distract Morales.

Turrin lunged through the door, slamming into Garcia and spinning him backward across the floor. Turrin launched a roundhouse punch that clipped the kidnapper across the side of his wet, scalded face. Garcia's legs got tangled in a wooden chair and he went down. As Turrin moved by, he snatched the M-16 from the injured man's unresisting fingers, crossed the narrow passage and ran for the door on the other side of the main room.

Turrin hauled open the door and went through, finding himself in the open. He blinked his eyes against the hot glare of the noon sun, taking a quick look around.

Beyond the small house the land lay exposed and dusty, dotted with a few scrawny trees and patches of scrub and mesquite. To the far west Turrin could make out hazy mountains. His rudimentary geography of the area said they were the Sierra Madre Oriental, which would place Nuevo Laredo off to the north.

His choice was made.

Turrin cut north, keeping the mountains on his left. He picked up the pace, knowing that his captors weren't going to quit as easily as that. His main problem was that the terrain was open, and while not exactly flat, provided little in the way of cover. All Turrin could do was keep moving, hoping he could find at least some rudimentary concealment.

He had gone a few hundred yards when he heard raised voices. Someone demanding he give himself up. That they would kill him if he didn't. The demands drew a thin smile from Turrin. Did they think he was that stupid? To believe they were going to give him a medal for escaping? He knew damn well they could easily kill him if they wanted. The other side of the coin begged the question—if they had wanted him dead, why had they not killed him as soon as they got him away from the hotel? As before, the reason for his abduction filtered through all the other matters crowding Turrin's mind.

What the hell *did* they want him for?

"YES, HE HAS escaped. Because he did. Do you think we let it happen because we were bored? Listen, just send some help. You can point the finger later. Right now we need to get him back, before Huerta and Salazar return. If we still don't have him it isn't going to matter who let him go, because we will all be fucking dead. Yes, he has a weapon. He took an M-16. How do I know? When he starts to shoot, we will find out if he is experienced. Now get those bastards off their asses and send them. Oh, we need to get medical help for Julio. Because he is hurt. I will go after the American. He is moving north. How should I know why. Just get here. Quickly."

The man Turrin knew as Agent Morales, Benito Hayos, snapped his cell phone shut and pushed it into his pocket. He brought the M-16 under his arm into play, breaking into a trot as he followed the distant figure of the escaped American.

Hayos was both angry and feeling completely foolish. He was still uncertain how Turrin had managed to break free. His move with the coffee had been totally unexpected and he had stalled Hayos with that kick, giving himself time to take off, picking up Julio's rifle at the same time. This was going to take some living down, Hayos realized. His pride had been hurt, Julio was walking wounded and the American was making a run for freedom.

In the distance Turrin had stopped, turning to look back. Hayos saw him raise the M-16, aim and fire. The bullet kicked up dirt only feet in front of the Mexican, missing only because Turrin hadn't taken enough time to get his range. That certainly answered the question. The American *could* shoot. Hayos dropped to one knee, shouldering his own rifle and drew down on the distant figure. He fired, triggering three fast shots and saw Turrin jerk back. Close but not close enough. But at least it stopped the American from firing again. At least for the time being.

Hayos climbed to his feet and took up the chase. He looked back over his shoulder. Julio was making slow progress. His burned face was giving him problems. Hayos had told his partner to stay in the house, but Julio had refused. He blamed himself entirely for the escape and wouldn't back down. He had a persistent streak that had overcome many obstacles during his life. It was going to be the same this time.

TURRIN KEPT moving north, aware now that the pursuit proper had started. The brief exchange of gunfire had been akin to the opening challenge in a skirmish, a matter of defining the roles of each protagonist. Neither was in the position to make a killing at that moment, but proving to the other that this was no game of bravado.

Life or death was no contest. In the end it would come down to that chilling moment when someone *would* die. In that fragment of time, when a man found himself staring at eternity down the barrel of a gun, pretense tended to fly out the window.

Turrin had been through too much and had survived on his wits too long to let himself end it all here and now in Mexico.

His trip here, in order to expose the deceit and double-dealing within both the DEA and the Mexican drug squad, had taken an unexpected turn. It had placed him in the spotlight, with unknown enemies gunning for him. It certainly wasn't the way Turrin had wanted things to go. If he had any hand in the matter, it wasn't the way he was about to let it end.

He reached a low rise in the land, where choking clumps of scrub fought to survive in the thin soil. Every step he took kicked up fine dust. Turrin was starting to sweat beneath the hot sun. He didn't let himself dwell on the discomfort for too long. It wasn't going to get any easier.

He followed the line of the scrub, using it as scant cover until he reached the head of the rise and saw a steeper drop on the other side. At the bottom of the slope the land merged into a dry creek bed that snaked its way across the land, and what was more important to Turrin, in a northerly direction. He went down the slope into the dry creek. The hard earth underfoot was baked and cracked. There was a great deal of scrub and mesquite growing along the creek bed. Turrin failed to understand why until he realized that although the creek bed was dry on the surface there might well be an existing water table below the surface. It might not be a great deal, but most likely enough to sustain the growth of greenery within its boundaries.

Whatever the reason for the vegetation Turrin was thankful for its cover. It would provide him with protection for as long as he stayed between the sloping banks of the redundant stream.

Turrin pushed through the scrub, trying not to attract too much attention by keeping his noise level down. The two Mexicans were most likely at home out here. This was their country and they would have a working knowledge of where and how far something like the creek bed might end up. Knowledge of the terrain could allow them to cut across country and lay in wait for Turrin farther along the creek bed.

That realization added caution to his mode of travel. He slowed and spent more time listening to what lay around him. This isolated piece of country had little in the way of indigenous life. Turrin hadn't even heard a bird chattering or seen any other animal. It was very quiet country, and Turrin saw the problems that might create.

With little extraneous noise around, any passing sound would be heard a good distance away, for both parties. Turrin would need to keep his movements as noiseless as possible. The advantage to him would be that noise from his pursuers might warn him that they were getting closer than he expected.

He remained in the creek bed, making frequent

checks that he was still heading north. He was hoping he might come across a highway, which would mean traffic, people, perhaps the opportunity to get help. It was a slim chance at the moment because he had no idea how far they had come away from the main highway. It was at least something to go for.

WHEN HAYOS GLANCED at his watch he was surprised to see that almost an hour had passed, and he was no closer to locating the American. He felt a slight rise of panic when he considered the penalty he might have to pay for letting Turrin escape.

Ramon Huerta wasn't a forgiving man. He hadn't reached his position in the drug-trafficking business through a benevolent attitude. The business itself was built on violence and intimidation. It ran the entire chain of command, and each level expressed its authority to the utmost. Hayos was no stranger to violence. It was how he maintained his own position, and he had no problems with that. Now he was under a potential threat himself—the condition didn't seem so attractive.

He tried to push the thoughts aside, concentrating on the pursuit. The American had located a dry creek bed and had been using it for cover. It was a smart move. He had taken himself away from the open terrain, utilizing the heavy growths of scrub and mesquite to conceal his movements. The dense thickets meant Hayos was forced to move slowly himself, staying alert in case the American decided to reverse the situation and wait in ambush for his pursuers.

Hayos had sent Julio along the open ground above the shallow creek bed, hoping his partner might spot the American from above. Julio, still in pain from the scalding coffee, was doing his best but he was suffering from the burns to his face.

Up ahead Hayos heard a crackle of dry vegetation. He paused and listened. The sound came again. It was a good distance ahead, the sound carrying in the silence. Hayos couldn't alert Julio, who was farther along the upper bank, without warning the American.

He moved on, the M-16 held ready. His finger stroked the trigger nervously.

There was a shout. It was Julio's voice.

Gunfire echoed along the creek bed. Shots rattled out…then silence.

TURRIN PICKED UP the sound of someone moving along the top of the creek bank. He crouched, checking the top of the rise, ears tuned to pick up any sound. He was sweating heavily, due to the heat trapped at the bottom of the creek bed. His shirt clung to his body, and his eyes were stinging from the sweat running down from his brow. Turrin sleeved it away, shaking his head to clear his eyes.

He caught a flicker of slow movement showing above the scrub that lined the top of the slope. Turrin eased a little farther back into the cover of the scrub. Despite the care he took his move created a scrap of sound. He saw the indistinct shape pause, turn in his direction, then rise above the scrub.

It was the man Turrin knew as Garcia. The American had no problem recognizing the younger man. The marks left by the thrown coffee had turned Garcia's face into a mask of angry, blistered flesh. He had to have been in agony, Turrin imagined, then dismissed any guilt. The Mexicans had taken him against his will, isolating him in this wilderness, so they forfeited any sympathy. And they weren't stalking him to offer the hand of friendship.

Garcia pushed forward, his M-16 sweeping the area. There was a moment when Turrin thought the Mexican had overlooked him. He was wrong.

Garcia pushed through the scrub, the muzzle of his rifle angling down at Turrin. He opened his mouth and shouted a warning, then pulled the trigger.

Turrin had moved the instant he saw Garcia's mouth form his yell. He threw himself to one side, hitting the ground, heard the sharp crackle of fire as Garcia started shooting. The earth just behind Turrin vibrated as the 5.56 mm slugs whacked into it. He felt the sting of stone chips against his back.

Turrin gathered himself, pushing up onto one knee, swinging his own rifle to his shoulder. He picked up the plunging figure as Garcia hurled himself down the creek bank. His finger stroked the M-16's trigger. He felt the rifle kick back against his shoulder.

The single slug caught the gunner in the left side, coring in to catch a rib bone. The bone splintered and the deflected slug angled off through Garcia's body cavity, puncturing a lung. Garcia grunted from the impact, losing his balance and slithering down the bank, the rough earth tearing at his clothing. The flesh of his knees was shredded as Garcia hit bottom. He fell, rolled and pushed upright.

Turrin was on his feet by this time, bringing his rifle to bear on Garcia as the Mexican plunged to the creek bottom, raising a cloud of dust in his wake.

He saw the man rear up, the M-16 suddenly jerking in his hands as he fired. Turrin felt a solid blow to his left thigh. The impact pulled him to the side, so Garcia's follow-up shots missed.

The little Fed returned fire almost automatically, his finger hitting the trigger in reflex, fired by his pain and anger. Not the best combination for accurate shot placing, but the range was short enough for Turrin to make a hit as he put three single shots in Garcia's direction.

He saw the slugs punch into the man's upper body, raising dust from his clothing, then saw the burst of red as they emerged from Garcia's back. The Mexican gasped, throwing his arms wide as he toppled over on his back, legs kicking in spasm, eyes staring at the bright sky. The M-16 cartwheeled from his grasp, turning almost lazily before it hit the ground feet away.

Turrin held himself from falling. He knew if he went down he wouldn't get up again. He looked at his leg and saw the hole in his trousers, blood starting to seep into the material. He could feel blood running down the back of his leg, too, realizing that the bullet had gone through. When he tentatively placed his weight on the leg he found he could stay upright. Despite the pain he was able to support himself. The bullet had missed the bone, but that didn't diminish the fact he had been hit. There would be damage to muscle and tissue, and that could be as severe as any other kind of wound. Shock and blood loss could be killers on their own.

Turrin needed time to tend his wound, even on a basic level, but he knew that wasn't in the cards at the moment. The shots would have alerted Morales. He would still be close. Turrin couldn't afford the luxury of first aid until he found some kind of sanctuary.

He moved off, favoring his injured limb and abandoning any caution now. He simply pushed on, trying to gain distance, and realized that his wound was slowing him. His survival instinct was strong, and the concept of surrender wasn't part of his makeup. If his enemies wanted him, they were going to have to come get him. He wasn't about to lie down. If they wanted a fight, he wasn't going to disappoint them.

And even if they did hunt him down he would make certain they paid one hell of a price.

CHAPTER FIFTEEN

A half hour on Turrin heard the approaching beat of a helicopter. He was moving slower now, blood loss weakening him. He had made the decision to bind his wound as well as he was able. Leaning against a jutting section of the creek bank, he ripped away the sleeve of his shirt and wrapped it around his thigh, covering the wound back and front. The pain almost made him cry out. He pulled his trouser belt from its loops and used it to hold the crude bandage in place, pulling it tight. It was by no means satisfactory, but it was the best he could manage.

The helicopter was getting closer now, making sweeps over the area and checking out the creek bed. It seemed that his pursuer had called in reinforcements. They seemed determined to get him back into captivity, while Turrin was just as determined to stay free. Right there and then he wouldn't have given himself good odds. Not that he was ready to hold up his hands and surrender. He would still give them a run for their money.

He heard voices behind him, closer than he would have chosen. Turrin kept moving, aware that the net was shrinking around him. He rounded a bend in the creek bed and shrank back into the scrub when he saw the hovering shape of the helicopter fifty feet ahead. It sank toward the ground even as he spotted it, the rotors dragging up dust and debris from the dry watercourse.

He was caught between two groups. His choice of direction was drastically reduced, too. He was going to have to move, and once he did he would show his position. Turrin decided he would leave his pursuers something to remember him by, a distraction to give him time to make his break.

Crouching in the scrub, Turrin saw the helicopter hovering a few feet above the ground. The armed figures dropped from the open side hatch. As the third took his jump, Turrin raised his rifle and took aim. He eased back on the trigger and felt the M-16 kick. The slug caught the exiting gunner in the right shoulder, knocking him off balance. The guy gave a scream of fright as he fell, hitting the ground hard with a solid thump. Turrin had already altered his aim. He triggered his shot at the chopper itself. His shot clipped the fuselage just below the open hatch as the pilot, reacting to Turrin's first shot, powered the aircraft away in a shallow turn.

Aware that he had given his position away, Turrin

pushed to his feet and headed up the creek bank. He dug in his heels, feeling the loose ground sliding under him.

A rifle crackled on full-auto, slugs plowing into the earth just short of his position. A second one opened up from another direction. Something clipped his shirt just above the waist. Turrin glanced up and saw the top of the bank only feet away. He set his teeth against the pain in his thigh and lunged forward, dragging air into his burning lungs.

He could hear pounding boots behind him, someone shouting his name, cursing.

He crested the top of the bank, felt the earth crumble under his feet and before he could do anything Turrin pitched forward, over the steep drop that lay on the other side of the rim. He threw out his arms to save himself, the M-16 slipping from his fingers. He hit hard, gasping for breath as he went down. The loose earth took him with it, throwing him to the bottom of the slope. Turrin came to a jolting stop, sucking dry dust into his mouth as he fought for breath.

Hands caught hold of him, roughly spinning him onto his back. Bright sun blurred his vision as he stared up at the ring of hostile faces and threatening gun muzzles.

"Go to hell," he said, his voice coming out as a harsh croak.

Someone laughed. Turrin recognized the man he knew as Morales. He leaned over so he was close to Turrin.

"No more games, my friend. It is time for you to come with us. Away from this place. If you had waited, all this wouldn't have been necessary. Two men dead and look at you. Such a waste of time for us all. Tell me, Turrin, was it worth it?"

Turrin pushed up onto his elbows, returning the Mexican's stare.

"Damn right it was. Every minute. Give me a chance, I'd do it all again."

Morales muttered angrily in Spanish.

"See if you like this, gringo," he said and slammed the butt of his rifle against Turrin's skull.

MACK BOLAN and Jack Grimaldi met Agents Diego Morales and Paco Garcia in a roadside café on the outskirts of Nuevo Laredo. They were shown the way there by Cal Walker, who had been liaising with the cops from the drug squad. Identification was shown so that there was no mistaking who they all were. Bolan was still using his John McCall cover. Grimaldi had a Stony Man 10, giving his name as Sam Loomis.

They sat at a table where they could see the door and the dusty window fronting the café. Morales had ordered coffee for them all and as they waited for it to arrive Bolan started the conversation.

"As far as we know, the only agency informed of Turrin's arrival was yours."

He directed his statement at the two Mexicans.

Morales held up his hands. "What can I say? It's the truth. Someone had tipped Huerta that Turrin was coming to look into links between the DEA and his organization. As far as we knew, Turrin had only spoken to our squad commander about his visit."

"That doesn't eliminate a leak in your office," Bolan said. "We need to check."

Paco Garcia glanced at his partner. It wasn't lost on Bolan.

"What?"

Garcia leaned forward, almost as if he were afraid they were being overheard.

"We believe we might have a lead. It's hard because the individual is a fellow agent. An hombre we have known for years."

"They're the ones who get overlooked."

"What makes you think it's this guy?" Grimaldi asked.

"Soon after we were told Turrin was on his way, Calverra started to get jumpy," Garcia explained. "Like he was sitting on something hot and couldn't wait to tell."

Morales nodded. "The day after Turrin went missing, Calverra, well, he was a man with something on his mind. Couldn't settle. Nervous. Not like him at all. One thing made us figure something was really wrong when he started to go out of the office to make calls from the pay phone in the hall."

"Significance?"

"It's always been a joke that Calverra never used his cell phone to make calls from the office. Always used the department phone. He was always being reprimanded for wasting the department's money on personal calls. So suddenly he starts using the pay phone."

Garcia waited as their coffee was brought to the table.

"It might not seem much to an outsider. But Calverra is a man who seldom changes his routines. It just seemed too much of a coincidence that he starts to act differently at the time Turrin arrives in town and then vanishes."

"Anything else?"

"Yes," Garcia said. "We set up a tail on him. Felt bad at first because this guy *was* a friend. But his behavior had been out of character, and coupled with what had happened to Turrin, we felt it had to be done. If it came to nothing, then it was one lead we could forget."

"And did it come to nothing?"

"Calverra had a meet with a man who works for Huerta. Tulio Mendez. He does all kinds of work for Huerta. He's suspected of a number of assaults, trafficking in illegal drugs. A general lowlife."

Garcia produced photographs. He slid them across the table to Bolan.

"Names on the back," he said. "Ramon Huerta and Mendez. Just so you recognize who you're dealing with."

Bolan took the photos and put them away. "Where does this Mendez live?"

"I wrote his address on his photo. In case you want to make an unofficial visit," Garcia said. "If he sees us, Mendez will vanish into the woodwork and let Huerta know we have been sniffing around. And Huerta's lawyers would make a field day of it."

"Don't worry," Grimaldi said. "Unofficial is our middle name."

"What about Huerta and Salazar?" Bolan asked.

"Haven't been seen," Cal Walker said. "I've been monitoring their progress the past few days. They dropped out of sight the day Leo vanished. Of course they might be back at Huerta's estate now."

"We'll take Mendez," Bolan said. "What are you going to do about Calverra?"

Morales made a slight gesture. "He's one of ours. We have ways of dealing with his kind. We'll keep him under surveillance. Find out what else he's been up to."

"Calverra has allowed our names to be used in a crime," Garcia said. "That I don't forget. Or forgive. He'll pay. Don't concern yourselves about him."

A SHORT TIME LATER they were back outside, standing by their respective vehicles.

"You want me to stay with the drug squad?" Walker asked.

Bolan nodded. "No offense, but I don't want you involved in this. It might not exactly be by the book."

"Okay. Just make sure you find Leo."

Bolan climbed in behind the wheel of the dusty Cherokee 4×4 he and Grimaldi had used to motor into Mexico. He waited until Grimaldi joined him.

"You want to go pay a house call?"

"Only reason I came all the way down here, Sarge."

TULIO MENDEZ LIVED in a run-down tenement building close to a large freight yard. The area teemed with people and busy streets. Bolan parked across the street from the building, and he and Grimaldi sat for some time studying the area.

"We get into trouble down here it isn't going to do much good calling for the cops," Grimaldi observed.

"Jack, such a bitter view from someone so young and innocent."

"I wish. On the other hand what's so good about young or innocent?"

"Cynical, too?"

"Maybe I'm keeping the wrong company."

Bolan grinned.

They kept up their surveillance for a while longer until Bolan decided he might as well do what he'd come for.

He wore dark slacks and shoes, a light shirt under a leather jacket. The Beretta 93-R was in a shoulder rig beneath the jacket. He checked the pistol before he moved.

"Stay hard, pal," Bolan said as he climbed out of the 4×4.

He crossed the busy street, having to dodge some of the local drivers who obviously saw pedestrians as potential targets. Grimaldi watched with a bemused expression on his face. If only those drivers realized just whom they were playing games with. He saw Bolan reach the sidewalk and step inside the tenement building.

He sat back, scanning the area, ever watchful.

And now the clock starts ticking, he thought.

BOLAN LOCATED the stairs and went up. The interior of the building was shadowed, the air heavy with the reminders of cooking and poor sanitation. The walls had once been painted. The coating was now faded, covered in scrawled graffiti, and peeling in patches.

He could hear the sounds of life as he went up the stairs. People arguing. Laughing. Babies and children yelling or crying. Radios blaring out and competing with TV sets.

He reached the first landing, stepping over a broken toy, and rounded the banister to take the next flight. Bolan made sure his jacket was open and he could reach the 93-R quickly if he needed. At the head of the stairs he turned along the poorly lit corridor, counting off the numbers on the doors as he went. As he passed one apartment, the door opened and a young woman, dark hair tumbling to her shoulders, stepped out. She stared at Bolan, devouring him with her deep brown eyes as he walked by. She was wearing a close-fitting cotton dress, off the shoulder, and struck a deliberately provocative stance as she eyed him. When he offered no response she leaned back against the doorframe, sighing with either disappointment or frustration. Moments later Bolan heard the door close and the click of her heels as the woman made for the stairs.

He reached the door to Mendez's apartment. It was scratched and one of the upper panels had a partial split in the thin wood. Bolan leaned into the door. There was no obvious sound coming from inside, which indicated nothing either way.

Bolan tapped on the door. His knock brought a flurry of movement from inside the apartment. He knocked again.

"Mendez? Open up."

Silence. A hushed conversation. Movement inside the apartment. A piece of furniture pushed to one side, across bare floorboards. A rapid conversation in Spanish.

Then Bolan heard the click of a weapon being cocked.

He pulled to the side, against the wall, and heard the boom of a shotgun. The upper panel of the door blew out across the corridor. Splintered wood showered the floor.

From inside the room a man began to yell in Spanish, his words of protest lost with the sound of a heavy blow.

Bolan turned and launched a hard kick to the door, the force tearing it from its hinges. He followed it, pulling the Beretta as he went in low, almost at floor level, the muzzle of the pistol tracking ahead. Bolan spotted the shotgunner, a beefy man with receding hair and a Zapata mustache. The guy was hauling a sawed-off shotgun toward Bolan's moving body.

Flame belched from the muzzle. Bolan heard the roar of the shot and felt the wind of its passing as the charge skimmed his head. He hit the floor, sliding across the boards, and triggered the Beretta. The triburst chugged out its 9 mm slugs. Two plowed into Zapata's left knee, tearing it apart. Flesh and bone mushroomed from the shattered limb, and Zapata screamed in agony, falling as his leg gave way.

Bolan rolled to his knee, keeping the falling shooter in his sight, and saw the guy go for the handgun tucked in his leather belt. The Executioner fired, his burst catching the beefy man in the chest, kicking him back. Zapata's gun arm flew wide, the heavy pistol slipping from his fingers. It described a wide arc, hitting the floor close to the second man in the room. He was down on his knees, head hanging, blood dripping in glistening strings from his torn mouth where he had been hit.

Zapata hit the floor, out of the game for good.

Turning, Bolan picked up the moving figure of the second guy. He had dragged himself to where the fallen handgun lay, reaching out to close his fingers around the butt. The guy snatched up the gun and turned his body around so he could see Bolan, the gun coming up from floor level as it was brought in line with the American.

The warrior took a long step, lashing out with his right foot, the tip of his shoe catching the barrel of the pistol as it tracked him. For the second time the gun was sent spinning across the room. It came to a stop against the far wall.

The guy on the floor clutched at his injured fingers, cursing in Spanish. He started to stand up. Bolan got to him first, reaching out with his left hand to grab the Mexican's grubby T-shirt. He dragged the guy to his feet, shaking him with the fury of a man tired of being set up and placed in the firing line. Bolan swung the man around and slammed him against the wall, the impact hard enough to bounce pictures off their hooks. Before the guy could catch his breath Bolan jammed the muzzle of the 93-R under his chin, digging it into the soft flesh until the man protested.

"You'd better understand English, hombre, because if you don't give me the right answer it's going to be your funeral," Bolan growled in a tone that couldn't have been mistaken for anything else except barely contained, unreasoning anger.

"Who are you? I do not know you."

"I believe you do. And I know you, Tulio Mendez. I know what you do and who you work for. And my job is to exterminate anyone who takes pay from Ramon Huerta."

"You are wrong, *señor*. I do not do what you say. I tried to help." Mendez touched his bloody mouth. "Look at my face. That loco one would have shot you if I had not interfered."

"More likely you didn't want it happening here. You wanted him to take me alive and do the killing somewhere else."

The expression in Mendez's eyes told Bolan he wasn't far off the mark.

"Maybe I'll finish what your friend started." Bolan pushed the Beretta deeper into Mendez's flesh. "You work out what a 3-round burst will do at this range. It will solve my problem, but you aren't going to like the result."

Sweat glistened on the Mexican's face. "What is it you want?"

"Where is the kidnapped American Turrin?"

"If I tell, you will kill me."

"Then take me there. Just remember one thing. Any tricks and the first thing I will do is shoot you."

Mendez held out his hands in submission.

"We go out of here nice and calm," Bolan said. "I have a 4×4 waiting across the street. We walk to it and get in the back. No games. I can kill you out there as easy as in here."

Bolan pushed Mendez ahead of him. The corridor was deserted. No one was curious enough to become involved. Bolan guessed that the sound of gunfire wasn't new to this neighborhood. He kept the Beretta against Mendez's spine, covered by his jacket.

The Mexican offered no resistance. He was wise enough not to create any fuss in his current situation. Any resistance and Bolan could have shot him without effort.

They negotiated the street, approaching the Cherokee. Grimaldi saw them coming and kicked in the engine.

"Open the rear door and get in," Bolan said.

He climbed in beside Mendez, pulling the door shut.

"Give him the directions."

Mendez guided Grimaldi for the next ten minutes until they were on the main highway, heading south out of the city.

"Stay on this road until I tell you," Mendez said.

MENDEZ HAD PUSHED into the corner of the seat in a sullen silence. He pulled up a corner of his T-shirt to wipe at the blood on his mouth. Bolan let him consider his situation for a while before he turned his attention on the man.

"We need to talk."

"If I don't?"

"Get something clear, Mendez. I really don't give a damn whether you live or die. Believe it. Don't make the mistake of thinking it's just talk."

"I said I would take you where they have Turrin."

"Why was he taken?"

Mendez hesitated, his mind working overtime as he struggled to find a way out of his current situation.

"Don't take too long," Bolan said, reaching down to touch the Beretta resting on his lap. "Right now I'm short on patience."

"When Salazar learned someone associated with the DEA was coming to Mexico he saw a chance to involve you, thought there might be a connection. He wants your head for what you did to his organization and the destruction of his business in Colombia."

"Son of a bitch," Grimaldi breathed. "He's mad at you, Sarge."

"I'm not exactly in love with him," Bolan said. "This is all a setup to draw me out. And Leo is caught in the middle."

"Salazar has a long memory," Mendez said. "He never forgives an injustice against him."

"Hell," Grimaldi said, "a drug trafficker with feelings. He'll be getting religion next."

"I hope so. It's time he was sent to meet his Maker."

THEY DROVE for a couple of hours, Bolan reminding Mendez not to play games and make certain they reached their destination. The Mexican began to take notice of their surroundings. He leaned forward, checking out the terrain on either side of the highway, and pointed out through the window.

"There will be a dirt road coming up. Take it. A mile or so in there is a house. It is where they took Turrin."

Grimaldi saw the turnoff and swung the Cherokee onto the rutted, dusty track.

"Better stop here," Bolan said.

Grimaldi eased the 4×4 into the scrub, set the brake and cut the engine. As it died they became aware of the silence.

"Why out here?" Bolan asked.

"Salazar and Huerta had a meeting to attend in Tampico. It was decided to hold Turrin here until they returned. And then he would be taken to Huerta's estate. Salazar didn't want anything to happen until he and Huerta returned. He thought it less likely you would find Turrin out here than at Huerta's estate."

"The man plays his cards smart," Grimaldi said.

"Not smart enough," Bolan said. "Are they back now? Salazar and Huerta?"

"Yes. At Huerta's estate."

Mendez led the way toward the house. When they were close Bolan called a halt. From the low rise, covered in mesquite, they were able to observe the old house. It was small, in poor condition. There was a great deal of trash scattered outside. A small generator was housed beneath a lean-to to one side of the building. The door to the house stood open. It looked deserted.

"How many guns guarding Turrin?"

"Only two."

Bolan looked at the Mexican, holding his stare until Mendez reacted.

"I told you the truth. Two. If you don't believe me, go to hell. I can't say what I don't know."

"Keep your gun on him. You know what to do."

Grimaldi nodded, easing his own handgun from inside his jacket. He pointed the Beretta 92-F at Mendez.

Bolan made his way to the house using all the cover available. The closer he got, the more certain he was that the place was going to be empty.

He reached the front wall and looked through the open door. The room inside was empty. Bolan slipped inside, making a quick check of the room. There were signs that it had been recently used. He crossed the room and the passage, reaching the back room where his friend had been held. Another inspection showed the room was clear. Bolan looked around. The bed had been used and there was a plastic tray on the floor near the door, with spilled food close by. Bolan saw a plastic cup by the door. There were marks on the doorframe where liquid had been splashed. Dark and grainy. He took another look around the room, saw the scattered magazines. There was nothing else to see.

Bolan walked back outside and scanned the area. He saw footprints in the dust, leading away from the house and heading north. There were other prints, as well. And tire marks. Too many to make much sense from.

If Turrin had been here, he was long gone. Bolan hoped it was to Huerta's estate. Salazar's plan had been to lure Bolan to *his* hunting ground. In that respect he had succeeded, because if Turrin was at Huerta's estate, that was where Bolan was going.

"Take Mendez inside," Bolan said to Grimaldi. "Lock him in that room. He can wait it out until the cops come for him."

Mendez didn't like the idea of being abandoned. He only needed to see the bleak expression in Bolan's eyes to keep his objections to himself. He submitted to the incarceration in sullen silence, deciding it was at least the lesser of two evils.

CHAPTER SIXTEEN

Huerta Estate

Hermano Salazar closed the door and crossed the shaded, quiet room. He stood at the foot of the bed where Leo Turrin lay and studied the sleeping American. The operation on Turrin's leg had been completed earlier that afternoon. Now the American was sleeping off the anesthetic. He would survive, Huerta's physician had assured the Colombian. All he needed now was rest. Salazar had needed to know that. The fact that Turrin might die soon made no difference. The man hadn't only escaped from his captors, but had also eluded recapture for some time, engaging Huerta's people and even taking out two of them before his eventual downfall.

Salazar admired true courage in any man. The American's determination, his tenacity, gained Salazar's respect. Even if Turrin was sacrificed in the end, he deserved his final time to be of as good a quality as could be provided.

Turrin had already been at Huerta's sprawling estate, close to the foothills of the Sierra Madre Oriental, when Salazar and Huerta had flown in from their meeting. It had been a successful one, concerning a deal that involved himself and Huerta buying into a consortium planning to build a luxury hotel complex in Merida on the Yucatán Peninsula. This deal was to be the first in a series of financial arrangements that would build hotels all around the Mexican resort circuit. From Yucatán to Baja California to Tampico, the Salazar-Huerta partnership would usher in a new era of high-class hotels that would offer anything and everything the *turistas* could dream of. Drug money would finance the construction, being laundered in the process, and would eventually come back as revenue. It was an ideal situation as far as Salazar was concerned. Money to make more money. He liked the idea.

But first there was the matter of Belasko to take care of. He was here in Mexico, now masquerading as John McCall. The American was nothing if not versatile. News had filtered through concerning the destruction of Deacon Marley's Jamaican operation. Salazar's informants had told him that not only was Marley dead, but also Fedor Trechenko. There had been a violent confrontation at Marley's Blue Mountain residence that had resulted in their deaths. Marley's coffee-processing plant and his car-rental business had also been hit. As far as Salazar had been concerned, his problem in the Caribbean was solved. The removal of Marley and Trechenko left the way open for him to step in and take over completely. The other drug traffickers in Jamaica were far less organized than Marley and would offer little resistance now that the island's main drug lord had been removed.

The good news had been tainted when further reports came through to blunt the edge of Salazar's pleasure. First he learned that the *Caliente,* along with its crew, had been destroyed, blown out of the water so that all remaining was matchwood. Then he learned that his hit team in Jamaica had also been wiped out, Santana, his torture master, included. Plus the loss of the laptop that had held vital business information. Names and contacts, routes, delivery points. Salazar had broken all contact with those people and places until he was able to work out fresh details. He had taken himself and his best protection team and had accepted Huerta's longstanding offer to visit with him in Mexico. Worse to come was the attack on Salazar's dock facility. First his hit team, waiting for Belasko, had been taken down and then his warehouses, apartment complex and part of his dock had been totaled by some high-tech helicopter. As a final insult, Salazar's pilot and helicopter had been hijacked by Belasko for a second time. He had flown to Salazar's own airstrip and had reduced the control tower to rubble.

Salazar had received all this in utter silence. He was,

for the first time in years, left with nothing inside except pure, white-hot rage. So stunned by the sheer audacity of Belasko that he had no words to express himself. He had taken himself off to Mexico and had pushed ahead with his deal with Huerta.

His first piece of good news came when Asa Randal informed him of Leo Turrin's possible visit to Mexico. The information came through and confirmed that Turrin had been in contact with Belasko throughout his mission to Russia and Jamaica. It was obvious that Belasko was working through Turrin, so it seemed the logical next step was to snatch Turrin and put him under threat. Belasko would come looking for him, especially if Turrin's capture was linked to both Huerta and Salazar. Randal's contacts, the ones open to cash incentives, detailed Turrin's trip. Huerta used this information to prime his contact within the Nuevo Laredo drug squad, and once the time and place of Turrin's arrival were known, there was no difficulty in arranging for two of Huerta's people to go to Turrin's hotel, posing as the genuine drug squad cops, and take the American captive.

It had seemed the sensible thing to keep Turrin on ice until Salazar returned with Huerta from his business trip. Plans had been in place for too long to change anything, so Huerta's kidnap team had taken Turrin to the isolated house the Mexican drug lord had used frequently when he needed somewhere out of sight to have talks with errant employees or troublesome intruders.

There were more than a few unmarked graves around the house where disposals had taken place.

Turrin hadn't taken his kidnapping well and despite the situation, had broken out. The rest was history....

Salazar satisfied himself that Turrin was comfortable before returning to the spacious lounge where Ramon Huerta and Asa Randal were discussing courier routes into the States. Randal was proving to be an asset, after all. His knowledge of DEA and Border Patrol procedures allowed him to show Huerta the least protected places along the Mexico-U.S. border.

"Offer enough money, we could get someone to phase out the electronics along this stretch," Randal said, indicating locations on the map of the border country.

"This could be done?" Huerta asked.

"Enough money and you can buy anything," Randal said.

"True," Salazar agreed. "Mine bought you, Asa."

If the remark hurt, Randal didn't show it. He simply smiled at Salazar, then returned to educating Huerta.

The Mexican, a stocky, fit man in his early forties, though wealthy and wielding great power, wasn't an overly sophisticated man. Huerta used the tried and trusted, old-fashioned methods of business. Brutality followed hard on the heels of terrorizing, coercion and intimidation. Huerta was proud of his success, and even Salazar couldn't argue against the methods Huerta employed.

The Mexican's huge, sprawling estate covered a wide

tract of land. Huerta ran a stud ranch and had a reputation for breeding world-class horses. He had a prize herd on his range and took great pride in becoming involved with the animals.

The main house stood in splendid isolation on a low hill, overlooking the working ranch a quarter mile away. The ranch employees, some with their families, lived on the ranch.

The big house was a rambling, two-story affair. Traditional both outside and in, the house also boasted every modern convenience available. There were large-screen TV sets in most rooms, including the bedrooms and the kitchen. The entire house was wired with hidden speakers so that Huerta could have music wherever he went. Expensive paintings adorned the walls, and Mexican sculptures were all over the house. The place screamed money, valuable contents, but not a great deal of class. If Salazar had taken over the house, he would have removed Huerta's art and burned it in the middle of the yard. He kept his thoughts to himself, not wanting to offend his partner. Huerta's lack of sophistication could be overlooked. His way of doing business impressed Salazar, and he wasn't going to do anything to spoil the relationship.

"Hermano, why don't you settle down. We are safe here. If that fucking American shows his face, my people will deal with him. He won't even get close. The security cameras will pick him up first."

Salazar said nothing. Huerta's claim sounded comforting, but all Salazar had to do was remind himself that the combined forces of Marley and Trechenko had failed to stop Belasko. He touched the SIG-Sauer P-226 holstered on his hip. The gun gave him some comfort.

Some.

But he still felt unsettled at the thought of Belasko showing his face. The American had a habit of walking through opposition like some phantom. Salazar wanted Belasko dead and buried. He just didn't want the problems that the man created whenever he showed up.

The Colombian crossed the room and went through to a smaller room that Huerta had as a home movie theater. It was equipped with deep leather recliners facing a huge plasma TV screen. There was even a full surround-sound system installed. Salazar's hit team was installed in the room, watching a Hollywood blockbuster movie playing from the high-tech DVD player. His team was taking the opportunity to relax, leaving the security of the house and grounds to Huerta's own people.

Salazar leaned over one of the recliners and spoke to the man seated there. The Colombian immediately turned away from the movie, giving his full attention to his employer.

"Is something wrong?"

Salazar placed a hand on the man's broad shoulder.

"No panic, Rosario. With all respect to our host, I still feel we should take a few more precautions. Take two of the team and go check out the landing strip. See that the plane is secure. Do a sweep of the area. Keep in touch using the radios."

"Yes. Of course."

Rosario pushed up out of the recliner and alerted two of the team. They joined him and followed Salazar out of the house. On the wide porch that ran the length of the building, Salazar gave them their orders. With the onset of darkness floodlights had automatically come on, bathing the house and the immediate area with light.

"Keep it low-key. We know Belasko is in the country. Once he finds out we have Turrin here, he will come looking for him. Let us be ready this time. One way or another, this matter will be settled soon."

Rosario sent one of the men to bring a vehicle. Huerta had a number of Jeeps he kept for moving around the large expanse of his property, and he had extended the use of these to Salazar and his people. When the Jeep arrived, Salazar stood watching as his three-man team drove out of sight into the darkness beyond the floodlights.

The rich aroma of a Cuban cigar reached Salazar's nostrils. He knew Huerta was standing behind him.

"You are still concerned, my friend?"

Salazar turned to confront Huerta.

"Ramon, please do not be offended. Understand what this man has inflicted on me recently. I don't doubt your security will keep him away. But it does no harm to be cautious."

"You are my guest. Free to do what you wish, and why should I be offended when you place your own people at my service? You know me, Hermano. I am a man who enjoys the peace and quiet of his home. Let your men do their job. Now come back inside and let us relax."

Salazar nodded, placing an arm around Huerta's shoulders as they returned to the house.

HUERTA'S PRIVATE landing strip was located a mile from his house. Bolan's earlier recon had established the presence of Hermano Salazar's Gulfstream jet. It sat at the end of the strip, close to where Huerta's pair of helicopters stood on a separate pad. A Jeep was parked nearby, and Bolan counted at least five armed men lounging beside it.

Once Bolan had located the strip and assessed the opposition, he withdrew and made his way back to where Grimaldi waited in the concealed Cherokee.

"Strip's that way," Bolan said. "About a quarter mile east. Salazar's jet and a couple of choppers. A Jeep and a five-man squad."

"What about the house, Mack? I still—"

"We've been through this. You handle the strip. Deal with the guards. Take out what you can. Wait until I call on the radio. Then we both make it a go."

Grimaldi offered no further argument. Bolan had his mind set on the night strike. Earlier he had carried out a detailed study of the house, concealed in a patch of scrub, checking the area out with a pair of powerful binoculars.

His recon furnished him with vital information.

Huerta had the property ringed by TV cameras, mounted on steel poles. The cameras were rigged to make regular sweeps, covering both the house and the adjacent open ground. Once he had established the position of the cameras, Bolan checked out the squat building that stood some five hundred feet from the house itself. It had no windows, only vent grilles and a short steel stack coming out of the flat roof. His close-up view had identified shimmering heat waves coming out of the stack. That and the vent grilles told Bolan he was looking at the generator building that supplied the electrical power for Huerta's house and all the equipment inside.

There were several Jeeps parked beside the house. Some distance away were the luxury cars Huerta owned. The drug lord, in keeping with his lifestyle, owned a small fleet of vehicles, from top-of-the-range SUVs to a couple of new Cadillacs, BMWs and a sleek black Porsche convertible. The Jeeps appeared to be for the use of Huerta's crew. During the time Bolan spent watching the house, armed Mexicans came and went, driving off to patrol the estate.

Just before Bolan retreated, he spotted a familiar figure on the porch fronting the house. He focused the binoculars and brought the figure into sharp detail.

It was Hermano Salazar. The Colombian was standing with a glass in his hand, talking to someone just out of sight behind one of the porch support pillars. It was only when Salazar turned to go back inside the house that the concealed figure moved to follow him and Bolan had a clear view.

Asa Randal.

The rogue DEA man was still sporting a bandage over the nose Bolan had broken at their last encounter. Randal, in deep discussion with Salazar, followed the Colombian back into the house.

Bolan was able to make his way back to Grimaldi with at least a partial answer to things he needed to know.

His main targets were at the house, and Bolan had no intention of allowing them to slip away from him this time. Which determined that he was going to make his strike as soon as it got dark.

They spent the time prior to the strike making certain they were fully equipped.

The rear of the Cherokee held a selection of weaponry they had brought with them from the U.S. With their Justice Department credentials and the cooperation of the Nuevo Laredo drug squad, courtesy of Agents Morales and Garcia, they had been passed through the border control point without delay or inspection. The Mexicans had wanted to make up for allowing Turrin to be spirited away from them so easily, and part of that cooperation extended to allowing Bolan into the country without any questions.

Along with his standard arms, Bolan had brought a couple of LAWs, one of which he passed to Grimaldi with the suggestion it would fit nicely into a Gulfstream jet. Bolan also had a selection of stun and smoke grenades. He chose an MP-5, fitted with a double mag, and added extra loads to his blacksuit pockets, along with others for his Beretta and Desert Eagle. His secondary offensive weapon was an M-16 A-2, fitted with an M-203 grenade launcher. Bolan had a selection of incendiary and HE grenades for the launcher in his combat vest pockets. A Ka-bar fighting knife was strapped to his side. He also slung a pair of night-vision goggles around his neck, plus his binoculars.

Grimaldi, clad in camou fatigues, wore his 92-F in a hip holster and carried a 9 mm Uzi, plus a Mossberg 590 DA shotgun. The pump-action 12-gauge's double-action trigger gave the shooter the advantage of a pistol-type action that cocked and released the trigger, adding to safety, even after a fresh shell had been pushed into the breech. Grimaldi was using the model fitted with a 9-round magazine, plus a Side Saddle shell holder fixed to the side of the weapon with an extra six loads. He carried the Mossberg across his back on a nylon webbing strap. He also had a pair of NVGs.

They used combat-cosmetics to dull the skin of their faces and hands, then sat out the remainder of the dusk, waiting until full dark. There was a pale moon, too. Bolan checked his watch, Grimaldi synchronizing his. The last thing they did before moving out was to check the compact transceivers they carried.

"Time to move out," Bolan said. "You watch your back, pal."

"And you, Sarge."

They moved out, each taking the direction that would bring him to his individual target zone.

Bolan moved at a steady trot, keeping away from moonlit areas, using the deep shadows as cover, and reached his first position. He slid into a shallow dip in the ground, placing his weapons beside him, and took out the transceiver.

Grimaldi answered his call without delay.

"What took you so long, Sarge? I've been waiting."

"I had a little farther to go."

Grimaldi chuckled. "How's it looking?"

"House is pretty well lit up. Floodlights all around."

"Hitting that generator should deal with that."

"Let's hope Huerta doesn't have a backup in the basement."

"Soon as I hear your explosion I'll do my party piece."

"Hold it a minute. I see something."

Bolan placed his transceiver on the ground and used the binoculars to scan the front of the house. He had made out figures on the porch. His interest was aroused as he recognized Hermano Salazar in conversation with three men. One went to collect a Jeep. The others joined him and they drove off, Salazar standing watching until the figure of Ramon Huerta joined him. They spoke for a moment, then went back inside the house. Bolan tracked the Jeep and realized it was heading in the general direction of the airstrip. He picked up the transceiver again and spoke to Grimaldi.

"A Jeep with three passengers just left the house, Jack. It looks like it could be heading in your direction."

"Thanks. Hey, Sarge, you ready to go?"

"Just keep listening, flyboy."

BOLAN TOOK the LAW and pulled the safety pins to open the end covers. He extended the inner tube, the action cocking the firing mechanism, and positioned himself on one knee as he placed the launcher over his right shoulder. He had already assessed his target distance at around two hundred yards—well within the LAW's effective range. He settled the sights on the front wall of the generator building, taking his time to be sure he had a good lock on his target, then fired. The 66 mm rocket, with its HEAT warhead, streaked across the target range and struck the generator building. The detonation demolished the entire frontage and brought the roof down, collapsing the building and destroying the diesel-powered generator. The blast extended to the rear of the building, puncturing the fuel storage tank outside and set off a fuel burn that boiled skyward.

With the explosion, the floodlights and those in the house went out.

THE EXPLOSION RATTLED windows in the main house, the vibrations knocking pictures off hooks and toppling ornaments from shelves. The immediate glare from the explosion was followed by the house being plunged into darkness as the power was cut.

In the room at the rear of the house where the camera images were viewed, the loss of light was followed by the monitor screens turning blank as the cameras were lost.

Ramon Huerta, to his credit, remained calm. He stood up and rapped out orders to his men. With the moon and the shimmering blaze casting light in through the windows, they moved to cabinets built into the walls, arming themselves with loaded weapons.

"Hermano, have your men join mine. You wanted your battle. I believe you are going to get it."

Salazar took the 9 mm Uzi the Mexican offered him. Asa Randal, autopistol in his hand, joined them.

"I owe that fuck," he said.

"Such hostility," Huerta said. "Don't let it cloud your judgment, hombre."

"Judgment, my ass. I'll show you how it's done American style."

EVEN THOUGH he had been expecting the explosion, the heavy boom of the detonation caught Grimaldi off guard. He recovered quickly, prepping his own LAW. He had worked his way in close to the edge of the strip, and the gleaming lines of the Gulfstream jet were slightly less than one hundred yards in front of where he lay in the deep grass and scrub. Grimaldi shouldered the launcher and took aim, locking on to where the fuselage joined the wings. He touched the firing button and felt the LAW jerk slightly as it fired, the rocket streaking across the relatively short distance to target.

The missile hit, detonated and subsequently blew the fuel tanks. The resultant explosion lit up the strip. The fireball it caused enveloped the stricken aircraft, throwing burning fuel in all directions. Grimaldi watched as the jet disintegrated in the midsection, collapsing in a flaming mass of twisted metal.

"There goes thirty million bucks," he muttered.

The Stony Man pilot discarded the LAW carcass, pulled his NVGs into place and adjusted the goggles until he was able to scan the area. He brought his Uzi into play, cocking the 9 mm SMG before moving away from his place of concealment, coming in around the blazing wreck of the Gulfstream.

As he rounded the tail end of the aircraft, Grimaldi spotted two men on foot, weapons up as they combed the area. He knew this was going to be a locate-and-kill exercise as far as the Mexicans were concerned. There would be no questions asked this time. The moment they saw him they were going to start shooting.

He dropped to one knee, shouldering the Uzi, and pulled back on the trigger the moment the first guy moved into sight. Grimaldi's burst caught the Mexican in the upper chest, the impact of the 9 mm slugs knocking the guy back a couple of steps before he tumbled.

Just beyond this guy a second armed guard brought his own weapon around, firing a little too quickly, so his burst hit the ground to one side of the kneeling American.

Grimaldi adjusted his aim, waiting that extra second

before he fired, and caught his target with a burst that put the guard down flat on his back.

The moment the second man went down Grimaldi gained his feet and changed position....

BEFORE BOLAN MOVED he loaded an HE grenade into the underslung M-203.

There was a lull of inactivity from in and around the house. It lasted only as long as it took the defenders to acknowledge what had happened and to initiate a response. Bolan made good use of the moment, pushing to his feet and sprinting across the open ground that lay between him and Ramon Huerta's house.

He had covered half that distance when he picked up the beat of a powerful engine. Bolan turned and saw a large SUV barreling across the open ground in his direction, headlights catching him in their beams.

The sound of a muffled explosion reached Bolan's ears, and he knew that Grimaldi had joined the war.

Someone leaned out the passenger window and opened fire with an autorifle.

Bolan had already anticipated hostile fire and he dropped prone to the ground, then raised himself enough so he could shoulder the M-16 and offer a response. He felt the rifle's butt nudge his shoulder as he pumped a succession of single shots at the oncoming vehicle, aiming up at the windshield. He remained where he was as the SUV bored down on his position, maintaining his steady rate of fire.

The windshield blew out under the concentrated on-slaught of 5.56 mm slugs. The driver reeled back under the hail of glass fragments burning into his face. Then two of Bolan's shots hit him in the right shoulder, tearing away a chunk of flesh and bone. The driver lost all control of the SUV, his world dissolving into bloody pain. The speeding vehicle hit a hump in the ground, the front wheels spinning, and the SUV flipped over on its side.

Bolan rolled the minute he saw the windshield shatter. He only just avoided being caught by the crushing weight of the heavy tires, and as he came to his knees, he saw the vehicle tip on its side. The weight of the SUV dragged it for a few yards before it lurched to a stop, rocking before it settled. The engine was still racing.

Bolan could hear someone screaming. He moved to the far side of the vehicle and saw the driver's upper body exposed while the rest of him lay crushed under the deadweight of the SUV. The guy's right shoulder was a torn mess of flesh and bone where Bolan's slugs had hit him, and his face was a bleeding mask. He was flailing about in agony. Bolan ended his misery with a single mercy shot to the head.

Sound above Bolan's head caught his attention. He looked up and saw the gunner pushing into view from the passenger window. The hardman still had his auto-rifle in his hand and he dragged it around to take a shot. Bolan hit him with three 5.56 mm slugs from the M-16, knocking him back against the window frame, where he hung and died.

Bolan used the SUV as cover while he made a quick check of the house. More armed figures were starting to emerge, and as they consolidated for a moment, he heard a Jeep engine bursting into life, headlights coming on. The Jeep raced across the open ground, heading in his direction. Bolan eased the NVGs into place, scanning the oncoming vehicle and seeing four men inside as it bounced across the uneven ground. One of the rear passengers was attempting to bring the swivel-mounted light machine gun into play.

Bolan brought the M-16 into target acquisition, finger on the trigger of the loaded M-203. He waited until his NVG vision was steady, then triggered the launcher. The HE grenade hit the front grille of the Jeep and blew the vehicle apart, turning it into a blazing wreck that continued to roll across the grass for twenty feet before it came to rest. None of the crew survived.

The Mexicans on foot skirted the stricken Jeep, still advancing toward Bolan's defensive position.

The soldier saw and accepted it was make-or-break time. There was no more waiting to be done. He braced himself against the rear of the overturned SUV and shouldered the M-16. He saw his targets, still in a tight cluster, and used their immobility to his advantage.

The M-16 began to crack single shots, each placed with methodical precision by a man who had been trained as a sniper. A man taught to make the best from any situation. To take the fight to the enemy, and not to waste time on ethical dilemmas. That could come later, if it needed to be analyzed, but at the moment of the kill there was nothing else.

Bolan's first shot hit his target. The man went down, fatally hit. By the time the others realized what was happening the Executioner had fired a second and a third time.

Two more down.

Huerta's men broke apart, each going his own way, but none of them remembering they were on open ground. There was no cover, and the shots kept coming.

Five, six and seven.

Three more bodies struck the earth, blood pumping from wounds. Life expiring.

The few survivors had scattered, turning in the direction of the house, eager to find cover from this almost invisible sniper who seemed to hit everything he fired at.

Bolan used the break in the action to move closer to the house, staying low, his black-clad figure merging with the ground shadows. He was within twenty yards now, close enough make effective use of the M-203 launcher. From his prone position on the ground he fired an incendiary grenade, dropping it on the front porch. The grenade detonated, the incandescent burn igniting the wood and sending flames up the front wall of the house.

Moving again, Bolan circled, bringing himself closer to the house, away from the blaze on the porch. He took one of the HE grenades and slipped it into the M-203, turning the launcher in the direction of the extreme corner of the house. He laid the grenade at the base, and the ensuing blast took a ragged bite out of the walls. Bolan moved in closer, unclipping a smoke grenade. He pulled the pin and threw the canister through the gap opened by the HE grenade. Moments later the grenade detonated and thick smoke began spreading through the room.

Bolan kept up his assault, moving constantly, using his smoke grenades at each opportunity. With the house well saturated Bolan retreated, waiting.

A trio of gunners broke from the blazing porch. They covered a wide spread of the frontage with their weapons as they stumbled, coughing from the white smoke drifting out the door they had opened. They started shooting as they emerged, firing indiscriminately. From his prone position on the ground Bolan was able to pick them off one by one, tumbling them to the ground with well-placed single shots from his M-16.

He moved again, a flitting shadow stalking Huerta's men. Striking, retreating into the shadows, using every natural feature to hide himself from the rapidly depleting and frustrated enemy.

Mack Bolan was in his natural habitat. Taking on the opposition on their home ground. Meting out his individual brand of retribution to those who had stepped over the line, distancing themselves from considerations of mercy and forgiveness. All Bolan had to do was recall the damage these people did with their poisonous merchandise. And the peripheral harm they created as they bought and bribed and brutalized, dragging in individuals who were only involved by capricious twists of fate. There were too many, too often, and the cycle went on.

Bolan crouched behind the cover of the parked cars of Huerta's fleet. He ejected the spent mag from the M-16 and snapped in a fresh one, cocking the weapon, and crawled to the front of the silver BMW he was hidden by.

He could hear Huerta's men calling to one another, their voices betraying their emotions, their anger.

Peering around the fender, Bolan spotted one of the Mexicans, wielding an M-16 as he turned right and left, seeing nothing, hearing nothing. Bolan tracked in with his own rifle and put a single 5.56 mm slug through the back of the guy's skull, pitching him facedown onto the ground. Bringing the M-203 into play, Bolan lobbed another incendiary grenade onto the roof of the house, where it flared into white-hot fury. Bolan withdrew and slipped an HE round into the launcher, then worked his way along the line of the parked cars until he reached the far end.

An armed figure stepped into view, moving along the parked vehicles. The guy was too late spotting Bolan. The American had already locked on to the man, aided by his night-vision goggles. He lunged up off the ground, his M-16 slashing around in a short arc. The butt cracked against the guy's jaw, slamming him to his knees. Bolan swung the rifle a second time, directly into the guy's exposed throat, crushing it. The Mexican started to choke, dropping his M-16 as he clawed at his throat, trying to suck air into his lungs. Bolan was on him in an instant, snapping his right arm around the man's neck, using his left hand to push the guy's head forward, increasing the pressure. The Mexican began to thrash around, arms and legs flailing. Bolan upped the pressure until the struggles ceased and the Mexican slumped in his grip. He lowered the man to the ground, took the discarded M-16 and made his way along the side of the BMW.

A number of figures formed in the general direction of the parked cars, unsure where their target was. Bolan leaned out, set the M-16 on full-auto and held the trigger back, targeting the advancing figures. The sustained burst scythed back and forth, 5.56 mm slugs finding yielding flesh. Two men went down, clutching shattered limbs. A third took a burst of slugs in his lower torso. He doubled over, gripping his body against the rising pain.

One guy stood his ground, returning Bolan's fire. The slugs thudded into the body of the BMW, tearing ragged holes in the silver panels. A brake light exploded, plastic shards filling the air. Bolan felt one slice his cheek. He held his position, adjusting his aim, and placed the final burst from the M-16 into the gunner's chest, kicking the guy off his feet.

Bolan tossed aside the borrowed M-16 and brought his own rifle back into play. He backed away from the parked cars, circling around until he could lose himself in the shadows, away from the illumination of the burning generator building, pausing only to fire the HE grenade at the parked cars, seeing the resultant explosion as the grenade turned the BMW into a pyre. The fuel tank blew and spread flaming gasoline over the area. A second grenade increased the carnage, blowing flaming debris across the ground.

Bolan continued his circle around the perimeter of the damage he had caused, then angled in back toward the house....

JACK GRIMALDI MET his enemies head-on, the Uzi crackling as the Stony Man pilot fired. His burst narrowly missed the Mexican guard. The guy twisted his body, firing in return as he confronted the American. Grimaldi felt the impact as the slugs chewed at the ground inches from him. He triggered the Uzi again, held the SMG steady and saw the other guy fall back, the front of his shirt blossoming red. As the guy went down, Grimaldi hit him again, a short burst to the head that laid the man down for good.

He heard the sound of an approaching engine and recalled Bolan's warning about one of the Jeeps heading in the direction of the strip. The sound increased as the vehicle, headlights piercing the darkness, came into view.

Guards ran out to meet it, clustering around the Jeep as it coasted in.

Grimaldi slung the Uzi from its strap and brought the Mossberg into play. He knew that if the combined force got its act together, he was going to find it difficult to handle them once they split apart. His best chance lay in a concentrated attack, taking them as a group. At the same time Grimaldi accepted what he was about to do was close to reckless, but he had never been accused of being cautious.

He jacked the first round into the breech and ducked into the shadows, swinging around to come at the Jeep from the side.

Grimaldi hit the group on the run, triggering shot after shot into their midst. The powerful charges from the Mossberg hit with devastating power, the concentrated impact tearing into flesh and metal alike. The attack never faltered. Grimaldi gave in to the adrenaline rush, loading and firing without pause, ignoring the noise and the screams, the flying debris. His assault continued until the shotgun locked on an empty breech. The last shell case clattered to the ground, rolling to a stop against the side of Grimaldi's boot.

Grimaldi plucked the reserve cartridges from the Side Saddle and fed them into the slot. When the sixth shell was in place, Grimaldi worked the shotgun's slide, feeding one into the breech.

He had no need. His assault had taken the Mexican and Colombian traffickers off guard, the firepower of the Mossberg reaping a deadly harvest. Grimaldi was the only one alive at the strip. He surveyed the result of his attack, shaking his head at what he saw.

"Jesus Christ," he whispered, unsure whether he was

simply expressing his feelings or saying a prayer for the dead.

"WHERE IS THIS damn American?" Ramon Huerta yelled above the din. "Show him to me and I will deal with him myself."

"Go stand on the porch," Asa Randal suggested. "He'll come to you fast enough."

The Mexican drug lord spun, eyes blazing.

"And handle him as you did? I do not think so."

He shouldered his way past Randal and headed for the front door to the house. He caught the handle and pulled the door open, only to be forced to step back from the fire spreading along the porch.

"This is madness. Who is this Belasko? Where is he?"

Huerta's remaining calmness vanished as he was confronted by the realization that his house was about to fall down around his ears.

HERMANO SALAZAR had retreated to the far end of the house, along with his armed bodyguards. His instinct warned him it was going to be in his best interests to withdraw from the situation as it stood. Remaining inside the house would only lead to disaster. Salazar had experienced Belasko's interference on two occasions, and each time the American had walked away virtually unscathed. Staying here, inside Huerta's so-called protected house, wasn't the answer to survival.

"Get us outside," Salazar ordered his bodyguards. "If we stay in here we'll burn."

As they pushed through the double doors leading to the main dining room, the lead bodyguard stepped inside, checking out the area. He turned and nodded to Salazar. The drug lord pushed by, indicating the sliding doors that comprised the end wall.

"There," he said.

His bodyguards spread out before him.

The crackle of an autoweapon sounded from the other side of the glass doors. The panels exploded into the room, glass showering Salazar and his team. One of the bodyguards stumbled, dropping his weapon and clutching at his head. Even in the faint light Salazar saw the gleam of blood on the man's fingers.

A figure dressed in black from head to foot breached the open frame of the sliding doors, the muzzle of a 9 mm Uzi tracking in on Salazar and his team.

The man was wearing NVGs. Not that it mattered. Salazar knew who it was.

Belasko.

"Kill him," he yelled at his bodyguards.

Before his words were fully out of his mouth, Belasko's Uzi stuttered, the SMG spitting fire as the American ducked to the side and turned the muzzle on the bodyguards. They were struggling to pick him out, hampered by the shadows in the room.

Salazar heard the meaty chunk of bullets hitting flesh, heard the stunned grunts that burst from the mouths of his stricken men. The thump of their bodies on the hardwood floor told him he wouldn't be calling on their help any longer.

He swung up his own Uzi, firing indiscriminately, the streams of 9 mm slugs hitting the walls as Salazar swept the room, back and forth, until the magazine was exhausted. He threw the weapon aside and pulled out the SIG-Sauer P-226.

"Show yourself," Salazar demanded. "Stand up like a man."

His words were greeted with silence.

The Colombian swept the room with the P-226, eyes peering into the gloom.

He could feel sweat popping out over his face. It ran into his eyes, stinging. The taste was salty in his mouth. For the first in a very long time Hermano Salazar experienced fear. Here, now, his power and authority meant nothing. Nor did his extreme wealth. Money wouldn't buy off this man. Not as it had with Asa Randal. This American would never be bought. Or scared off. He was, like death, inevitable.

Salazar pulled the trigger, sending a 9 mm slug at a moving shadow. He heard the bullet strike the wall. Then a faint whisper of sound. The drug lord turned hastily, fired again. Nothing.

He could hear his own breathing. Harsh in his chest. Sweat was dripping from his chin. He wiped it away with the back of his hand.

Damn you, Belasko, where are you?

As if in answer, Salazar felt something cold glide

across his gun hand. There was a sharp burst of pain, and he knew he had been cut with a knife across the knuckles. The cut was deep, the pain increasing almost instantly, and he felt blood welling from the wound. His fingers slackened their hold on the pistol. He tried to maintain his grip, but the knife cut had gone too deep and he felt the weapon sagging.

And then a hand reached out of the darkness, fingers knotting in his thick hair. Salazar felt his head being jerked back, pulling his throat taut, and in the instant before it happened he knew—

The keen blade bit deep, slashing everything in its path from one side to the other. Blood began to pulse from the severed carotid arteries, bubbling from the rest of the deep, great wound in his neck. He cried out, only uttering a wet gurgle, feeling the flood of his own life-blood washing down his shirt, soaking through the expensive material.

And then he heard the soft whisper of death itself, the words adding a final chill of terror to his dying moments.

"Time to go and meet all the innocent souls you sent to hell, Salazar."

Mack Bolan released his hold on Salazar's hair and pushed the Colombian away. The drug lord dropped to the floor, his body shuddering in spasm as his blood spread out from beneath him in a widening dark pool.

Bolan put the Ka-bar away and unslung his Uzi, moving out of the dining room and down the passage, his NVGs illuminating the darkness with a green glow.

Twice he was confronted with armed men struggling to see their way in the gloom. He hit them with short, killing bursts from the Uzi, driving them to the floor. The house was still misty with drifting smoke from the grenades he had lobbed inside. He reached the wide staircase leading to the next floor, and as he did a stocky figure blocked his path.

Bolan recognized Huerta from the photo he had been shown.

Ramon Huerta, Uzi in his hands, peered at Bolan through the smoky gloom.

"This is as far as you go, gringo. First you die, then your friend up there."

He was still leveling his Uzi when Bolan triggered his own weapon, driving a burst of 9 mm slugs into the Mexican's chest. Huerta spilled backward, hitting the floor on his back, fingers reaching for the weapon he had dropped.

"No second chances, hombre," Bolan said coolly, and put another burst into Huerta's skull. "You've had yours."

He went up the wide, polished wood stairs reaching a wide landing with corridors leading off in either direction. An indication of where Turrin might be came when a Mexican stepped into view from his right. The guy rushed at Bolan, reaching for the pistol on his belt. It was an error he didn't get a chance to correct. Bolan stepped forward to meet his lunge, left hand sweeping up to knock aside the gun hand, then drove his right fist into the Mexican's face, crushing his nose in a bloody strike. The Mexican grunted, momentarily stunned from the blow, and Bolan caught his gun by the barrel, twisting it savagely. The guy cried out as his trigger finger was snapped, flesh tearing as Bolan wrenched the weapon from his grasp. Continuing his move, Bolan slammed into the Mexican and shoved him against the rail edging the landing. He leaned hard on the man, bending his spine until the man groaned.

"You understand English?" Bolan asked.

"*Un poco.*"

"Where is the American, Turrin?"

The Mexican pointed down the corridor. "The third door."

"Is he alone?"

"No."

"How many?"

"One. Randal."

Bolan wasn't surprised at that answer.

The Mexican stared up at the grim-faced American as Bolan pulled down the NVG goggles.

"I go now?"

"Oh, you go," Bolan said and swung the man over the railing.

The Mexican hit the floor below as Bolan turned and headed down the corridor, discarding the binoculars and the NVGs from around his neck. He put down the

Uzi and the M-16, leaning them against the wall, not wanting the extreme firepower they possessed within the confines of a room. He eased the Beretta from its holster, setting the selector for 3-round bursts, and held it in his hand as he counted off the doors.

The door to the room he wanted was standing partway open. Bolan pushed it wide with the toe of his boot, letting it swing back to give him an unobstructed view of the interior.

The first thing he saw was a bed, with Leo Turrin lying in it. Standing beside the bed was Asa Randal, a pistol in his hand pressed to the side of Turrin's head.

"Damn, I knew you'd cut your way through those assholes. Fuckin' knew it."

Bolan stepped into the room and stood to one side of the door, his back to the wall. He kept his gaze on Randal, ignoring Turrin. The 93-R hung loosely at his side.

"Now we got us a dilemma here, don't you think?"

"I can't see that."

"No? It's like this, Mr. Justice Department asshole. I've got the guy responsible for upsetting my little game *and* the son of a bitch he sent to take me out. You see my problem, Belasko? Who do I off first? You or the fuckin' ER extra?"

"If that's all, Randal, we don't have a problem."

"Oh? The fuck we don't."

Bolan's gaze didn't waver. He held Randal transfixed. The rogue DEA agent had no comprehension of what Bolan was about to do until the last moment, and by then it was far too late.

The flicker of realization showed in Randal's eyes a split second before Bolan's right hand came up, the Beretta settling on his head. The Executioner stroked the trigger and placed a triburst just above Randal's right eye. The slugs punched in through his brain and out the back of his skull. The rogue agent died before he even had time to touch the trigger of his own weapon. He fell back against the blood-streaked wall, sliding down to hunch on the floor.

"For the mo-ne-y," Bolan muttered as he crossed to stand over Leo Turrin.

Turrin raised his head and stared at the bloodstains on the cover over him. He looked up at Bolan.

"You had to do it the hard way."

"With you in the damn field there isn't any other way."

Turrin raised his shoulders. "Okay, I get the message, pal."

"You had better, *pal.*"

Turrin flipped back the bed covers to expose his bandaged limb.

"Souvenir?" Bolan asked.

"Not what I intended. Caught a bullet. Tell you about it later."

"Desk job from now on, Leo. No more playing around. Mister, you are grounded."

Bolan took out his transceiver and keyed in for Grimaldi.

"Sarge."

"You okay?"

"Getting there. All clear at this end."

"What the hell is that noise?"

"I borrowed one of Huerta's choppers. Should get us out of here a little faster."

"Push up the speed, Jack. The sooner we get out of here the better. We have a burning house here and a Justice agent with a leg wound."

"Can he walk?"

"Maybe I'll boot his ass down the stairs and find out."

"What about Huerta and his home boys?"

"All accounts squared here. Colombian, DEA and the local problem."

"I see what you mean about the fire, Sarge. You and Leo haul ass out of there and I'll pick you up on the front lawn."

"You got it."

Bolan took Turrin's arm over his shoulders and helped him out of the room. He retrieved his Uzi and M-16, handing the SMG to Turrin. They made their way down the stairs and out of the house. There was no offer of resistance if any of Huerta's crew were still alive. The bodies sprawled around the area suggested that Bolan had handled the problem fully.

The helicopter swung down out of the night sky, the underslung power light illuminating the area. Bolan slid open the side hatch and helped Turrin inside, then followed himself.

"Let's get out of here, Jack—I'm bushed."

As they overflew the house Bolan saw that the fire was spreading, flames showing at most of the windows now.

"This thing fitted with a radio?" he asked Grimaldi.

"Yeah, why?"

"Try that frequency Morales gave you. See if you can make contact. If you do, ask them to call the local firehouse and tell them they have a job."

"Yeah, I'll do that. Then where, Sarge?"

"Across the border, Jack. Get us back home."

BOLAN SLUMPED in the seat beside Turrin. He stared out through the side window, not seeing anything, but letting his thoughts go back to the start of the mission when he had first spoken to Turrin and accepted the job. It seemed a long time ago now. A great deal had happened, and he had confronted the enemy and walked away yet again. He had inflicted some telling damage on the drug trade, and it would take time for the business to rebuild. He knew it would. He also hoped that the different law-enforcement agencies would take advantage of the knowledge that had come their way and use it to push forward their battle. He didn't have to ask Turrin what he would do. The man would make certain that the guilty officials and agents would be dealt with, and he would do it to the bitter end.

Bolan reminded himself that he needed to have a talk with Hal Brognola at Stony Man. He hadn't forgotten the unexpected weapons cache he'd found in the hold of Deacon Marley's ship, and the two dead men in the Jamaican's office. There was something odd about that part of the setup that required further investigation. But that was for another day.

Bolan glanced across at his friend from Justice. Turrin returned the Executioner's gaze and raised a hand in a simple salute. It had all started with Turrin and now it was back with him.

The circle was complete.